Johnnie Finds
A
Dead Body

DS WHITAKER

This is a work of fiction. Names, characters, businesses, places, events, locales, and incidents are the products of the author's imagination or used in a fictitious and satirical manner. Any resemblance to actual persons, living or dead, or actual events is purely coincidental. Certain long-standing institutions, agencies, and public offices are mentioned, but the characters involved are wholly imaginary. The opinions expressed are those of the characters and should not be confused with the authors. Also, please do not feed wildlife.

Author photo by Diana Lang
Cover Design by DS Whitaker

To Tim for his love and support

To my Beta Readers with much gratitude

To Stumpy, may you live forever in our hearts

Prologue

In the pale moonlight shimmering on the wet sand, an unusual form below caught Stumpy's eye. It was a creature, but not moving. Just lying there, gaze upward. He descended from his roost and zigzagged over to the new thing on the water's edge. It smelled human and also like saltwater. He fit his jaw around one finger, tugging at the skin. It was bloated and didn't taste good.

In a couple more hours, when the sun returned, the nice man with the round metal-framed eyes and brown boots would arrive, possibly offering a crunchy treat. Until then, he could allay his churning stomach with sleep.

He climbed a tall palm tree using his thin razor-like claws, resting at the top, gazing across the bay at the twinkle of lights in the distance. A cool breeze tickled his leathery skin. Sometimes, his phantom tail would ache, as it did now. Losing it to that terrible machine all those years ago still pained him.

As Stumpy closed his eyes to slumber, he thought, "Someday, I will have my revenge."

Chapter 1

Dear Diary,

Today was different, finding the dead guy in the surf at Hawksnest. Luckily, I found him before sunup. He didn't have an ID, but I called him Bob, cause, you know.

Bob had a strange look on his face. Like surprised, but that could be because he died.

The police asked what I did, and I said 'nothing'. Chief Tobias gave me that look he always gives when he doesn't believe me. Said I shouldn't leave the island. But I never leave, so that was dumb. Not like I have a million dollars. Or anywhere to go.

Anyway, I went back to work afterward and none of the tourists were jerks, except for one guy at Cinnamon Bay who wouldn't turn down his car stereo in the parking lot, but I counted to thirty and only spat in his direction once when he wasn't looking.

I didn't see Cud today, which is weird. But maybe he was spooked by the dead guy.

Bob had a cool Bugs Bunny key chain sticking out of his pocket. It jogged a memory of the hospital, so I took it before Tobias arrived. So Happy Birthday to me a day early, I guess.

Sweet dreams, Johnnie.

* * *

Johnnie leaned on his rake, scratching the scar along his collarbone. Not too much seaweed today. And no mushy dead guy like yesterday. The early morning surf lapped gently against the sand. The horizon was a pale blue with hardly a cloud or a breeze. Three sailboats were moored in the distance, dotting the horizon line. The sun broke over the hills behind him in a yellow glow. He consulted his phone to review his daily list of tasks and any specific directions via text messages from his boss, Kemper. Two texts from last night read, "Tobias needs you to call him," and "Trunk Bay repair latch men's WC."

Johnnie hit 'delete' on the first and flipped down his round, amber-lensed sunglasses.

Stumpy ran up to him and eyed him with his head cocked and swished his chopped-off, ringed tail making grooves in the sand.

Johnnie took a baggie out the pants pocket and threw two cheesy puffs to his buddy. The iguana ate one, held the second in his mouth and scampered away.

His other friend, Cud, was sleeping under a swath of mangroves.

To his right, a patch of sand was newly disturbed, appearing like a round depression about eighteen inches in circumference. Might be a sea turtle nest. If it was, he needed to report it and keep people away. He liked keeping people away from stuff. But turtles must be birdbrained, or at least this one was, because it was smack dab in the center of the crescent beach, where most of the tourists trampled and kids made sand castles. But he wasn't allowed to move the eggs. Only put some stakes and rope around it and hope for the best.

He walked east, through the trees and brush, over to Cud's nest. His long-haired friend was awake, sitting on a broken boogie-board, rubbing his eyes with his tanned and bony fingers. His blanket—a discarded Sponge Bob beach towel and recent addition to his stash—rested on his lap.

Johnnie said, "Yo, man. How was your night?"

Cud, which was a nickname—because who names their kid that— was his best friend. Cud was older, but never said his age, and homeless, although he didn't need to be. Johnnie's sister told him she read an article about Cud once in Time Magazine, but that was years ago. Cudlow Loughton was a former investment company CEO and self-made billionaire. A decade ago, he mysteriously left his job in the Bahamas and gave up all his worldly possessions to live off the land in

St. John.

Maybe that's why Johnnie liked him. They were both damaged and misunderstood and didn't enjoy being around lots of people. But most of all, Cud was nice. All the time nice, not just nice when people are looking. And Cud didn't waste his time with jibber-jabber or personal questions. Yeah, Cud was okay.

"My man." Cud pushed his long locks behind his thin shoulders and rolled his neck; the grinding of his bones was clearly audible. "I was having the best dream. I was on a roller coaster and then I was flying over the water. Also, I was naked the whole time, and no one cared." He stretched his arms to the sky and let out a long yawning grunt. "I have some beef jerky and banana figs for breakfast. Want some?"

Cud's beard was at least a foot-long and white. His hair was also long, falling nearly to his waist, although he tied it back with bits of fishing line. The result looked like a cross between dreadlocks and a disheveled, fraying rag mop, with a few dead leaves stuck in the tangled mess. Cudlow picked at the brown, brittle leaves and dropped them on the ground.

"I'm good. Hey, I've got a few granola bars. They're in the side bag on my scooter. Help yourself."

Cud brushed the sand off his faded brown tank top and cut-off pants. "Thanks, Johnnie. Can I help you this morning before I go?"

Cud had a schedule. Or perhaps it was best called a routine. Sleep on the beach overnight, collect native fruits in the morning, walk into town or a resort to sell them in the afternoon, swim in the evening as the sun sets, and repeat. Some mornings, before his search for fruit, Cud kept Johnnie company during his chores at Hawksnest Beach.

Johnnie said, "Maybe. Hey, yeah, can you scan the parking lot for trash? I've got to report a nest."

"A turtle nest? Wonderful. Show me."

The men walked over to the sunken area of sand. The birds were waking up to the sun, squawking in the canopy above.

They stared at the sand, as if it might do a magic trick. Johnnie said, "I didn't know you liked sea turtles so much."

"I appreciate all new life. It's the only thing making this planet worth a crap. I haven't seen a turtle come up on this beach in two years."

Johnnie took off his cap and scratched his head, feeling the half-moon-shaped raised skin above his right ear. "I guess. Hey, that reminds me, did you see the dead guy yesterday?"

Cud clasped his hand over his mouth. "Oh, yes. Terrible."

"What time?"

"Before you arrived. I heard a commotion out on the water the night before. Probably a boat. I got up to take a piss about an hour before you arrived and he was face up staring at the full moon. Only he wasn't really seeing."

"Cud, where were you? You should've told Chief Tobias."

"You know I don't get involved." Cud dug his hands into the pockets of his cutoff cotton trousers, his fingers poking through holes at the bottom. On his leather belt was a black sheath with a black-handled knife. Only Cud didn't own a belt or a sheath.

"Where d'you get that?" Johnnie pointed to the belt.

"Found it."

"*Found it*? Where?"

Cud looked at the ground. "I don't get involved."

"Oh, Jumpin' Jehoshaphat!" Johnnie shook his head. "You took that off Bob?"

Cud furrowed his brow, "Bob?"

"Bob. The dead guy."

Cud blinked. "You knew him?"

"No. I just call him that."

Cud's mouth gaped open. "Oh! I get it now. He floated—that's not very nice."

"The belt. Where—"

"What can I say?" His long-haired friend shrugged. "I needed a new knife. Mine's as dull as butter from slicing coconuts. And he didn't need it anymore."

Johnnie sighed and walked over to retrieve his rake where he left it, leaning against a palm tree. "Man, you know what? That means you're involved."

He smiled and clapped Johnnie on the back. "Not if you don't say anything."

Johnnie gnashed his teeth and closed his eyes. This was a quandary. His sister Robin said he needed to always tell the truth. But Cud was his friend. He could pretend he didn't know about the knife. And besides, Cud wasn't the only one who took a souvenir off Bob.

"Fine, I didn't hear or see anything."

"Good man!" Cud waved and headed to the parking lot.

The beaches were open twenty-four hours a day, but most folks arrived after eight o'clock, with peak activity at noon. Johnnie tried to get his tasks at Hawksnest done before seven-thirty or eight, which included trash removal, combing the beach, inspecting and cleaning the restrooms, and small facility repairs. At that point, he got into the National Park Service pickup truck and repeated similar chores at Trunk Bay and Cinnamon Bay.

He pulled out his phone and called Supervisor Snow.

A female voice answered. "Hi, Johnnie. I was going to call you."

"Hi Kemper, I found a turtle nest. At Hawksnest Beach. Think it's a nest."

"Okay, I'll send the biologist later today. In the meantime, stake a ring around it."

"Will do, boss." His stomach felt queasy and his heart rate quickened, realizing he'd wanted to ask Kemper for the afternoon off, and had forgotten. "Boss, is it okay if I take off early today? It's my birthday. Robin's taking me to lunch."

He heard her grunt with exasperation. But not in a mean way. "Sure, just make sure you do all the trash pickups and restroom cleanups. How many hours of leave should I put down on your timesheet?"

"Four. Can I put it down as sick leave?"

"Are you feeling sick?"

"Kinda." He coughed into the phone for good measure.

"Fine. By the way, Chief Tobias wants you to call him back. He said you aren't answering your phone."

Talking with Tobias was like negotiating with a brick wall to move out of your way after your brakes fail. Nothing good could come from it. "I told him everything. Nothing more to say."

"I don't think you get to decide that. Call him back now. That's an order."

"Yes, ma'am." Johnnie sat at one of the picnic tables and ended the call. Stumpy came over and brushed against his leg. He leaned over to face his scaly friend. "What do you want? More cheesy puffs? I don't have any more. And they ain't good for you." It was true. He wasn't supposed to feed wildlife. And junk food wasn't good for people, no less iguanas. But Stumpy was old and somewhat broken. Stumpy's skin was a dull gray-green and crusty looking; a swath of dorsal crests on his back were missing in a noticeable gap. His defining feature, though, was his chopped-off tail, the reason for his moniker. Giving Stumpy treats was technically bad, but not the *worst thing* he could do.

Stumpy gave him a side-eye and blinked. [Maybe I just want to say Happy Birthday!]

"Well, thank you, Stumpy. You are more polite than most humans, I think."

[And more handsome. What about some fruit? Got some fruit?]

"Sorry, no fruit. Do you want to go to lunch later with me and Robin?"

A large woman in a small bathing suit walked by and stared at him.

He gave her the finger when her head was turned. Some folks called him crazy for talking with Stumpy. Since the incident in Afghanistan where he lost two centimeters of brain mass, he talked to lots of things. But it was no one's business but his own. And he understood Stumpy talking back was only in his imagination. Unlike that time in Miami when he became psychotic. That was not a good scene.

He also received strange looks because of his eye-wear. According to Cud, his round, wire-framed prescription glasses, with flip-up tinted lenses, made him look like the human fly or a steam-punk airship captain. But he liked them anyway. And the convenience of an all-in-one pair meant he no longer threw money away on misplaced sunglasses because of his poor memory.

Robin said he shouldn't worry about strange looks. Most of the time he didn't. But when the looks were nasty, it bothered him. And when he got bothered, sometimes he got angry and said or did very wrong things. His therapist said fits of anger were common in people with brain injuries and wasn't really his fault. But that didn't excuse him from 'doing the work', meaning, using his coping skills and trying to behave.

His phone rang. *His landlord.*

"Morning, Gertie."

"Blessed morning, Johnnie. Happy Birthday! I won't ask your age, but I have a present for you. I'm going to leave it in your apartment, and I know you don't like your place messed with. So, I'll leave it on the counter and won't touch anything else. Is that okay?"

"Aw, Gert, you didn't need to do that. What is it? Another bookmark?"

"No, something different. A small surprise. But I hope you like it."

7

In the corner of his eye, he spied an infraction. Three boys in their early teens were standing on the rocks on the east side of the cove. Against park regulations. They looked like jackasses because they were throwing stones up at a tree. Meaning, they were likely harassing a bird or an iguana. "Sorry, Gert. Got to go. Thanks for calling."

As he walked the three hundred feet to the other end of the beach, Johnnie counted. *1, 2, 3...*

He took the stack of cue cards out of his back pocket. The top one said, 'relax muscles' and the next 'breathe deeply'. With every step, he inhaled for a two-count, inflating his chest, exhaling for another two-count. A squawking bird erupted from a tree branch and the boys, now looking in his direction, dropped their stones.

As he reached them, the ache behind his eyes subsided. Johnnie looked at the sky and said, "Young men, standing on the rocks and harassing wildlife are both against park regulations. Please refrain." He didn't wait for a response and began walking back to the picnic pavilion.

Behind him, he heard laughter. Mean, mocking laughter. They called him 'Harry Pot-Head'. Johnnie knew he shouldn't look back. Shouldn't take note of their faces or clothing. Nothing to recognize them later for some kind of revenge. Or get the contraband fishing spear out of the tool shed and chase them into the water. No, those would be bad decisions.

Today was his birthday. These assholes weren't going to mess it up for him.

Chapter 2

At ten o'clock, Johnnie had finished his chores at Cinnamon Bay and returned to Hawksnest, where he parked the white government pickup truck, locked it, and changed out of his uniform. Now wearing cut-off jeans and a green T-shirt, he called the day quits. He drove his scooter west to Cruz Bay, the commercial hub of the island.

His red scooter, a 2007 Piaggio Fly 50, with a top-speed of 39 miles per hour, was nicknamed the *Flying Pig*. But mostly just *the Pig*. Robin gave it to him when he moved to St. John, after his alleged incident in Miami.

He didn't intend to hit that crowd of people with his car. He was lucky no one was badly hurt. Only some scrapes. His expensive lawyer got the toxicology report thrown out on some kind of lab protocol error and convinced the jury that the brakes failed. Also, the jury may have been sympathetic because of his Purple Heart.

Johnnie couldn't tell the jury the truth; that he was drunk and out of his right mind, somehow seeking to recreate the incident in Kandahar. *Perhaps hoping for a different outcome?* They would have had him committed. Johnnie stopped the binge-drinking after that. Nevertheless, once he moved to St. John, his sister decided it was best if he drove a less lethal vehicle.

Johnnie arrived at The Yellow Parrot at 10:30. It was an outdoor square-shaped bar with a red-tin roof near the ferry dock. It was usually filled with mainlanders who didn't know the better hangouts. Not his favorite people. But the bar was conveniently located near Robin, who worked a couple blocks away.

Mandy, the daytime bartender, was bubbly and smiled with gleaming, perfect white teeth. She was medium height, had a full figure, long dark braids down to her back, and wore a baseball cap with a New York Mets logo. She always wore a tank top and athletic spandex shorts. Johnnie found her very attractive as a person, although she was a little

9

young for him. She was twenty-five. Today he turned forty-five. But he still admired her from a distance.

He walked up to the bar, but didn't see Robin. Decidedly, it was a good opportunity to have a beer before she could criticize.

"Johnnie," Mandy said, "the usual?"

"Yep. You see Robin?"

Mandy wiped down the wood bar in front of him. She leaned forward and whispered, "No, but the Chief is looking for you. What did you do?"

Earlier, at Cinnamon Bay Beach, Johnnie saw Chief Tobias pull into the parking lot. He should have talked with the Chief. Get it over with. But he hid in a clump of mangroves, behind some rocks, until the Chief left. He didn't know why. Maybe afraid of confrontation and saying something wrong. At one point, Tobias walked within ten feet. Yet undiscovered, Johnnie heard him cuss and mutter under his breath, "Mother-loving Johnnie Crosswell. I don't need this shit."

Johnnie didn't need shit either. Why was Tobias so hot to talk with him? There was nothing left to say. It wasn't like the dead guy spontaneously woke up and told him the story of who killed him. That would be weird. Other than taking the key ring, he didn't touch the guy. Well, he brushed tiny crabs off the guy's legs, but only out of respect. It wasn't like they'd find his DNA on Bob.

"Mandy, I didn't do anything. Other than find a dead guy."

She turned to fill a glass with Blackbeard Ale at the tap. "Heard about that. Any word on who it was?"

"I don't know and don't care." Those words came out of his mouth and he realized they came out cold. Like he was a monster. Truth was, he had nothing against Bob. In fact, he felt bad for the guy. "What I mean is, I just found him. I don't know what else I can tell Tobias." He tried a smile, but it felt forced, so he stopped.

She placed a cardboard coaster under his frothy pint. "Count this one on me. I heard it's your birthday." Mandy winked, and before he thought to say thanks, she walked across the bar to another customer.

The bar was only half-filled, which seemed right for a Tuesday at ten-thirty. Admittedly, he was early for lunch because Robin said she'd be there at eleven, but it was a special day and it made no sense to delay his celebration. And he was grateful for his timing, because a cool breeze kicked up, and from the darkening sky, it looked like they were in for some punishing rain. Robin was going to get soaked.

He drank his beer and peeled back the label, attempting to remove it in one piece. The beer was cold and smooth and reminded him of the time before. When he had all his brain matter. When he could go to a bar and remember everyone's name and flirt with women and not get anxious or angry watching strangers have fun. When he had a life. Not that he remembered all that well. Only in flashes. Or maybe these were false memories, based on stories his friends told him in the rehab facility, before they decided he was too much of a project.

Cool air whipped around his arms and sideways rain hit his lower legs, despite his position near the center of the structure. A hundred yards away, dozens of people coming off the ferry scattered and yelled, trying to outrun the torrential rain, which was impossible. They ran anyway, looking for whatever shelter they could find, lugging suitcases and shouting at their spouses about why they didn't call a taxi ahead of time. A group of people ran straight to the bar, with no doors or barriers to slow their arrival. They shook with cold and wrung out their T-shirts and wiped the water off their faces. The kids wanted to play in the rain, but scowling parents dragged them back.

Johnnie tried not to make eye-contact with them. Because, soon, they would ask questions. So many questions. Like how to rent a car or where to buy an umbrella. He wasn't a God-damned concierge or tourist office. All he wanted was to drink his beer in peace. *Should he just leave?* Robin would understand. Or maybe she wouldn't. So, he stayed, head down. No eye contact. He placed his hands over his ears. *Hear no evil...*

Someone tapped his shoulder.

Johnnie yelled, "I don't know the number for the taxi company." He turned sideways on his bar stool to face the idiot tourist. But it was Chief Tobias. He froze.

The Chief sneered. "Hmmpf. Where have you been? Didn't you get my messages?"

Tobias was a large man. Nearly half a foot taller than himself. About six-foot three, over two hundred and thirty pounds and clearly worked out from the defined muscles straining the fabric of his short-sleeved police uniform. He had an odd face, like someone hit him with a shovel, because his nose was crooked and flat and he had a big scar on his chin where the skin seemed to have healed misaligned. And Tobias was serious. The kind of person who doesn't laugh unless he's bested you at something. From the first time they met, Johnnie decided he didn't like

Tobias.

"Sir, sorry about that. I've been busy. Didn't you hear? It's my birthday. Can I get you a beer?" He tried a smile again. It still didn't feel right.

Chief Tobias crossed his stocky arms. "Look, I need you to come to the headquarters at one o'clock or I'll find a reason to arrest you. You understand?"

Johnnie straightened his back and saluted. "Sir! Yes, sir!"

Tobias grunted and walked away into the rain, putting up his umbrella with military precision. Lightning cracked across the sky, followed by booming thunder. It seemed as if on cue, signaling Tobias' grand exit, like the Chief commanded the earth and sky like Zeus. But maybe this was his mind playing games on him.

Johnnie reached in his pocket and pulled out the key chain. Bugs was in a pose like a pugilist, with yellow shorts and boxing gloves. On the metal ring were three keys. Two looked like house keys—there wasn't any writing. One was small with an engraving. He cleaned his glasses with the end of his t-shirt, then tried reading the print.

Mandy came back to check on him.

"Hey Mandy, can you read this?" He handed her the key. "The print is too tiny for me."

She examined it. "Hmmm. Wait." She took her cell phone from her canvas waist apron and turned on its flashlight. "I see it now. I think it says 'Carib Bank'.

"Huh." *Maybe a safe deposit key?* He'd never owned anything valuable enough to have one, but wrote a note in his phone to ask Cud about it tomorrow; he would know about bank keys.

"Can I get you another?" She gestured to his near-empty glass.

He ordered another beer.

Not long after, Robin arrived. On her petite frame, she wore a white suit jacket and navy skirt, in keeping with her usual work attire. Her shoulder length wavy black hair seemed damp, despite her umbrella. She was holding a tall red gift bag.

"Johnnie, happy forty-five!" She reached around his shoulders and gave him a hug while he remained seated. She placed the bag in front of him. "Open it."

"Thanks, Sis. Am I taking you away from important business?"

"Not at all. Dottie cleared my calendar." She sat at the stool next to him.

He opened the greeting card first. An Amazon gift card for a hundred dollars was taped inside.

"Thanks."

She shook her head. "I would have gotten you some books, but I can't keep track of what you've already read."

Since his accident five years ago, his ability to read and comprehend words came back slowly. Reading, once a frustrating exercise, eventually became his primary solace and escape from his own thoughts. He read nearly every evening, mostly fiction and across many genres except for horror. As much as he loved books, he had to be mindful of eyestrain, which led to migraines.

Johnnie held the package. It had white tissue paper. He pulled out the contents. A box of Mallomars. There was something else at the bottom. An automotive headlight for his scooter.

She smiled, her blue eyes shining. "I know how you love Mallomars, so I got someone on the mainland to ship them. And I don't want you driving in the dark without a headlight anymore. You'll go around a curve and bounce off a donkey."

It was true. His headlight broke a month ago and he couldn't find the part he needed at the local auto parts store. So he gave up. Which wasn't smart, but he trusted his driving skills. He'd driven in worse conditions during deployments, even in sand storms. At least here, there weren't IEDs or mobs with grenade launchers. Robin was right though; there were stray donkeys and chickens wandering the roads, particularly near his place. Sometimes they sauntered out of the way of moving vehicles. Often, they didn't. Still, the gift showed she cared, and it was better than another pair of socks.

"Thanks. Do you want to get a table?" He looked around. The rain subsided and the tables further from the center of the bar now seemed safe from the former deluge.

"Nah, we can eat here. I'm going to get a burger. How about you?"

"I was thinking the same. Hey, I saw the Chief. He wants me to come in at one o'clock."

"Really? Does he want to ask more questions about the dead body?"

"He won't say. But he said he'd arrest me if I didn't show."

"Do you want me to come? As your lawyer?"

He almost said yes. His sister was technically a lawyer, although as

13

one of the fifteen senators in the US Virgin Islands' legislature, she hadn't been in private practice in seven years. "No. It will be fine. But can I ask you something? Hypothetically?"

She sat back and interlaced her fingers on her lap. "Sure." She closed her eyes.

"Why are you acting like I'm going to say something bad?"

She opened her eyes. "Maybe because you never talk in hypotheticals."

"Fair enough. I'm asking for a friend. Is it considered a crime to take something from a dead guy?"

"Oh, for crying…what did you take?"

"I said *a friend*. What if a guy took a belt and a knife off a dead guy? Is that stealing?"

"Short answer, yes."

"But the guy is dead. He can't own it anymore."

"Right, but on his death, legally his estate and belongings transfer to his heirs, or if there aren't any heirs, to the state. In actuality, you are stealing from them."

"Huh. No shit."

She slapped her hands over her ears. "Don't say anything else, because it's best if I don't hear it."

Mandy came over and handed them menus. "Senator, can I get you something to drink?"

"I'll have whatever Johnnie's having."

"Do you folks want a few minutes to look at the menu?"

Johnnie said, "We'll both have burgers. Mine medium-rare, hers medium-well. And two more beers."

Mandy smiled and took away the menus. "I'll put it right in."

His eyes must have lingered on Mandy as she walked away because Robin said, "A bit young for you."

"She's nice. That's all. So, hypothetically, if the item was small, and the family didn't know about it, it wouldn't be a problem, right?"

"Maybe. It's best not to bring it up."

"Right."

Johnnie liked the key ring. It was plastic and cheap, but it was fun and he loved Bugs Bunny as a kid. Bob's family probably wouldn't know or care, and if they did, how would they know it didn't fall to the bottom of the bay?

And maybe, if someone asked, he could say he found it washed up a few days later. How was he supposed to know it was Bob's?

That seemed like a good plan. Better than telling Tobias about stealing. The Chief wouldn't be cool with that.

Yeah, best to hide the key chain for a few days and not say a word.

* * *

Dear Diary,

My birthday was good except for talking with the Chief. He told me the guy had stab wounds in his back. I asked, what does that have to do with me? The Chief showed me a file with an old police report from that time in Miami where I stabbed a dude. But I told him that was before I started therapy. And the guy was a douche harassing this woman on the beach and I told him to stop. The other guy with him had a throwing star and hit me square in my left shoulder blade as I walked away. Which means they started it.

Anyway, I don't carry weapons anymore.

Chief asked me if I knew Doug, the owner of the marina. I kind of know him, but everybody does. Doug is always running newspaper ads and his face is plastered on lots of benches in town. So, I asked the Chief, is Doug the dead guy? Chief wouldn't answer.

Then he gets in my face, saying the DNA results will come back tomorrow, and do I want to tell him anything. Like, even if I killed Bob, that wouldn't scare me. Tobias is an amateur compared to the Army interrogators I used to know. I laughed, although I know that was a wrong response.

In other birthday news, Gertie embroidered a pillowcase for me with flowers and the words, "Home is Where the Heart Is". Then she asked if I could help her re-hang the shutters this weekend.

Goodnight Diary. Sweet Dreams, Johnnie.

Chapter 3

He saw her at daybreak. The goddess of the water. That's what he called her because he didn't know her actual name. On calm days, she glided into the bay from the East on her paddleboard and eventually made a U-turn.

Despite her distance from shore, he could tell the Goddess was tall. Maybe over six-foot; taller than him. Her hair was shaved close on one-side, her remaining hair fell a few inches below her shoulder, blonde nearly white, with loose waves. The sun sometimes glinted off her dangly metal earrings. Toned and tan, wearing a black shorty wetsuit, she traveled across the waves effortlessly, like she and the board were one.

She seemed otherworldly, like a mythical creature, and as elusive as Snuffleupagus. In a rare land sighting, Robin said she saw the Goddess last year in the parking lot at Maho Bay and was with a guy with hair like Fabio. But Johnnie never saw the Goddess on dry land, which added to her mystique.

He often daydreamed she would paddle in and he'd be brave enough to say hello. But after that, he didn't have a clue of what to say to her. Still, just seeing her pass through was a good omen for the day.

Johnnie continued his chores, picking up some trash at the pit toilet restrooms. The smell was gross. He never used them, waiting until he got to Trunk Bay to use the flush toilets. Not that he was a sissy about dirt and feces. But once, overseas, his phone fell out of his pocket in a latrine, causing an unspeakable scene. His memory of the past wasn't great. But that one stuck.

Next, he got a broom and swept out the sand out of the changing rooms. The spider web in the corner had grown since last week in the dank space. He couldn't let it go any longer. Someone left a glass bottle on the floor in one of the stalls. Glass containers were strictly forbidden, but he was accustomed to people breaking rules.

16

As he gathered the trash bag and his broom, Cud walked up. A dirty and torn fisherman's net style bag hung around him cross-body. The bag contained coconuts and some banana figs. Cud peeled the skin off the top of a mango with a pocket knife. *Bob's* pocket knife. "Good morning, Johnnie. How are you on this blessed day? Want some mango?"

"Hey, Cud. Nah, I'm good. I had a breakfast sandwich earlier."

"I saw the Chief looking for you yesterday."

"Yeah. I talked to him in town after lunch with Robin. He thinks I stabbed Bob. What a dickweed." He carried the trash and broom to the back of the pickup truck in the parking lot. Cud followed.

"Tobias lacks imagination. Any word on who the unfortunate soul was?"

Johnnie told him about the conversation with the Chief. But there was a more pressing matter on his mind. He leaned on the truck's tail-gate and flipped up his sunglasses. "Cud, look at this." I held out the small key. "It says Carib Bank. Is it one of those safe deposit box keys?"

"I reckon so. They have a branch here. Where'd you find it?"

"In the seaweed earlier this week." Technically true, although it was in Bob's pocket and Bob was in the seaweed.

"Do you think it belonged to the dead guy?"

Johnnie looked Cud in the eyes. "Did you know it's legally considered stealing to take something off a dead body? You should be careful with that pocket knife. Maybe hide it."

Cud laughed. "I still say finders' keepers."

Johnnie walked to the tool shed, "Follow me."

Johnnie opened the shed door's padlock. "I tell you what, maybe you should swap out the knife. You take this one." He took a folding survival knife off the wall. "It's much better for cutting fruit. Even coconuts. I'm not allowed to use it, and it's no use here. But, in return, I need your help."

"Sure." Cud did a little dance in place, swishing his hips.

"Why are you dancing?"

"Why not? This new knife is very cool."

Johnnie sighed. "I have to run an errand in town at noon. Might take an hour, ninety-minutes tops. But I'm supposed to be repairing and sealing the picnic tables here this afternoon. If you go out on your fruit scavenge this morning, could you be back to cover for me? That way, if Kemper or Merv comes around, you can tell them…shit, I don't know."

He searched his brain for a plausible answer. Maybe he was making this more difficult and complicated than it needed to be.

"I'll just tell her you had to sign for a package at the post office."

Johnnie beamed. The post office on the island was notoriously slow and could explain his delayed return. "Yes. That works. Thanks, Cud."

"You know, I used to be adept at subterfuge. How about an additional quid pro quo?" Cud started shimmying in place again.

Johnnie laughed. "What would you like?"

"A frozen Snickers would be heavenly."

"Sure."

Cud saluted and danced away toward his usual nesting spot. "Wonderful. See you later!"

* * *

Johnnie sat at the picnic table, still in his uniform, watching the time change on his phone. *Cud should be back by now.* Going to the bank was dumb, but maybe he'd learn more about Bob and why he was stabbed to death. A bird flew under the pavilion roof and landed on the table, pecking at some crumbs of bread left by the last occupant. It was diminutive and fluffy, with a russet chest. *A Mangrove Cuckoo.* The bird eyed him suspiciously while continuing his feast. "Hi, little bird." The bird didn't reply. Moments later, two larger birds, brown Thrashers, swooped in and scared the small one away. Johnnie swept his arm across the table, forcing the intruders to scatter. *It wasn't right.* He muttered, "Pick on someone your own size."

When Cud arrived, satchel empty, he said, "Sorry, I'm late. I had a bumper crop today. I made almost twenty-five dollars." He beamed. "Mostly mangoes. One guy bought a dozen."

"That's nice. I'll be right back." Johnnie got up from the table. He quickly changed into civilian clothes, shorts and a plain T-shirt, and hopped on the Pig. "I'll be back soon," he said to Cud as he fastened his helmet.

"Don't forget my candy bar, Johnnie," Cud said, waving.

A few minutes later, Johnnie parked his bike two blocks from the bank, just to be sure no one would read his license plate if things went sideways. He checked his phone. It was 12:20.

The bank building was in a strip mall, with wide windows at the front and an ATM by the door. He walked inside the rectangular space. It had commercial vinyl tile and a dropped ceiling with fluorescent lighting. The walls were covered with posters depicting smiling families with information about home mortgage rates, or faceless people in suits promoting small business accounts. The teller window structure was red Formica and had three service counters, but it looked like only one was in use, because the other two were filled with brochures. He walked up to the counter.

The teller, young, in a pink suit jacket with a gold name tag, looked bored; her chin resting on her palm. A floor fan behind her rotated back and forth.

"Good afternoon, miss. I'd like to check on my safe deposit box." He used his most pleasant tone, like he was happy, but his heart was racing and beads of sweat formed on his neck. A security camera behind the counter seemed locked on him. Not that it was moving, which meant it was probably his own paranoia. He resisted the urge to turn away.

She got on a phone, speaking into the receiver, "Good afternoon. Samuel, customer here for the boxes." She pointed. "Sit there, he'll be out soon. Lunch time and all."

He walked over to the guest chair, sensing eyes on his back. The modern IKEA-looking desk with two monitors had a nameplate, "Mr. Samuel Jameson, Bank Manager".

Johnnie lifted a brochure off the desk describing money market accounts and began reading. Not that he was interested, but it gave him something to occupy his mind and calm his nerves. More sweat poured down his back. Was he having a panic attack? Or was the air conditioning out?

He turned his head toward the teller. "Miss, is it hot in here or is it me?"

The woman fanned herself with a yellow folder. "Lord, have mercy! I told Mr. Jameson to get it fixed. I'm about to walk out, to tell the truth. It ain't right."

"Um, okay." He went back to reading about the different investment accounts. He had a checking account with only a couple grand in it. His rent, though reasonable for the island, was still fifteen-hundred a month. His therapy sessions and medications came to about five hundred a month. Plus, there was the lawyer's bill he was still paying off in installments. There was no money left for investing.

A tall thin man in his 40s with a dark pimpled complexion, wearing a short-sleeved dress shirt with a purple tie, came into the room from the back. His name badge read S. Jameson. This was the guy.

"Sir, I'm Samuel Jameson, the bank manager. How can I help you today, Mr…"?

Johnnie didn't want to give his actual name. "Um. Just call me Bill."

"Well, Mr. Bill, you have a box with us?"

"Um. No. It's my sister's. She passed away."

"Oh, I'm so sorry. My condolences. Did you get the box as an inheritance? Do you have the probate order with you?"

"Um, no, it just happened. I have a key. Box 33."

"What is the name on the account?"

He wiped the sweat from his neck with the top part of his T-shirt. His brain got foggy and there was ringing in his ears. "Name? Er, Bob."

"Your sister's name is Bob?"

This wasn't going well. He rubbed his forehead and closed his eyes. "No. Um. That's my cousin. My sister's alive. Sorry, I need a minute."

Think! Think, dammit! Sweat soaked his shirt, plastering it to his back. His left knee bounced; he held it down with both hands, but it wouldn't stop. He had to get out.

"I'm sorry. Must be the grief or heat exhaustion. I'll come back with the paperwork." Johnnie bolted off the chair. "Thanks for your time." He headed to the door without shaking hands goodbye or looking back.

The door chimed as he exited. He lengthened his stride down the sidewalk, as fast as he could move without running. Johnnie kept going until he reached the Pig. He unlocked her and hopped on, not looking back, gunning the weak engine up the hill out of town.

Stupid, stupid, stupid. He should have had a plan. What was he thinking? Was he so brain-dead now?

As he approached Hawksnest Beach, he realized he'd forgotten to buy Cud's Snicker bar. He'd have to make it up to him another time. *Why couldn't he remember one goddamned thing?*

He parked his bike in the lot. Cud was sitting on a picnic table under the pavilion. Johnnie looked at his forearm, at the two healed, raised linear marks. Bob's knife was in the shed. Part of him wanted to. The other part heard his sister's voice quietly say, "Don't".

Still in his civilian attire, he walked past Cud and toward the shore. He reached the water's edge, the mid-day sun beat down, kids frolicked in the surf chasing ghost crabs.

He threw his glasses onto the sand and stormed into the water, sneakers and all, and kept walking until his chin touched the surface. The water felt cool. Like a rebirth or a baptism. He wanted all his mistakes washed away. Johnnie remained there, near floating, nudged by gentle currents, allowing the universe to control him like the tides, so he couldn't be held responsible anymore. So he couldn't disappoint himself anymore.

Johnnie let out a guttural scream toward the sky. "I hate you! I hate you!" He inhaled deeply, bent his knees and dipped below the surface; closing his eyes, curling into a ball. Counting in his head. *1, 2, 3…*

The beating of his heart grew louder. He kept counting. At one hundred, he opened his eyes. The water was clear. Not too many fish at this depth. He kept counting. 105, 106, 107…

At 165, his lungs burned.

Johnnie scrambled back to the surface for air. He coughed and took in precious oxygen, treading water, his feet looking for purchase. Facing the beach, the tourists appeared serene as they lay on the sand. Like they didn't have a care in the world. *Had he been that way once?*

He swam a few feet towards the beach, found his footing on the sea floor and pressed his legs through the water toward dry land and considering his next move. His wet clothes clung to him, hair dripping, his sneakers filled with squishy sand. Wiping the salty water from his eyes, his self-hatred turned to determination. He found his glasses and dusted off both sets of lenses.

Maybe he just needed a better plan.

Because—as much as his brain was broken—he was no quitter.

After a long day at work meeting with constituents for five hours straight, Robin arrived home to her one-bedroom condo on the hillside overlooking Cruz Bay. Built in the nineties with stucco exterior and rounded columns, her place had nice views of the ocean. Not that she ever spent time appreciating the view.

She closed the front door behind her, turned on the lights, strode to the bedroom, opened her walk-in closet and kicked off her high heels. Then peeled off her suit. She threw her bra in the hamper, put on a thin cotton night dress, and clipped up her dark hair. At the bathroom, she washed her face and applied a pale green cleansing mask. Assessing her reflection, she looked like Shrek's sister. Not that it mattered. Why was she concerned with youthful skin when she would die alone, married to her job?

All day long, people wanted things from her. Issues with insurance companies or building permits or school funding. Sometimes more personal matters, like she was a family counselor. Those might be funny if the stories weren't so tragic. Although one guy wanted to know about the zoning regulations for raising guinea hens on his condo terrace. She needed her assistant Dottie to do some research on that, but it made her day.

While the mud-mask worked its magic, she went to the kitchen to make dinner. Ironically, after the discussion about hens, she was making a roast chicken with some vegetables. Enough food to provide a few meals over the rest of the week.

As she placed dinner in the oven, her phone rang. She shook off her oven mitts and fumbled for her phone in her handbag. On the seventh ring, she put it on speaker. "Hello, Robin Crosswell." She felt her face. The mask was almost stiff, ready to take off.

A gruff voice said, "You need to control your insane brother."

She picked up the phone and walked to the sofa. "Who is this?"

"Chief Tobias. Is he off his meds again?"

She froze. Whatever he was going to tell her couldn't be good. "Hold on." She ran back to the kitchen, opened a drawer, and pulled out a pad and pen. "Can you tell me exactly what happened?" She held the pen, poised to write word for word.

"Senator, look, I just saw some bank security footage. Your brother was at the Carib Bank around twelve-thirty. The bank manager was concerned by his strange behavior."

What did Johnnie do now? Hopefully not naked... "What did he do?" Robin returned to the sofa and clutched a throw pillow to her midsection. She drew shallow breaths through clenched teeth.

"He told the manager his sister died and left a safe deposit box key. But then he said it was his cousin, Bob."

Good, not naked. "Did he break any laws or hurt anyone?"

"No, but the manager thought he might have been casing the bank and chickened out. That's why he called me. Then I saw the footage and knew at once it was Johnnie. We've talked about this. I can't spend all my time babysitting his antics."

Robin let out a deep breath. "So, he did nothing illegal. Just some crazy talk. Is that right?"

"Yes, but you know as well as I do, this is how it starts. Remember that time three years ago when he jumped on the ferry in the buff? And the time he scratched that tourist's car with his rake? I'm not paid enough to deal with his shit."

She leaned back and closed her eyes. "I understand. I'll talk with him. Thanks for calling." She hung up, fell sideways on the couch, and buried her face in the bottom cushion. Her fists pounded the soft fabric. "Why, Johnnie?"

She pushed herself back up and noticed a new green smudge where her mud mask transferred to the expensive linen. *Great.*

Robin strode to the bathroom and removed the mask, revealing pink skin. She splashed water on her face, continuing even when no longer necessary, lost in her thoughts. She just had lunch with Johnnie yesterday. He seemed fine. A little down, but *not* manic, wired or suicidal. Although, he appeared apathetic about his headlight. *Was that a death wish?*

Robin went back to the sofa and looked at the notes she just took. In her distress, her handwriting was illegible. Something about her being dead, a safe deposit box and a bank robbery.

Johnnie had significant debt, but he wasn't a bank robber. Or hadn't been. She'd told him many times that if he got into a financial bind, he could come to her. Not that she was made of money, but she lived comfortably even on a government salary.

It had been a long day. She didn't want to get in her car and drive across the island in the dark. The last time she drove out there, she nearly hit a donkey, and a flying pebble left a quarter-size radial crack in her windshield. Praying this wasn't a complete crisis, she dialed his number.

"Hey, Johnnie, it's Robin. Did I catch you at a bad time?"

"Hi, not at all. Thanks for lunch yesterday. And the Mallomars."

"Johnnie, I want to say…" *What could she say?* Don't rob banks? Have you lost your damned mind? "Well, you know I love you more than anyone in the world. Even if you are a butthead."

She heard silence.

Johnnie said, "What is it?"

"Chief Tobias called me. He said you were at a bank today."

More silence.

"John, are you there? I'm not mad. Tell me what's going on."

She heard him curse under his breath.

Finally, Johnnie said, "Um, what did you hear?"

"Something about a safe deposit box and you thought I was dead."

"Um. Yeah, I'm sorry."

"Do you want to talk about it? When was the last time you talked with Doctor Phillips?"

"Shit, Robin. It's nothing. I got confused. I'm better now."

"I can come over if you want to talk." She meant that, but hoped she didn't have to.

Another long silence.

"John?"

"Really, I'm fine. I woke up this morning and something told me I needed to check out box 33 at that bank. It was dumb."

This wasn't adding up. "Like a dream?"

"Yeah, sort of."

"And you *didn't* think I was dead?"

"No, I...I was just trying to see the box. I woke up and remembered a voice—like God or Oprah or someone—saying I needed to open the box and it had something to fix my brain. But after I got there, I realized I must have made this up in my head and went back to work."

"You weren't casing the bank to rob it later?"

"Jumpin' Jesus, Robin! I don't rob banks."

"You were asking about stealing at lunch yesterday. Did you take something from the dead man?" She held her breath. "Please, you can tell me anything. Anything. I can help."

Johnnie sighed. "Had nothing to do with it. Cud found something on the beach. I thought it belonged to the dead guy. That's all."

Her mind raced. There had to be a better explanation. *If the daily physical exertion and dealing with the public at his job was wearing him down, causing problems...* "Is your job stressing you? I can always pull some strings to get you a quiet job with the post office."

"Hell no. Look. I'm fine. My job is good. And Dr. Phillips says walking and sunlight are helpful for regulating my moods. I don't want to be in a cell all day babysitting sorting machines."

"I know, but I'm worried about you. If you are over-extending yourself…are your meds okay? Are you taking them regularly?" The oven timer went off. "Look, I have dinner in the oven. Can you hold?"

"No, you go have dinner. Like I said, I'm fine. I'll call Lou tomorrow. Scouts honor. Love you, bye." Johnnie hung up.

Robin stared at her phone. "Crap."

She removed the chicken from the oven and lifted the foil. It smelled great, but now she wasn't as hungry. Robin placed the pan into the refrigerator. Instead, she plucked a handful of grapes and placed them in a small bowl and went to her bedroom. She snacked and read a few pages of a vampire romance novel before turning off the light to sleep.

Staring at the ceiling fan in the dark, she thought about what Johnnie said. And she had only one conclusion.

Whatever Johnnie was up to had to be some next level bullshit.

Because she didn't believe a single word.

✱ ✱ ✱

Dear Diary,

I did a dumb thing today. Robin is pissed and I can't blame her. I promised to call Dr. Phillips, but I'm busy this week, so I'll call Saturday.

After my foul-up, I had dark thoughts. Like the time before I got my meds and the dog in the neighbor's apartment whispered demonic shit. But I feel better now, and I didn't drown or reach for any knives.

I did some thinking and I have a new idea, but I have to convince Cud to help.

Tonight I worked in the yard alongside Gertie. She sang the entire time, but it was sort of nice. She is always so happy and I wonder if that's normal. Afterward, she gave me a hug for helping and it didn't freak me out, but I told her don't do that again without asking first. She asked, if next time, could she could thank me with home-baked cookies and I said that was a much better idea.

Good night Diary, J

Chapter 4

At sunrise, Johnnie had just finished raking the beach and emptying the trash at Hawksnest and began to sweep the pavilion floor when he heard Cud yawning in the distance. He put down his broom to check on his friend. "Good morning, Cud. How did you sleep?"

Cud was sitting cross-legged next to his cooler, drinking a bottled water. "Good morning. Same as always. It rained last night."

"How is your tarp holding up?" The last time Johnnie saw it, the tarp was badly faded, with a few holes and the edges frayed. It was folded up under the cooler at the moment.

Cud scratched his head. "It's seen better days."

"I can get you a new one. Any size."

"Don't worry about me. I'm sure I'll find a replacement. All kinds of things wash up around here. Or get left here."

It was true. Cud was the unofficial lost and found at Hawksnest. His campsite, although camouflaged well, included brightly colored amenities. In the last couple of months, Cud obtained a new camp stove, three beach blankets, two bottles of sunscreen, ten flip-flops—all mismatched and different sizes—and the biggest prize, a hard-sided cooler with a cracked lid.

"Really, it's no problem. It's easy to order tarps. I, um, have another favor to ask."

Cud stood up and stretched his back, swinging his torso right and left, like an old Jack LaLanne video. "Johnnie, you're a good friend, but I don't like that look in your eyes."

"What look?"

"Like you're hatching a scheme." Cud stood feet apart, touching his toes with alternate hands, like a windmill.

Johnnie was hatching a scheme. Maybe an elaborate one. And it had inherent risk. His sister would call it foolhardy and illegal if she knew the truth. He inhaled deeply. "Cud, do you want to help me investigate the safe deposit box?"

"What do you mean, investigate?"

Johnnie motioned for Cud to follow him to the pavilion. They sat at a picnic table to discuss the plan. Cud was unconvinced about its success considering all the preparation needed. Ultimately, Johnnie said, "What else do you have to do that is more exciting?"

Cud scratched his head. "I don't like wearing shoes."

"It's only for an hour. Aren't you curious?"

Cud relented. It would take a day or so to get Cud fixed up, but that could be an interesting part of the challenge.

Yes, Johnnie thought, *time for Cud's extreme makeover.*

After work, Johnnie and Cud got on the Pig and headed east to Coral Bay to see Miss Sheila. Her rates were reasonable, and she took walk-ins. It was close to three when they arrived.

Her place was small, with cracked wood siding, faded green paint and a roof with some shingles missing. But the yard was covered in bright flowers and fanciful metal garden sculptures, and you barely noticed the house for all the splendor. A hand-painted shingle, hung on a post in the front yard, read, "Sheila's Place". If you were a tourist, you wouldn't know if it was a restaurant, a bed-and-breakfast, a boutique, a salon, or just the name of her house. The ambiguity was intentional. She didn't like non-islanders. Which made it the best place for Johnnie and Cud to go.

He parked his bike on her white-rock driveway and they walked around the path to the back. A woman's voice shouted, "Oh, no you don't." The screen door flew open and Sheila stood there with her hands on her wide hips. "Johnnie, you know we all love Cud, but I can smell him from here." She pointed to her outdoor shower. "No offense. There's soap in the shower. I'll get some towels." She disappeared back into the house.

Cud looked up at Johnnie. "I knew this was going to be a problem. Maybe we should reconsider." He held up a swath of his long hair. "I don't know if the fishing line will come out."

Cud bathed in the ocean every night. He wasn't too scummy. But through the lens of Miss Sheila, Johnnie realized that perhaps Cud was an acquired taste. He looked Cud up and down. "You know, why don't you shower at my place and you can borrow some of my clothes. It's only another fifteen minutes down the road. Then we'll come back."

"That is the wisest thing you've said all day." Cud walked back towards the scooter.

Johnnie called out, "Sheila, we'll be back in an hour. We'll fix…um, you'll see."

* * *

On the drive to Johnnie's place, Cud second guessed the whole crazy plan. He enjoyed living under the radar. His hair embodied his current life: wild, free and off-putting. Having normal hair again might snap him back into his old self, his small-minded, money-centric existence. When they arrived at Johnnie's place, he had half a mind to say he wanted out of their deal. *What was in it for him?*

Still, the mystery of the deposit box and a needed change of routine spurred him on. *Would it kill him to cut his hair and play a part for a day?* He was curious about whether he could pull off a normal demeanor after these ten years. And his friend seemed so obsessed with the box. Since Johnnie arrived four years ago, he didn't feel so alone, so ostracized. And John was always looking out for him, like a son; but unlike his actual son, who had disowned him.

Johnnie steered the scooter off the road into a stone driveway. The house in front was a one-story, ranch-style structure in a faded yellow color with more brightly colored patches where shutters should have been. The steel standing-seam roof was dark green, and the house appeared to have shiny new replacement vinyl windows. Notably, the property was situated on a flat plot; unique for its hillside location. The front of the house faced the ocean with an unobstructed, stunning panoramic view. Even in its diminished state of upkeep, it was intact. Other homesites they passed on the journey were rubble or mere foundations.

He followed Johnnie to the white cinder-block garage, turned apartment, to the left of the main house. The front facade—where a double garage door should have been—was boarded up with painted plywood with a three-foot-wide vinyl window at the center. The entrance was on the right side. As he glanced around, a woman in a flowered housecoat was gathering something, some kind of green vegetables, in the backyard garden. The woman with the dark complexion and pulled-back hair waved and smiled.

Cud asked, "Johnnie, *who* is that?"

Johnnie inserted his key into the doorknob. "My landlady, Gertie. Come on."

Cud stopped and waved back. She had a striking aura about her. Since his change of lifestyle, he became adept at reading auras. At first, he thought he was going insane, seeing colors like that. After the first year of living off the land, he accepted his talent as normal and not the sun baking his brain. Still, he didn't like to talk about auras. It sounded crazy. And people took him for crazy as it was, looking at him with pity or contempt.

"Can you introduce me?" he said.

Johnnie huffed. "Okay, but let's be quick. We need to get to Sheila's before she closes and I don't know how long it will take to unravel *that*." He pointed to Cud's hair.

They approached the sizable vegetable garden. "Gertie, I'd like you to meet Cud."

Gertie got up and dusted off her knees. She extended her hand. "Nice to meet you. Will you be staying for dinner?"

No one had offered him dinner since he arrived at the island. Yes, the aura was strong in this woman. And she was beautiful. Curvaceous, copper brown skin, graceful, caramel eyes you could melt in. "I would love dinner. Everyone calls me Cud, but you, sweet lady, can call me Cudlow." He reached for her hand and kissed the top of it.

Gertie blushed. "Well, that settles it. I'll open a bottle of wine. I can have dinner ready at six."

Johnnie said, "Thanks, Gertie. We have a few errands. Make it six-thirty?"

She smiled. "Of course. See you boys later."

Cud grinned at being called a boy. And he liked how Gertie smiled at him. Her entire face lit up like a sunrise over the hillside. It felt like love at first sight. But perhaps he was just sentimental and lonely. He would need to take things slow. Because, now, he needed to cut his hair and shower properly to impress Gertie. Or at least make his best effort at normalcy and see where things went.

Johnnie's apartment was a square-ish studio. His clothes—including two extra park uniforms—hung on an open metal rack by the entrance.

No rugs on the polished concrete floor except a mat at the front door.

A double bed with navy blue linens against the far wall, a kitchen with a microwave, sink and a tall narrow refrigerator, a living area with a television and an old gray velvet sofa. It was orderly and clean, and would have been deemed minimalist except for the abundance of books. A dozen worn paperbacks rested on a leather trunk in front of the sofa. A thick photo album in a green felt cover lay on a side table next to a lumpy pink ceramic mug that looked like a five-year-old made it. Cud wondered about it. *Did Johnnie have a kid?* Or was it something from his own childhood?

A black-framed photograph of Johnnie with Robin at a bar was displayed on his nightstand. More stacks of books, a sizable number, lay in a mound on the floor next to his bed. Had to be at least a hundred.

The only decoration on the beige walls consisted of an Audubon calendar and a small watercolor painting of some palm trees and surf. The overall mood was like a cave occupied by a transient loner. Cud understood about being a loner, but this kind of depressing environment seemed intolerable.

Johnnie took off his boots by the door and called out, "Alexa, playlist one." Classical music, a piece Cud recognized as Largo al Factorum, played softly over small speakers on top of the refrigerator.

"You surprise me. I never took you for a classical man."

"I used to like the Rolling Stones. Still like them. But my doctor said some classical music might be good for my brain."

"Oh, like babies in the womb?"

"Something like that. I don't know if it helps, but I told my doc I'm up for anything, as long as it isn't more medication." Johnnie pointed to the back wall. "There's the bathroom."

Cud opened the door and peered in. It was tiny with a three-foot, pre-fab stand-up shower. The walls were painted cinderblock with a two-foot wide awning window above the sink. A single bare bulb on the ceiling lit the dark space.

Johnnie said, "I think our best course is to take some length off first. Let you get the shampoo in deep and Sheila can shape it later. Okay?" He retrieved a pair of child's safety scissors from the vanity drawer.

Cud held his hand out. "I'll do it. You can wait outside." This could be emotional and he didn't need an audience. Not that Johnnie would tease him or be unsupportive. But, just in case he began to sob or break down, he didn't want anyone's pity. It was just hair to most people and they wouldn't understand.

He shut the door for privacy. Preparing for the first cut was like standing on the edge of a rocky cliff and while deciding to jump thirty feet into a raging sea. He grit his teeth, braced his mind, and sheared off the first chunk. *There. It was done. No going back.*

He decided shoulder length was the best compromise. The first section hung up on the fishing line and he had to trace it back to cut again. The mass fell to the floor, not in splinters, but in a tangled mass like a furry octopus. He picked it up and held it in his hands. Thoughts raced through his mind of wanting to bury it ceremoniously, like a dead cat. Instead, he took a small snippet and put it in his back shorts pocket as a memento.

It got easier after that. Most of the fishing line became dislodged as he worked around the back of his head. He couldn't rightly see what he was doing, and it was probably very uneven, but it was only the first phase. Sheila would do the rest.

He turned on the hot water in the shower and waited for the temperature to rise. Johnnie had just one brown bath towel on the back of the door. He made a mental IOU to replace it with a new one later. Which would mean calling Jackson, his grandson and acting estate manager. Jackson was a good kid. Guilt coursed through him, realizing he should call the lad more often.

Cud stood under the warm water lathering for five minutes. At first, the water swirling down the drain resembled dark bone broth. He looked at his arms. He discovered white skin he hadn't seen in years. If he was under less time pressure, he would have spent more time scrubbing. But he needed to save time for the biggest battle, shampooing his hair.

The first round of shampoo was a mere suggestion. His hair resisted and his fingers couldn't get through to his scalp. He worked up from the bottom. A little more success there. With the second round of shampoo, he gained the upper hand. His fingers now touched his scalp, although the hair was coarse and still a little clumpy. The third application of shampoo was the charm. His wet hair laid down flatly against his head with no lumps. He jumped out of the shower through the mist and opened the bathroom door a crack, "Johnnie," he yelled, "Do you have any conditioner?"

Johnnie called back, "Under the sink."

Cud opened the vanity door and found a tube of hotel-sized conditioner. It would have to do.

A few minutes later, Cud wrapped the brown towel around his hips and exited the bathroom. "Ta da!" He threw his hands in the air like a ringmaster.

His host was sitting on the sofa, reading a paperback. The Ruslan and Ludmilla Overture danced playfully in the background. Johnnie looked up from his book. "Cud, you look…clean."

"Yes, I had dirt in places…well, best not to tell. And I'm sorry about your towel. Do you have clothes for me?"

Johnnie inserted an embroidered bookmark into his novel, got up and crossed the room toward his clothing rack. A stack of neatly folded T-shirts—sorted by color and large earth tones—lay on the top metal shelf. He handed a bundle of clothes to Cud. "Keep the towel if you want. I have another on the clothes line. These should fit. Hey, thanks again for doing this. I know change can be difficult." Johnnie reached into his pocket. "Here's some cash for Sheila."

Cud appreciated Johnnie saying that. Sometimes his friend could be brusque and cool. Other times, he was caring and emotionally intelligent. Change *was* difficult. But perhaps Johnnie was talking about himself.

A small circular mirror hung on the wall by the apartment entrance. He estimated it was eight inches in diameter. Cud pointed. "Thanks. Why don't you have a mirror in the bathroom? How do you see yourself in this small thing?"

"Who says I want to see myself?" Johnnie sat back down on the sofa and put his nose back into his book.

He'd seen that look before. Johnnie was in a mood. Not an angry mood. He recognized those. But sullen and a touch withdrawn. "Did I do something wrong?"

"No. Kemper just called. Chief Tobias said Bob's brother wants to meet me tomorrow. Jesus, I just found the guy. Why can't everyone leave me alone?"

"Does this change the plan?"

"I don't know. I guess not."

Cud sat down on the sofa next to Johnnie. "This is Bob's safe deposit box key, isn't it?" It came out as a declaration, not a question. "Maybe you should give the key back to the family."

"Cud, I can't explain it. This whole situation is off. Like, there were times we'd be on patrol at night, and you just knew there were eyes on you. Eyes that wanted to hurt you. I felt the same way yesterday when I talked to the Chief. I don't trust Tobias and something fishy is going on. We stick with the plan."

"What do you think is in the box?"

Johnnie stood and went to the kitchen. He took a bottled water out of the fridge. Taking a sip, he cleared his throat and said, "Damn-it! I don't want to steal anything. I just need to know what's in it. You go, find out what's in there and leave. That's all."

"Man, don't get testy with me. I'm your friend, but I don't take people's attitude. Now, settle down. Let's get that haircut and have a nice dinner afterward, okay?"

Johnnie closed his eyes, held the water bottle against his neck, and seemed to be counting to himself. After a moment, he put the bottle back in the fridge and said, "Sorry. I wasn't mad at you. You know that, right? As my therapist says, I have trouble explaining myself. I don't like it and get frustrated."

"Yes, I know." He headed back to the bathroom with the clothes. "That conditioner has quite a pleasant fragrance. Can I keep the tube?"

Johnnie smiled. "Sure, Cud. Now hurry. You won't want to be late for Sheila or to Gertie's dinner. It's fried chicken Thursday."

No, he certainly did not want to be late to either. Having the attention of two fine women in one night, albeit platonic, was going to be a wonderful diversion from his routine.

And he would enjoy the sweet scent of jasmine in his hair while doing so.

Chapter 5

Johnnie couldn't believe his eyes. When Cud stepped out of Sheila's salon, he was unrecognizable. About ten years younger looking with his smooth silver locks, catching the breeze like a celebrity in a shampoo commercial. Or maybe it was Cud's smile. So broad it seemed his face could split apart. Visible now that his beard was gone.

"Jolly good, mate, I'm starving. Let's go."

Johnnie stood transfixed. "Cud, your hair…"

"I know! Sheila is a doll. Really listened. Kept it long on top but a bit shorter in the back. She said I look like an older Hugh Grant. I can't stop running my fingers through it. Oh my, we should have taken before and after pictures. But come on, I can't wait to show your landlady, Gertie. Is that short for Gertrude? I knew a Gertrude once. A maths teacher at University. A real sour puss. But Gertie seems nothing like that battleax. So, tell me, was she ever married? Would it be rude to ask her? I want to know everything…"

His friend sure was chatty. But all Johnnie could think about was the bank box and their scheme. He needed his friend to focus.

Cud continued. "…Do you think we'll have cornbread tonight? I miss it so. My wife, bless her, she used to make the best mince pie and always served it with corn bread. The stuff of the Gods…"

Johnnie took a deep breath and yelled, "Cud! Stop! Just get on the damned scooter."

"Sheesh, man. You don't have to yell. I'm determined to enjoy this miraculous evening." Cud stared at him and crossed his arms. "I know what you need. You need to smile."

Johnnie shook his head. "Look, I'm not trying to be a jerk, but my head hurts."

"Smile or I walk home and forget your little heist." Cud grinned.

His cheek twitched—not much—but he felt it. "You'd walk in the dark all the way back across the island? And they say I'm nuts."

Cud pinched Johnnie's cheeks, "Smile. Come on. You'll feel better." He released him, stepping back, gesturing him to try.

Johnnie bared his teeth with exaggerated curled lips.

"Oh, good Heavens, you look like a braying donkey. Forget it." Cud shook his head, donned his helmet and got on the back of the Pig.

✻ ✻ ✻

Cud was excited to show Gertie his new hair. He walked behind Johnnie into Gertie's place and surveyed the interior. The front door opened to a living area, with terracotta floors, white walls, and a vaulted ceiling with white-washed beams. A white rattan ceiling fan hung in the center of the open space. Small framed needlepoint scenes of flowers and birds hung on the front wall next to the picture window.

To the rear was a u-shaped kitchen with countertops covered in two-inch square cobalt tiles. The appliances were a mix of black and stainless, and the cabinets were standard-looking with a light oak finish. Delicious smells wafted from the kitchen.

The dining area was a zone to the right of the living space, demarcated by a sisal area rug. A delicate lace table cloth, tall candles, wine glasses and flower-patterned china plates adorned the table. Fresh flowers of yellow, pink and blue in a white ironstone pitcher completed the picture. The table looked like a feature spread in an expensive home and garden magazine.

Gertie took off her yellow apron. She wore blue eyeshadow, pink blush and a magenta lipstick. Her natural black hair was loose and wavy, framing her russet complexion. Beneath her apron, she wore an olive-green mid-length dress with a V-neck and that accentuated her waist.

He couldn't take his eyes off her. Yet, he didn't want to stare. *Was this how Johnnie felt about the Goddess?*

She said, "Welcome. Cudlow, I love your hair."

Cudlow ran his hand through it. "I feel transformed. Thank you for dinner. It all smells wonderful."

Gertie hung her apron on a hook next to the double wall oven. "It's no trouble. I enjoy having new guests."

Cudlow beamed at her. "And I enjoy being here. Tell me, can I assist?"

"You can pick the wine and help me bring the food over." Gertie pointed her head toward the counter.

Cud joined Gertie in the kitchen.

"I love your dress." He inspected the two wine bottles. One was a Zinfandel, the other a Merlot. He chose the latter.

"This old thing?" She gave a sly smile, as if she rightfully knew how the dress suited her to perfection. "So, Cudlow, I want to know all about you."

His heart stopped. *What could he tell her?* And why hadn't he prepared a suitable answer, knowing certain questions would arise. "What do you want to know?"

From the living room, out of view, Johnnie called, "Is there anything I can help with?"

Gertie called back, "Just take a load off." In a quieter voice she asked, "Where are you from originally? I detect an accent." She stirred mashed potatoes in a tall pot on the stove, put down the spoon and went to the refrigerator.

Had he slipped back into his British accent again? "Oh, I was born in London. We were poor, but I studied my best. After university, I moved to the Bahamas." With the cork screw, he worked at opening the wine. It had been many years since he'd opened a bottle himself, always having staff for such things, and it showed, because he struggled with it, unsure of how to extract the cork.

She took milk out of the fridge and poured a couple dashes into the steaming potatoes, stirring with force. "London. I've always wanted to go. Can you put the rolls on the table?"

He put down the bottle and picked up the rolls. They smelled heavenly. "You should! How about you? Are you originally from St. John?"

She didn't stop stirring. "I moved here twenty-five years ago. I was a school teacher. But I'm retired now. So, Cudlow, are you married?" She asked this matter-of-factly, like it was a job interview, not like she was flirting. Still, the question rattled him.

A lump lodged in his throat. "I was. Happily." He needed to change the subject to something less sad. After taking the rolls to the table, he asked, "Are those carrots from your garden? They're simply massive." He gambled on a joke and chuckled. "Is the soil radioactive?"

Gertie smiled. "You know, I used to be a black thumb. But once you learn about the pH here, it's easy to grow food." She walked to the wine bottle and opened it in two seconds. "Well, I think everything is ready." She wiped her hands on a dish towel. "Time to bring the rest over."

A few minutes later, with the table set, Gertie lit the tapered candles. "Let's say Grace." She reached her open palms across the table to both Johnnie and Cud.

Gertie said to Cud. "Would you like…?"

Cud smiled and took her hand. Her skin was soft. A mixture of excitement and happiness washed through him. "Yes, please." He bowed his head. "To our Creator, we give thanks for the bounty before us, and for new friends and old, and may we strive each day to be worthy of Your love and honor all Your creation. In the name of the Father, the Son and the Holy Ghost, Amen."

She said, "Cudlow, that was beautiful."

He blushed, not wanting to let her go of her hand. "I'm inspired by your kindness."

Johnnie tucked a cloth napkin under his chin. "Gertie, this smells great."

After their meal, she said, "Now, tell me what 'no-good' you boys are up to."

Johnnie asked, "What…what makes you think we're up to something?"

"A woman can always tell when men are up to mischief."

Cudlow looked at her. "We do have a scheme. But it's top secret." He twisted an imaginary key in his mouth. "Tick a lock."

She said, "Hmmm. So mysterious. Nothing bad, I hope."

Johnnie said, "No. Nothing bad like murder."

Cudlow laughed. "Yes, hardly."

"I should hope not!" she said, adding a chuckle.

Cud said, "It's best if we don't say anything."

Gertie said, "Well, how about dessert? I made a pecan pie."

Cud leaned back in his chair, rubbing his swollen belly. "I'm sure it is delicious, but I couldn't eat another morsel. This was the best meal I've had in a solid decade." It was true. He'd not eaten to this level of satiety in years. Another bite might not keep down and that would be a travesty.

Johnnie got up from the table and grabbed Cud's plate and his. "Yeah, we have work to do anyway." He took the plates to the kitchen and scraped the food remnants into Gertie's compost can.

When it was time to say goodbye, Gertie grinned and said, "Have a good night. If you need a getaway driver, let me know. I could use some excitement."

Cudlow laughed. "Yes, at our age, just waking in the morning without hip pain can seem exciting."

"Speak for yourself, sweetie," Gertie smiled. "I still have things going on." She sashayed her hips and snapped her fingers.

"Yes. Yes, you do." Cud took her hand and kissed the top of it. "I've so enjoyed dinner tonight."

Gertie winked at him. "I've enjoyed it too."

* * *

Johnnie walked into Gertie's and hardly recognized her. She looked like a movie star. Nothing like the woman in the flowered house-coat, kneeling in the garden, her cheeks smudged with dirt. It felt eerie, like he was in the Upside-Down, and everyone got a makeover but him.

Why was he feeling like the third wheel on a romantic date? Gertie and Cud chatted in the kitchen like he didn't exist. Maybe that was okay, because not existing was usually a good thing in his mind. His cheek began twitching again. Something to read would steady his brain. A needlework magazine on the sideboard caught his eye. It was better than nothing.

A few minutes later, after they sat down at the table, Gertie asked Cud to say grace, and she reached her hands to both him and Cud.

He hated holding hands. Or being touched. But making a fuss would be worse. He took her hand and Cud's, counting in his head. It felt like he was hooked up to electrodes, even though he knew the discomfort was really a manifestation of his own awkwardness.

Glancing at Cud's hand, he noticed Sheila had given him a manicure. Thankfully Cud thought of that. What was the point of a haircut to impress the bank manager if his hands looked like crud?

Cud said a prayer, and Gertie seemed impressed.

Johnnie pulled his hands away, focusing on the bowls in front of him. He reached for the long wooden spoon in the mashed potatoes. "Gertie, this smells great."

They ate and conversed about the weather and recipes. Or at least Gertie and Cud did.

Johnnie noticed Cudlow kept giving Gertie adoring looks. She appeared to reciprocate, laughing at his jokes and touching Cud's arm. He felt like a fly on the wall. Like he could evaporate into smoke and they wouldn't notice. When Gertie asked about dessert, he felt relieved Cud declined. All this sitting around chatting wasn't productive. "Well," he said loudly, "time to go. Thanks, Gert."

On the short walk to his apartment, Cud wiggled in a strange dance-walk, like a praying mantis in a Robert Palmer music video. "Johnnie, your Gertie is really something."

"Yes, but we need to discuss the plan. Snap out of it."

They entered the apartment and Johnny closed the door behind them. Cud said, "You never answered my question earlier."

"What's that?" Johnnie went to the kitchen and got some Ibuprofen from the cupboard and a glass of water. *Would his headache ever go away?*

"Gertie? Was she married? Divorced? Widowed?" He wrung his hands.

Cud seemed lovesick. The last thing he needed. "You really like her, don't you?" He swallowed two pills and chased them with a gulp of water.

Cud hugged himself and closed his eyes. "Johnnie, like is not the word. I'm having feelings…I haven't felt in a long time."

Johnnie didn't understand infatuation between old folks. "Maybe it's just your new hair."

Cud exhaled and looked at himself in the small mirror by the door. "You know, the old Cudlow was a terrible man." When he turned, his eyes were misty. "Going to a bank might…"

Johnnie put his glass in the sink. "Might what?"

"I don't know. But it scares the hell out of me."

✳ ✳ ✳

Dear Diary,

I can't write too much because I have a guest tonight. Cud is staying over. I've always offered he could bunk with me instead of sleeping on the beach, but this is the first time he said yes.

During dinner, Cud was making eyes at Gertie, and she him. Not sure how I feel about that. Usually I get upset seeing other couples happy, (I'm working on that) but I didn't mind them. Maybe it's progress.

Cud looked different after the haircut and shave. Before bed, he said it reminded him of his evil twin. I think he was talking about himself. But it made me feel like a bad person for making him do this favor. Anyway, he's tucked in on the sofa and looks happy now.

Cud said I should smile more, but I don't know how. It's been a month since I talked to Dr. Phillips and I should make another appointment, but she says I need to be totally honest which means I'd have to talk about Bob, and I'd rather not right now.

We watched The Simpsons tonight. It was funny. I like Lisa the best because she's suspicious like me. But Cud is like a cross between Homer and Bart. Happy with simple things but rebellious, which is a weird mix, but that's how it is.

Tomorrow, Cud goes undercover. Wish us luck Diary.

Love, Johnnie

Chapter 6

It was Friday, which meant a work day. At five, Johnnie and Cud were up and out the door before sunrise. As they got on the bike, Johnnie said, "First, you need to get a suit. All I can give you is a hundred. Can you work with that?"

Cud shook his head. "Don't worry. I have a plan for clothing. Keep your money."

"Really? Fine. You should probably take my scooter for the day. Do you know how to drive one?"

Cud thought hard. He hadn't driven a car, no less a scooter in a couple decades. In the time before, he always had Terrence, his chauffeur, to take him places. "Maybe you could give me some pointers? How about we clear the beach first and get all your assignments out of the way and we'll practice in the parking lot?"

It made sense. The stores wouldn't be open until ten. "Okay."

They arrived at Hawksnest Beach at five-thirty. The sun would rise in thirty minutes. Enough time to comb the seaweed, inspect or fix the barrier tape around the nest and deal with any over-night trash and mayhem. Because the park never closed, sometimes folks would have parties and leave all kinds of artifacts in their wake.

Once they arrived, Cud said, "I'll check for jellyfish and glass."

"Thanks." Johnnie got his rake from the tool shed. He stopped by the turtle nest first. All looked well.

He raked the seaweed for about fifteen minutes when Cud ran up. "A bumper crop!" He dangled three rubbers in Johnnie's face.

"Eww, dude! Not cool. Get away."

Cud chuckled. "Ha! You need to lighten up. Everything will be fine today. Stop with the sourpuss."

Johnnie shook his head, not sure whether to feel disgust or gratitude. One of the worst parts of beach maintenance was picking up used condoms. Not only were they disgusting and unsanitary, but the sea

41

turtles mistook them for jellyfish, ingested them, and died. He was lucky when people used the brightly colored ones; he could spot and pick them up with his grabber tool easily. The clear ones, when mixed with seaweed or on wet sand, required close inspection which was too gross for words.

The rest of the morning was uneventful. Next week was Easter break and off-islanders would descend like a hoard of locusts. It was the calm before the storm. Around ten, Cud and Johnnie finished most of the chores and Cud asked about his driving lesson. Johnnie scanned the beach for any infractions in progress. Finding none, he said, "Okay. Ten minutes."

The parking lot was full at this point. Not ideal for Cud to learn how to make full 180 degree turns. Johnnie handed his key ring to Cud. The Bugs Bunny one, which now contained his personal house key, bike key and Bob's deposit box key. Cud straddled the Pig and donned a helmet.

"What now?"

Johnnie turned the key and showed him the throttle and brake. "Just take it slow. Ease into it."

Cud gripped the handlebars tightly, causing his fingers to turn white. He gently accelerated; Johnnie jogged beside. All was going well.

A car entered the lot and came directly at Cud.

In an apparent panic, when Cud should have braked, he accelerated wildly. To avoid the car, he steered right. Now heading towards a parked sedan, Cud reached out to push off its trunk. The scooter wobbled and he held on, driving it off the pavement into some shrubs, where he toppled over.

Johnnie ran up. "Are you alright?"

Cud spat out some twigs. "Just a little dust up. I'll get it next time."

"Are you sure?"

Cud grinned. "Just like riding a bicycle. You'll see."

After more practice, Cud got the hang of it. After remaining upright during a tight 180-degree turn, Cud shouted, one fist in the air, "See, I'm King of the World!" He came to a stop and turned off the bike next to Johnnie. As he lifted his leg to dismount, the bike fell, bashing the inside of his calf.

"Ow! Bollocks!"

Johnnie caught the scooter mid-fall. "Cud, the kick stand! Are you okay?"

"Oh, right." He said sheepishly. "Yes, I'm fine. I'll remember next time."

A vehicle entering the parking lot from the other end caught Johnnie's attention. The Police Chief's SUV rolled in…like the Death Star…or a Borg ship. He expected to hear an ominous John Williams overture. The *last* thing he needed.

Chief Tobias parked in the open handicapped space. He and another man got out of the vehicle. The unknown man was tall, like Tobias, medium build, with a crewcut, black button-down dress shirt, and black pleated dress pants. He looked like the kind of guy that goes door-to-door with a clipboard trying to sell solar panels or life insurance. His clothes didn't match his demeanor, as if he were playing dress-up for a role he wasn't enjoying. *Was this Bob's brother?*

Cud, sitting on the bike ready to leave, stopped. He parked the bike and came over to Johnnie. He whispered, "Watch out."

Johnnie grimaced, his adrenaline ready for a battle. "Why? What?"

Cud grabbed Johnnie's arm. "The other guy? His aura is black as night. I saw it right away. Don't let him rile you."

Johnnie sighed. He didn't believe in the aura stuff. But he didn't want to argue. Cud really seemed to be a true believer. "You'd better get going."

Cud nodded and went back to the bike.

Ten seconds later, Tobias and the unknown man walked up. Tobias said, "Crosswell, glad I found you this time. Who's your friend?" He pointed to Cud, who was motoring away.

The Chief didn't recognize Cud. Not that he could blame him. Cud was often invisible to regular mortals and now with the helmet, shorter hair and clean clothes, it was unlikely anyone would figure it out. "Good afternoon, Chief. He's just an old friend from Miami."

"What's his name? He looks familiar."

Johnnie needed to change the subject because lying always got him in trouble. The secret to lying is *remembering* the lie. And his memory was not up to the task. "Who's *your* friend?"

"This is the deceased's brother."

Johnnie put out his hand. "Sorry for your loss. I'm Johnnie. What's your name?"

The man didn't shake his hand back. "Mark. I was wondering if you found anything *else* when my brother washed ashore."

"What do you mean, *anything else?*" Johnnie studied Mark's face. This was not a grieving relative.

"You know, anything in his pockets. The coroner showed me his effects. So just wanted to know if you saw anything. I mean, not that I'm accusing you of taking anything. Sometimes things show up later, you dig?"

The hairs on Johnnie's neck stood on end. This 'brother' character was not adding up. He squinted, focusing on the edge of Mark's face, looking for the black aura. *Nothing.* Not if you didn't count dirty smirks or razor stubble.

Johnnie shook his head. "I didn't find anything but your brother. Were you two close?" Without waiting for a reply, Johnnie took a half-step forward and smirked, "Did your brother have any enemies? I mean, Chief here said he was stabbed a few times. Someone must have *really* hated him." After he said this, he knew he stepped in it. He was antagonizing this goon, hoping for a reaction. Hoping for a fight to wipe the smug look off his face.

Mark leaned forward—planting his face almost close enough to meet the bill of Johnnie's park service cap—with his lips curled and jaw lifted. "Are you insulting my dead brother? Because I don't think you want to do that." Mark stabbed his index finger into Johnnie's shoulder.

Some of Mark's spittle landed on his glasses. Johnnie knew he should back down. He owed it to Robin to behave. The last thing he needed was to throw a punch, especially in front of Tobias. It would mean lock-up for sure. Stepping backward three feet, he took off his glasses and wiped them with a cloth from his pocket, keeping his head down. After replacing them on his face—fitting the curved temple tips securely around each ear—he continued looking at the ground, gritting his teeth; he placed two fingers to his carotid artery. He counted towards fifteen, in a voice slightly above a whisper, swaying back and forth on his heels. Johnnie took deep breaths between numbers, glancing up occasionally to make sure Mark didn't sucker punch him.

Mark shook his head, pointing his thumb at Johnnie. "Chief, is this guy okay? Cause I don't know if he's a punk or a looney."

Tobias crossed his arms. "I ask myself that all the time. Come on, let's go."

Johnnie kept gazing downward until he heard their voices drift away out of earshot.

But their voices went toward the water. A hundred feet away, the men were examining the spot where Bob washed up. The Chief seemed to be carving out an outline in the sand with his heel.

Johnnie stared at the men for a spell while he contemplated having lunch.

Stumpy ran up to him and rested his front feet on his right boot. [Johnnie, what did they want?]

"Hey Stump. They were just being jerkwads."

[Any cheesy puffs today?]

"Sorry, I forgot. I've got a lot on my mind."

[What's more important than snacks?]

"Did you see Cud? He looks great, right?"

[I liked the old Cud. He gives me mango and breadfruit.] Stumpy blinked at him, raising a front foot in the air.

"All right." Johnnie walked to his scooter, where he stored his insulated lunch bag in the helmet compartment under the seat. He had half an ear of corn leftover from Gertie's dinner. He put it down on the concrete for Stumpy."

[Thanks, Johnnie! I knew I could count on you.] Stumpy attacked the cob; it rolled around as he dislodged soft kernels with snaps of his jaw.

A rival iguana ran out from under a bush and tried to take the cob away. It became a battle. The two locked their sharp mouths together, the rival smacking Stumpy repeatedly on the head with his longer tail. It was an unfair fight in that regard. Smidgens of blood formed where their jaws met. A man and woman walking along the path moved sideways to give the fighting creatures a wide berth.

A teenage girl, gangly, maybe thirteen, sitting on a beach blanket with her parents, noticed the scene and walked over. She stood shoulder-to-shoulder with Johnnie as they both watched the intense commotion. The girl said, "I didn't know they could fight like that. Shouldn't you stop them?"

The kid had a point. Johnnie felt bad for instigating the fight, albeit indirectly, by feeding Stumpy. He retrieved the half-eaten cob, and the iguanas stopped fighting, riveting their eyes on their object of desire. The rival with the long green tail sprang onto Johnnie's leg, digging his sharp claws through his pant legs into his flesh, climbing him like a tree. Johnnie threw the cob across the sand in a knee-jerk reaction to the pain. Stumpy led the chase, but the fight between the animals continued twenty feet away.

The girl looked down at Johnnie's leather boots. "You're bleeding."

Johnnie inspected the damage. There were small holes in his pants, but a thin stream of bright red liquid flowed from under his green pant hem onto his boot laces. He said to the girl, "This is why you should never feed wild animals." He pointed to the clearly written sign next to the walkway outlining the park rules. "Now go back to your parents."

The girl shook her head and walked away. "Whatever."

Johnnie retrieved the first aid kit from the tool shed, finding antiseptic and bandages. He sat at a picnic table and inspected his leg. It felt worse than it looked. He was wrong to give corn to Stumpy. Technically, he should report his injury to Kemper, but it was idiotic and his own damn fault.

As he finished tending his leg, he scanned the beach. The Chief and Mark were gone.

He thought about the look on Mark's face when he asked about finding anything else. If he had said yes, would Mark claw him like a corn-crazed iguana to get it back?

Possibly.

That guy was bad news.

He hoped Cud would be back soon.

Because now he *needed* to know what was in the box.

And do everything in his power to make sure Mark never got it.

Cud enjoyed the breeze blowing across his chest as he crested the hill and descended the winding road toward Cruz Bay. The whine of the engine intensified up the steep hills; the scooter slowed during the climbs, crawling and clawing for every foot of ascent. Conversely, the downhills were like an amusement ride; but with more inherent danger.

He regarded the worn narrow path of missing grass next to the road, the same walking path he took every morning to sell his meager fruit haul. Now, driving the scooter, he wondered how he hadn't been killed several times walking along these roads. Between the truck drivers who acted like they had nine lives by crossing the median without a care, and the tourists forgetting to drive on the left, his walks on the shoulder seemed like lunacy.

All these years, he told himself that traveling by foot was preferable. Walking miles every day made his legs and heart strong and added to his self-reliance. Now he wondered if he'd only been headstrong and foolish. The early months living on the beach made him doubt his sanity. In fact, he muttered to himself almost constantly, scaring himself and others. Thankfully, his will to live came back and his rantings ceased.

But he didn't linger on self-doubts. He was enjoying the ride on the Flying Pig and his strange and mischievous task ahead. *A mystery to solve!*

Once in town, he parked the red scooter at the Marketplace, a boxy structure with shops, restaurants, and offices. On the third floor, he found a payphone. They were rare to non-existent on the island now. But he paid attention of their locations, because they were his lifeline to call his grandson. Normally, he called on major holidays or birthdays. Today would be different.

He dialed the number and followed the automated menu to make the collect call to Nassau.

After a few seconds, a young man's voice on the other end replied in a British accent, "Hello? Paw?"

Cud said, "Jackson! How are you, lad?" He responded using his native-born London accent. Not his Americanized informal mode of speech he adopted when he became Cud the recluse instead of Cudlow E. Loughton the fourth.

"I'm fine. Pawpaw, are you alright? I must say, I'm surprised but happy to hear from you."

"I'm perfectly dandy. In fact, I met a lovely woman last night. But I need you to do some things for me and not ask questions."

Jackson sighed. "Hold on. Let me get some paper."

Cud waited until Jackson was ready and said, "I need you to send two dozen roses to Miss Gertie Brown, 1812 Spring Garden Road, Calabash Boom. There aren't any florists on the island, so you must purchase them on St. Thomas and send them across on the ferry. Hire someone to deliver them the entire way so they don't get lost. And don't put my name on the card. I intend to be a man of mystery. Did you get that?"

"Yes. What else?"

"I need you to transfer ten million dollars into a new money-market account at the Carib Bank on St. John under my name. Don't tell your father."

"Why?" Jackson asked.

"It's none of his concern. Please, right away. I'll wait by this pay phone so you can call me when you're finished. And I need clothes. A suit, shirt, tie and dress shoes, the whole ball of wax. You know my size. Have someone deliver them to me on the third floor of the Marketplace. Something classy yet understated. But don't fret, they can be off the rack."

"Pawpaw, what in blue blazes are you up to? Have you decided to come back to civilization? Dad would be so happy. We can take the jet to St. Thomas and meet you for dinner. What do you say?"

Cud was afraid of this. "No, sorry, I'm just working on a project today. Nothing has changed. In fact, if all goes well, I'll ask you to transfer the funding back to the family trust soon after."

Silence on the other end. Then Jackson sighed. "You need all this right now? This very moment? A little notice would have been helpful."

"Sorry, things come up. Tell you what. Work on the suit first, then the money and later, you can work out the flowers for delivery sometime over the next few days. Does that help?"

"Marginally, Paw. As long as I'm getting you a suit, can I get you anything else? New underwear? Toiletries? Anything to make your camping more pleasant?"

Cud had lied to his family when he left those years ago. He said he was camping at an eco-tent resort on the southern end of the island. A sort of 'glamping' in a wood-framed cabin with a canvas roof, solar-powered lighting, and rain-water gravity showers. They had no idea he was living and sleeping under a moldy tarp on a public beach.

Cud thought for a moment. He had enough toothpaste and recently bought a new toothbrush and floss. Saving up for better footwear was one of his goals, but not entirely necessary given his cache of abandoned flip-flops. "I'd like a nice hat. Maybe canvas or straw, with a chin strap. A good sturdy comb and lip balm. And some jasmine-scented shampoo and conditioner. Also, a cloth, cross-body satchel for carrying fruit."

The more he thought about the things that would make life easier, he realized the list could go on forever. Sleeping on Johnnie's sofa yesterday—with a pillow and clean sheets—was a bittersweet respite. He missed pillows perhaps most of all. Still, more physical possessions would ultimately encumber him, driving him back to a life indoors. And that could lead to falling back into his old ways. No, he couldn't let that happen.

"I think that will do it. I'll wait here at the Marketplace. Cheerio, Jackson." He hung up the phone and doubts seeped in. He was entering dangerous territory.

As a matter of habit, he checked the coin return. *Nothing.* He sat cross-legged next to the wall-mounted phone and watched shoppers duck into the various shops. The shoppers appeared happy, ogling trinkets and magnets at the gift shop across from him. The store window showcased bright paper flowers, mugs, shot-glasses, T-shirts that said 'Don't Hassle Me I'm On Island Time', copper wind chimes with sailboat or shell motifs, hand-painted spoon rests, and plush mongoose toys with blue satin bows.

No, he decided, he didn't need that kind of happiness.

As soon as his task was complete, he'd head back to the wild.

Chapter 7

Curled on the floor, Cud woke, startled by someone calling his name. "Mr. Loughton?"

A thin woman, dark-skinned and short, stood over him. She was young, maybe in her twenties, wearing a crisp white hotel uniform with a name badge the read "Denise". She was smiling—a good sign—and had a gray vinyl garment bag draped over her arms.

He shook his head to clear his thoughts. "Yes, dear. I take it that is for me?"

"Yes, sir. Your grandson said I could find you here. If you'd like, I could drive you to the resort where you could get changed properly. It's only a five-minute trip. We have a tailor on call to assist if you'd like."

He had wanted to keep things simple. And he couldn't blame Jackson for adding certain amenities, but still he wished he hadn't made such a fuss. "No, dear. I'm eager to get my project started. Did Jackson say anything about the account?"

"Yes, everything is set up. I wrote the account number and the branch manager's name and placed it in the jacket pocket. I put my own business card in there also, in case you need further assistance."

Cud squinted at Denise. Even in the uneven lighting, he could make out a green aura around her. Intelligent and quick—a powerful combination. Jackson had selected a good emissary.

His back ached as he grabbed the hand rail on the wall to ease up. He dusted off his shorts and raked his hand through his newly cropped hair. "What do you think of the hair cut? I think Miss Sheila did a superb job."

Denise laughed. "My mom goes to Sheila's. Jackson sent me your picture — so I could find you. The hairstyle in that picture was a bit severe. I like this one better."

"I do, too." He ran a hand through his hair again, relishing the silkiness. He thought about what picture Jackson could have given her. Probably one from his old life. When he wore it slicked back like Gordon

Gecko in Wall Street.

"The other items, the hat and toiletries? We are still working on those. Can I messenger them later to your Eco Tent residence? Can you give me the building number?"

"Um. No. Tell you what…meet me here same time tomorrow and I'll pick them up in person. Does that work for you?"

"It's no trouble, sir. I'm happy to deliver—"

"No!" He couldn't risk Denise finding out the truth and somehow relaying his state of habitation to Jackson. "Sorry, I mean, it would be more convenient for all if you could kindly bring them here tomorrow."

Denise nodded. "I understand. This time tomorrow."

Cud smiled to make amends. "Well, Denise, it was lovely to make your acquaintance. But I have to be going. Thank you for your prompt service." He gave her hand a quick squeeze after he took the garment bag.

He headed to the public rest room.

Ten minutes later, he was decked out in his new attire. He hadn't worn underwear during the last five years, but Denise included crisp white boxers in the garment bag. *A civilized gentleman wears underwear*, he thought. To pull off the disguise, he needed to dress the entire part.

He fiddled with the tie. It was red silk, reminiscent of those he wore in the time before. Momentarily, he wondered if he'd forgotten how to tie a Windsor knot, but it came back to him with pure muscle memory. The first attempt was no good, because his neck was thinner now. He got the length correct on the second try.

His heart broke a little seeing himself in the restroom mirror. He looked like his old self. The self that took and kept taking, who hurt people, stealing away homes from families, raiding their retirement accounts for his own gain.

Cud stepped closer to the wall mirror, gazing into his own green eyes. Were these the same eyes? Or was he different now? A better person? Was hiding from the world the right move? He admitted to himself that he avoided self-examination, fearful that the old demon was still lurking.

The man in the mirror had set aside his fortune, hoping to make amends. But it felt like an empty gesture. Giving up comforts was a start. His father had always said the path to true salvation was through active measures, as in good deeds.

His excursion to snoop inside a dead man's safe deposit box didn't seem like a good deed.

Cud backed away from the mirror, his head down. He'd committed to the plan. It was too late to back out now. And besides, perhaps they could solve the case and bring Bob's murderer to justice.

Walking to the bank, he found the note in his jacket pocket. He examined the piece of paper with the account information. In his worn canvas billfold, he noticed his driver's license from the Bahamas had expired three years ago. Normally, a competent bank manager would laugh him out the door with such a pitiful form of identification. But no bank manager would eject a customer with a ten-million-dollar account.

Along the sidewalk, he recognized some folks walking past. He gave them knowing looks, searching their eyes for an unspoken greeting. They didn't acknowledge him. His disguise was effective.

A minute later, the bank was in sight. Cudlow practiced his greeting, using his native accent, whispering to himself. A Brit in a nice suit would surely impress them.

He walked in, his shoulders back, chin up, his suit jacket buttoned. At the teller's window, he asked for the manager. The teller directed him to a guest chair near the front and told him to wait.

Cudlow tried not to fidget. The collar of his shirt strangled him. The sharp unbroken leather of his cognac-stained dress shoes dug into his ankles, despite the slight buffer provided by his thin black socks. He'd forgotten antiperspirant and he could feel the wet circles forming under his jacket. As a reward for his sacrifice, he decided he must get a gelato afterward.

The bank manager appeared and took his seat at the desk, smoothing his tie. "Good afternoon, sir. I'm Samuel. What can I do for you today?"

The man was thin, wearing a short-sleeved white dress shirt and a pink tie with palm trees embroidered on it. His hair was short, his skin dark. He had a gold watch, but not an expensive one. Under the fluorescent lights, he couldn't surmise the man's aura color accurately. This wasn't unusual. Whoever invented this kind of lighting was a monster. Aura colors appeared distorted. Green looked yellow, pink looked purple. He'd need to see Samuel in sunlight for a true reading. But without the aura, he could tell Mr. Jameson was a gentle soul, with an inner glow. The small gold cross around Samuel's neck was a good sign.

Cud shook his head, knowing it was time for some serious play-acting. "Good day, Samuel. I'm looking to obtain a safe deposit box for my valuables. Is this something you could help me with today?"

"Certainly, sir. Do you have an account with us?" Sam looked to his computer screen.

"Why, yes! Cudlow Loughton. L-O-U-G-H…"

Sam typed as he listened. "I've got it here, sir."

Cud slid his driver's license across the desk and waited for the reaction.

Sam looked at Cud, then the screen, then the license, then back at Cud. "Mr. Loughton, thank you for coming in today. Can I get you some coffee or water?"

Cudlow grinned. "Well, a bottled water would be very nice."

"Absolutely." Sam snapped his fingers to the woman at the teller window. "A water for our guest." Sam made another hand gesture to the woman, but Cud didn't know what it meant. Probably something signaling an important customer was in their midst. Yes, it was working.

Sam continued, "Mr. Loughton, as a valued client, we'd be happy to offer one of our premium boxes free for the first year."

"Well, that's very nice of you. But I have what you might call an eccentric request."

"Sir, at Carib Bank we are always happy to accommodate our clients."

Cud smiled. "You might think me a bit daft when you hear this."

"Sir?"

Cudlow bit his bottom lip. This was where the plan become tricky. It was his own idea and he felt clever when he suggested it to Johnnie last night. But now in the light of day, he had his doubts. Still it was a much better idea than Johnnie's plan to simply bribe the man. And hopefully more fun. "Well, do you believe in the afterlife?"

"I believe in the heavenly Kingdom? Why?"

"My mother, deceased for several years now, speaks to me. She guides me in all my financial affairs. At first, I thought I was going off my trolley, you see, but she's always steered me to the best investments. I count her as the reason for my sizable success."

Samuel stared.

Cud assumed he had left the poor man stunned. "Well, yes, I know it sounds bonkers and you think I'm off my proverbial rocker. But the reason I mention this, I'd like to be left in the vault for a few minutes so my mother's spirit can guide me to the select the right box. And unfortunately, mother often won't communicate in front of strangers. If you could simply show me which ones are available, it shouldn't take more than five minutes for her to help me make the sound choice."

Sam looked side to side, around his desk, and at the ceiling.

In a soft voice, Cud said, "I assure you this is not a practical joke or one of those Candid Camera set ups. I understand your reluctance." He got up from the chair. "I can go to another bank if this is a problem."

Samuel burst from his seat. "No! I mean, Sir, this will not be a problem. Let us go look. Follow me."

The bank manager led him to the back and opened the vault room. He pointed to the boxes that were free and wrote their numbers on the back of one of his business cards. "Mr. Loughton, I can't leave the door open for security reasons, but please knock loudly when you are finished. Then we can do the paperwork."

Cudlow smiled. Everything went as he hoped. "Thanks, Samuel. You are a wonderful bloke for indulging me so. Yes, mother was right about you."

The manager scratched his cheek and blinked at him. "She's talked to you about me? Just now?"

"Oh, no. In a dream last night. She said I'd meet a delightful fellow at the bank today."

"Um. Well," Samuel directed his voice into the air, "thank you, Mama Loughton." Samuel looked around the vault and behind him. "I'll leave you now."

After the vault door closed, Cud took Bob's key out of his pocket. It was hard to make out the tiny engraved number. It looked like 33. Could have been 38, 36 or 88. Perhaps he needed reading glasses. He hadn't had a proper eye exam in years. Nor a physical. Yet, he felt more vigor and stamina than in his earlier life. Losing nearly fifty pounds could have that effect.

He tried the box numbers with two-digit sequences with 3's, 6's and 8's. To camouflage the noise, every so often he said loudly, "Mother! I seek your loving guidance! Speak to me!"

The key turned in number 88. He consulted the list of available boxes. Now for the difficult part.

He knocked on the door. "Samuel, I'm ready."

Samuel came in. "Did your mother communicate?"

"No, not yet. She likes odd numbers. Perhaps 89? Could I see the size of it? The interior?"

"Let me get my keys. Come with me."

Cudlow waited at Samuel's desk. The next step was madness. But he'd come this far.

Back in the vault, Samuel put both the customer key and the master key into number 89.

Cudlow took out a paper fan from his pocket and stuffed it up his sleeve. He turned and yelled, "Mother! You're here!"

Samuel turned to look. "Where?"

He pointed to the opposite corner by the vault door. "Don't you see her? The blue light?"

Samuel took a couple steps, tilting his head side to side. "I don't see anything." He returned to his keys.

Cudlow wafted a breeze across the back of Samuel's head and quickly folded and tucked the fan away.

"What was that?"

"Did you feel that? Her presence? Oh, how wonderful."

Samuel's eyes widened. "Yes. Dear Lord."

"Don't be frightened. She said he wants to say hello. Goodness, she never appears to strangers. A high honor. Go to the corner. Please. Shake her hand."

Trembling, the manager stared at the corner.

Cudlow nodded, "She won't bite."

The bank manager turned and put his hand out, scanning as if he was afraid to hit something.

"No take a step further. To the corner." With Samuel looking the other way, Cudlow switched the bank's master key into number 88 and added Bob's key alongside.

When Samuel turned, Cudlow said, "Oh, dear. She's gone again. Well, if you don't mind, I need to summon her again. Allow her to bless the inside of the box. Confirm the choice. Could you be a good sport and give me a couple minutes?"

Samuel grimaced. "Sure. I'll start the paperwork." He walked out of the vault and headed to his desk.

Cudlow opened Bob's box and scanned the contents. A thumb drive, a copy of the Washington Times dated two weeks prior, and a photocopy of a map showing the northern portion of St. John and the east end of Tortola. He took out the newspaper and a folded note fell out. It was addressed to a woman named Mary saying only he was sorry and he loved both her and someone named Robbie.

Should he take the note and somehow deliver it to this Mary person? In that moment, he wished he actually had a deceased mother that could tell him the correct thing to do. Truth was, his mother was living, 99-years old, in the Bahamas at an assisted living community. She'd disowned him when he gave up his fortune. He often assumed his mother survived on a mixture of sheer greed, pettiness, and stubbornness.

Cud took only mental pictures of the newspaper, note, and map. He pocketed the thumb drive.

From outside the vault, Samuel called, "Are you alright in there, Mr. Loughton?"

He raised his voice, "Yes, right as rain." He closed the box, while saying loudly, "Mother, are you with me? Just give me a sign! That is all I ask," to mask the squeak of the box on the metal drawer slides. He scanned the area to ensure no loose ends.

A few seconds later, he exited the vault. "Yes, Samuel, I'm ready."

"Did your mother approve the box?"

Cud said, "Well, wouldn't you know it. Mother wasn't decisive today. That happens sometimes. Well, I'll just have to see if she tells me in a dream tonight." He held up the paper with the box numbers and touched it to his temple with a smile.

"So, um, you won't be selecting a box today?" Samuel retrieved his keys from box 89.

They headed back to Samuel's desk. Cud picked up the bottled water and downed half of it. "Sadly, no box today. My grandfather's Rolex will need to remain in my domicile for another fortnight until Mother decides. She cooperates mostly on the new moon wouldn't you know it. However, Samuel, I would like to make a small withdrawal, if you could help me with that."

"Whatever you need, sir."

"I'll need ten."

"Ten? Thousand?"

"No, just ten dollars. Hmm. Maybe twenty. I plan to get an ice cream and reading spectacles. Yes, that sounds about right."

Samuel walked to the teller and came back with a twenty-dollar bill and a withdrawal slip. "Just sign here."

He signed. As he stood, he looked down at his tie. He couldn't wait to get the blasted thing off. He loosened the knot, pulled it over his head, unwound it flat, and folded it in fourths.

Samuel said, "Anything else I can do? We have some wonderful long-term CD rates." He smiled ear to ear and handed him a brochure.

Cud raised his hand. "No, thank you, Samuel. Here." He handed him the tie. "With great pleasure, I can say I won't be needing this. Perhaps you can make use of it. A gift from mother and me."

The bank manager took the tie and inspected the tag on the back. "Armani? Well. Yes, I will wear it fondly." He beamed and shook Cud's hand.

Cud walked out the door, his hand in one pocket, fondling the plastic orange thumb drive. He could hardly believe he'd done it. Samuel was so nice. Perhaps mother would have really liked him.

The sun beat down on him, heating his suit fabric like a microwave. Down the sidewalk, he stopped at a stone bench, took off his suit jacket, transferred Denise's business card, the thumb drive, and his wallet to his pants pockets, and untied his shoes. He stuffed the jacket and shoes in a rubbish bin.

After obtaining his gelato—mint chocolate chip—he sat on the grass under a nearby palm tree to savor it. Across the street, a steady flow of people sauntered by on the sidewalk. He rubbed the red marks on his ankles. They weren't bleeding but they would be sore for a few days.

What was on the thumb drive? Did it have something to do with Bob's demise? He had half a mind to call Denise and ask to use her hotel's business center. But no, he didn't have shoes now. He didn't want to embarrass her. Instead, he decided to get those reading glasses and drive the scooter back to the beach to see Johnnie.

They could figure out the next steps together.

Dear Diary,

Cud is staying with me again tonight, so I can't write much. The dead guy's brother is an imposter and a punk and I really wanted to punch him today. But I didn't. Plus, I didn't know iguanas liked corn so much. Remind me to bring cheesy puffs tomorrow.

At work, it looked like some folks trampled over the turtle nest, which isn't cool.

Cud did great today. I can't talk about it to you, diary, because it would be ill-advised to write it down. He wasn't supposed to take anything, but the stick thing got me curious. But the files needed a password and now I'm stuck. Cud told me about the map showing the north side but I don't know what it means. This is a real mystery.

Also, Cud talks in a British accent now. Not all the time, but it comes and goes. He's freaking me out and I told him this and he said he'd try harder to be normal. We cut off the sleeves and bottom half of his new pants and he said it made him feel better. Cud also got reading glasses today, and he asked if he could have one of my old paperbacks. He picked the weird novel about a pandemic spread by dogs.

Have a good night, Diary. Your friend, Johnnie.

P.S. It's now the next morning and Cud is still asleep. I need to make a correction. I yelled at Cud last night to stop talking British. It just came out but I think I hurt his feelings. He accepted my apology but then I almost cried, which was worse. After he went to sleep, I went outside to look at the stars and then I cried.

I'm a real rotten person, Diary.

Chapter 8

The sunrise was violently orange, like a volcanic eruption across the sky. As the sun ascended, the color eased into a bright yellow before turning pale blue. A donkey walked by Gertie's driveway with a bell around its neck, and kept walking, heading downhill on the dirt road.

It was Saturday. Johnnie's day off. But he liked to keep to his routine, waking before dawn. While Cud slept, he sat outside on a folding chair, drinking a diet soda, reading a book and watching the day begin. Roosters crowed on and off. The hill behind him was alive and wide awake, with birds and the clacking of crabs rolling downhill.

A few minutes later, Cud appeared, asking for a ride back to Hawksnest, saying something about an appointment in town later. Which was a good idea, because he wanted to pick up something from the tool shed.

They arrived at the beach at seven and there were a dozen cars in the parking lot. A man wearing a brimmed black canvas hat walked the beach with a metal detector, which was strictly forbidden anywhere within park service boundaries. A young couple was necking on a beach blanket by the east end; the sort of public display of affection that made Johnnie's skin crawl. Three middle-aged women on yoga mats talked and stretched their legs near the west end. The Saturday morning class was popular and more folks would arrive soon. A ranger crouched by the turtle nest; his face obscured by his felt Stetson style hat. With cordless power tools at his feet, the ranger tinkered with a molded-plastic box.

Cud said, "Cheerio," waved, and was gone.

Johnnie walked up to the ranger. It was Merv, an okay guy in Johnnie's book, although a little vain. Ranger Merv Hartley was a decade older and a former power-lifter who enjoyed talking about his daily push-up routine. Back in the day, according to Robin's accounts, Johnnie could do a hundred push-ups. Now, he'd rather have all his marbles than arm strength; though in reality, he had neither. Merv was bald, with a five-head and eyes that always looked like they were judging. But in reality, Merv was mostly concerned with himself.

Johnnie asked, "Whatcha doing?"

Merv looked up. "Hey, Johnnie. Kemper asked me to install this wildlife camera. To check for mongoose. Something was digging near the nest."

"Cool. Do you need any help?"

"Isn't it your day off?" Merv checked the batteries in the box, taking them out, inspecting the ends for corrosion.

"Yeah, but I don't have anything else to do." An ache of sadness pricked his thoughts, knowing how true that was. He didn't have a girlfriend. No friends—except for Cud, Robin, and Gertie—and no hobbies except for reading and spear fishing. If he'd had a boat, he would sail around the island every weekend. But owning and maintaining a boat was costly.

Sometimes he played chess online but only because his therapist said games were good for reinforcing neural connections. But he couldn't play role-playing games because of the violence, or poker because it made him angry when a douche sucked out with a lousy hand on the river. Doctor Phillips strictly forbid social media; it was a mine field of hate, intolerance, and stupidity. Or worse, people posted pictures of their glamorous, perfect lives; he hated them the most.

"Okay, if you don't mind. You can hold this in place against the tree while I cinch up the cable lock." Merv pointed up in the palm tree. "I need to point it towards the nest."

"Happy to."

They got down to work.

"Hey, did you see that guy with the metal detector? You should bust him."

Merv shook his head. "He said his wife lost her wedding ring yesterday. The dude looked like he might cry, so I gave him five minutes."

"When did you become a softy?"

"I'm not always a douche." Merv's voice registered annoyance. "The guy seemed like a basket case."

"Nice watch. Is it new?" Johnnie pointed to Merv's gold wrist-watch. It matched the chunky gold ring on his right hand, the one with the black opal center stone.

He quickly placed a hand over the dial. "Thanks. I...inherited it."

"Cool. Anything else I can do?" Johnnie asked.

Merv shrugged. "Nah, I got this. Go have some fun. It's a beautiful day."

Johnnie looked out over the water. No sign of the Goddess. More sailboats dotted the horizon. The holiday crowd was arriving.

"Yeah, I was thinking of doing some fishing." He walked to the tool shed and undid the lock. Merv followed him.

Johnnie took out a three-piece interconnecting spear-fish pole set, bundled together with some wire. The pole itself was fiberglass. The spear had five prongs, roughly six inches long.

"Jesus, Joseph, and Mary! Johnnie!" Merv yelled, his hands clutching his sizeable forehead beneath his brimmed hat. "You can't use that fucking thing in the National Park! Are you crazy?"

"I know." Merv was correct. The National Park's protected waters extended over a mile from the shore.

Merv pointed to the instrument. "Just having it in your possession in the park is illegal. A friggin' five-thousand dollar fine."

"I know, Merv! Fuck. Give me a little fuckin' credit. I confiscated it last week from some ass-hat. Mine broke so I'm taking it back home to Calabash. Unless you want to report me for that too." He bared his teeth at Marv, daring him.

Merv sighed and crossed his arms. "Did you report the guy to Kemper?"

"No. I try not to be a hard guy." Johnnie took a plastic garbage bag from a box in the corner of the shed and dropped the pole bundle inside, twisting the top of the bag and slinging it over his shoulder.

"Dude, you like cheated the government out of that fine money. You should have radioed me or one of the other rangers."

"The government will survive. Look, the guy begged me. And he hadn't used it yet. I caught him before he got two feet into the water. No harm done."

"Fine. I didn't hear or see anything. But you owe me one." He moved away from the shed, gesturing Johnnie to move so he could lock the door again.

"Really? What about the detector guy? Like you're Mr. Perfect?" He also remembered Merv got wasted at the employee Christmas party and demanded everyone challenge him at arm wrestling. It was dumb.

"It was just a figure of speech. Relax, Johnnie." Merv clicked the lock in place.

Johnnie reflected. Yes, he was too spun up. Being called crazy and being yelled at wasn't improving his mood. But Merv was a good guy. He didn't need to be so defensive. "Sure. Sorry. I've had a lot on my mind lately." He sighed. It felt like he was apologizing twenty times a day. Which wasn't wrong, but it meant maybe he needed to talk with Dr. Phillips.

"No problem, bro. See you later." Merv walked away, took his phone out of his pocket and appeared to be dialing.

Johnnie stopped, hoping to listen to Merv's phone call. Was he reporting Johnnie's rule-breaking? After five seconds, he heard Merv say, "Hey, yeah, it's me. Two hundred on the Steelers. Yeah. I'm good for it. I came into some cash."

Time for my exit, Johnnie thought. He walked towards the parking lot. The man in the broad-brimmed hat, the one metal detecting on the beach, walked parallel to him toward the lot, about fifteen feet away. But now, Johnnie recognized him. It was Mark, Bob's phony brother. The way Mark marched with his head down, he didn't seem in good spirits. He stomped the sand like a hippopotamus with a mood disorder.

Johnnie stopped and ducked behind the corner of the rest room. He didn't need another confrontation.

Mark approached a parked black SUV. He pulled out his phone.

Johnnie crept closer, finding some bushes nearby to hide and listen.

"Yeah, it's me. Couldn't find it. Nothing."

After a pause, and a few 'uh huhs', Mark said, "Look, it probably fell out of his pocket into the ocean. I'd say it's gone forever. You really didn't have a backup?... Oh, that was the backup. Well, that sucks. Anything else you want from me?"

Another pause, Mark nodded. "Carib Bank. Good find. I'll need some cash for the manager."

More 'uh huh's'. "Great. I'll check it out." Mark put his phone in his pocket, got into the SUV and sped away.

Johnnie walked to his bike. He strapped the plastic bag with the spear against the side. Only now, he had a decision to make. Go fishing and enjoy the day? Fishing always calmed him down. It would clear his mind and let him think. Or he could try to find some encryption expert to crack the thumb drive.

But where does one even find a computer security geek? He could ask Robin, but she would talk him out of his pursuit and force him to return the thumb drive to the bank. No, he needed to do this on the down-low. And the only person with the resources to help him and keep it quiet was Cud. And Cud was off on some other mystery errand.

He chose fishing.

Heading back to Calabash, along North Shore Road, he got stuck behind a slow, massive truck. Johnnie thought about zipping around the truck, but passing on the island, with the curves and hills, was like playing hot potato with a hand grenade. After five minutes, the vehicle, with its large knobby tires, pulled off toward the Annaberg area. He considered this odd because the area was well within the National Park. Large vehicles, other than Park Service, rarely visited this spot. As it turned, the words on the side of the truck became visible: *Island Engineering Land Surveyors*. After the hurricane, Kemper said some shorelines had moved. Perhaps they were re-surveying the beach.

He crested the next hill. A band of storm clouds to the south were moving fast in his direction. Was this a sign to turn around and hunt down Cud? Surely, the gods or fate wanted him to figure out this mystery.

The voices in his head debated back and forth about how to spend his day. One wanting to fish, the other wanted to find Cud, and a third admonished them both for not calling Dr. Phillips.

Something hit the top of his helmet. Around him, rice-sized shards of ice bounced off the pavement. *Hail.*

It almost never hailed in the Virgin Islands. Maybe once every thirty years. Was the universe trying to tell him something? He pulled his scooter off the side of the road under a tree. The hail grew larger and came down in a torrent, ping-ponging off the pavement violently. A car coming the other way braked, then skidded, nearly running off the road, and down the hillside. Other cars came to a stop. Drivers took pictures through their front windshields. Johnnie ducked further under the branches for protection. The air cooled. The frigid breeze formed gooseflesh on his arms. It seemed like Armageddon.

His phone rang. It was Robin. He hit accept, shielding the phone. "Hey."

"Are you seeing this?"

"Yeah, I was on my bike."

"Are you okay? People are losing their minds in town."

A loud crash of metal boomed.

"Shit. I have to go." Johnnie ran out from tree to discern the source. A stake truck rear-ended a stopped blue sedan. The sedan, now sideways in the road, was dented, its rear wheel at an inoperable angle. Its bumper, cracked and in pieces, laid on the ground. The truck driver got out and appeared uninjured, but quickly realized his mistake and dove back into this cab for cover. The driver of the sedan, a tan surfer-type dude with long blonde hair, did not venture out. A wise choice considering the chaos. *Was it Fabio?* Johnnie squinted trying to see if the Goddess was in the vehicle. But no, Fabio was alone. If it was in fact, *the* Fabio. He had no way of knowing.

After another minute, the hail stopped and heavy rain followed, with the intensity of a car wash. He wanted to get home, get out of his soaked uniform, put on dry clothes and read in bed. If he felt up to it later, he'd call his therapist. The thin rain poncho he stored under the seat of his scooter did little to help as he took King Hill Road to avoid the more well-traveled Centerline Road. Sideways rain plastered him in the face, messing up his glasses. He encountered more vehicles stopped in the road and wove around them. Drivers gave him looks of incredulity. One driver, Mr. Bravos from the local market, rolled down his window, shouting an offer of a ride home. Johnnie waved him off and kept going. In his mind, he berated himself for not installing the replacement headlight. *Was he even visible to oncoming vehicles?*

Twenty minutes later, Johnnie was home. Soaked like a drowned rat, but relieved. The rain had let up except for a few stray drops and the clouds to the south had dissipated with pockets of blue sky and beams of sunshine searing through.

Gertie watched him through her screen door, shaking her head. "Johnnie, do you need some towels?"

He focused his gaze toward the back of the house. His two bath towels, the ones he and Cud used this morning, were still hanging on the clothes line, evidently soaked. No one had expected it to rain. Still, one more dumb move.

Johnnie stowed his helmet in the under-seat compartment of his scooter and walked up to her door. "I would sure appreciate that."

She cupped her hand under his chin, "Let's look at you. Hmm, mmm.

Wet as a newborn." She released him. "Come in. Stay by the door." She disappeared into her bedroom.

Before he entered, he took off his yellow poncho and flicked the rain drops off. He wrung out his T-shirt and ran his hands over his hair, easing the water out. He stepped inside. A puddle formed on the floor around his sneakers. The house smelled like warm bread.

"Are you baking today, Gertie?"

She came back with two fluffy yellow terry-cloth towels and handed them to him. "I'm making lemon squares for the Church bake sale tomorrow. Would you like one?"

"No, thanks. Save them for a better cause. I'll wash the towels and bring them back tomorrow."

Gertie, wearing a floral blouse and white cropped jeans, beamed at him. "I didn't see you leave this morning. Is Cudlow staying over again? I find him charming."

"I think he's staying…at his own place tonight." *Did Gertie know Cud was homeless and living on the beach?* It wasn't his place to say.

"Well, tell him he's always welcome. Do you have his phone number?"

Johnnie unfolded a towel and wiped his face. "He doesn't own a phone." An accurate statement.

"No phone?" She rested her hand across her cheek and shook her head. "How does one reach him? I want to invite him to church tomorrow. Remember how he talked about God's creation at dinner the other night? I bet he would love Pastor Lillian."

He had no recollection of a discussion about god or religion, but he had been preoccupied and worried about their bank scheme. Maybe he had spaced out. Or maybe it was the delicious mashed potatoes consuming his attention. "If I see him, I'll give him your number."

She rested her hand on his arm. "Yes, would you? Thank you, dear."

He nodded, looking at the puddle on the rust-colored tile floor. "Sorry for the mess." In a circle around him, sprinkles of water penetrated the grout lines.

She waved him off. "It's fine. Go get dry."

Johnnie went to his garage apartment. Gertie's shutters—the ones she had painted kelly green—rested in a stack against the outside wall, reminding him he needed to hang them soon. He closed his door, turned on the overhead light, stripped off his wet uniform, and wrapped himself in the towels.

"Alexa, playlist three." List three was for his sullen moods. Not that he was sad. But he wanted something different from classical. The Bruce Springsteen song, Atlantic City, played softly, and he sang quietly along.

The thumb drive had to be super important. It was still inside his bedside drawer. But perhaps that wasn't secure enough. He scanned the room for a hiding spot. The thumb drive was ruggedized according to what Cud told him, meaning it could withstand nearly anything. As in, he could bury it in the back yard and it would be fine. But with his faulty memory, that wouldn't be a good plan.

He remembered how thoroughly that detective tossed his apartment in Miami after they arrested him for aggravated vehicular assault. Nearly every surface touched, every cushion torn open, every cereal box emptied.

But what good was having the thumb drive if he didn't know the password?

He knew nothing about Bob. Then it occurred to him. The one thing they had in common.

Could it be that simple?

He brought his laptop to his bed and propped up two pillows behind his back. He stuck the drive into his laptop. Accessing the drive, a window popped up asking for the password.

Trying several catch phrases, like 'Looney Tunes' and "Rabbit Season', he typed the correct password on the tenth try. A directory appeared, listing only one file, an excel spreadsheet file titled 'registration numbers'.

The spreadsheet had three columns of ten-character long, alpha-numeric numbers. No headings, descriptions, notes, or formulas. It made no sense.

How could this be so important?

Johnnie unplugged the thumb drive and taped it behind his wall calendar. The one item undisturbed during the Miami shake-down.

He didn't know what the numbers meant, but he hoped that Cud would know.

* * *

Dear Diary,

I started reading a new book this afternoon and forgot to call Dr. Phillips. Robin called tonight and said she won't help me the next time I get in trouble if I don't call by Monday.

So, I have to do it.

Hail fell from the sky today. Which made me wonder if the world is ending. Robin said it's just weather. She's probably right.

Gertie seems infatuated with Cud. Except I worry, what if it doesn't work out between them? My marriage didn't survive. And my parents got divorced. And Robin's divorced also.

Maybe people aren't meant to stay together. Although if I met the Goddess in person, I would try to win her heart. She takes my breath away. But I don't deserve someone as perfect as her.

Anyway, tomorrow I'm going to find Cud in the morning and tell him about Gertie's invite to church. And maybe he'll know what the numbers mean. It might be some kind of spy code. Cud said he used to be good at numbers. Since the accident, adding fractions messes me up. But that's another story.

Wish me luck with the doc tomorrow. And remind me to buy extra towels and install the new headlight.

Goodnight Diary, Johnnie.

Chapter 9

Cud woke with the sunrise. Hues of pink and pale blue lit up the sky, and birds chattered about everything and nothing. He eased up from the boogie board he called a bed and the stack of palm leaves he wove into a pillow. The wind whipped his hair across his eyes. Stretching his legs and arms upward, he heard his vertebrae pop.

He dusted ants and sand off his hairy legs and from between his knobby toes. Parched, he drank a bottled water he purchased with his fruit sales yesterday. His sales were high yesterday, hauling in twenty-one dollars. A strong sign that holiday travelers had arrived.

Cud brushed his teeth and rinsed out his mouth with bottled water. He hadn't been to a dentist in five years, and he paid close attention for any toothaches or gum bleeds. Arranging his last visit to the dentist was difficult, requiring Jackson's intervention. It was embarrassing and he never wanted another root canal. In his opinion, being homeless was one thing, but being homeless with rotten teeth was another. He still had his dignity.

He ambled down to the shoreline for his ablutions, wearing only his new boxers, carrying a 'found' beach towel and his new shampoo. Trunk Bay, less than a mile to the east, had public showers, but he wasn't a fan and the beach was often more crowded. One time he stepped on a piece of glass at the public shower, which also soured the experience. Bathing in the sea held more appeal.

Stumpy ran towards him, staging himself in Cud's path.

"Good morning, Stumps old friend."

The iguana gazed up, moving his head side to side, mouth gaping. He reached out with one clawed foot into the air.

"Come see me after. I need to wash." Cud pointed to the water and side-stepped to continue his trek.

Stumpy hunkered down in place, his stare glued on Cud.

Cud called back, "Good boy."

He dipped a toe in the surf. The water was cool, or perhaps it was the unusually windy weather that made it seem so. Cud squeezed a small dollop of the shampoo into his palm, which was reef-friendly and sulfate free. He left the bottle next to his towel and entered the water. He dunked his head backward, scrubbing his scalp. Even a tiny amount of shampoo made a noticeable difference in his hair.

Cud waded in further, relaxing into a floating position, facing the sky. His now silky locks floating around his face. Closing his eyes—his ears just below the surface—he drifted with the tide and gave thanks to the universe for another day to experience all Earth's goodness.

A few moments later, splashing and yelling disturbed his reverie. He righted himself in the shallow water and looked at the beach. Three young men in their 20s were throwing a football in the surf, only a few feet away, as if they hadn't noticed him there.

But another voice caught his attention. Johnnie was calling out, "Cud! Cud!"

Being Sunday, Johnnie wasn't here for work, evidenced by his casual attire. *What could he want?* Cud hitched up his wet boxers and pressed his feet against the sand, exiting the ocean.

"Good morning," he sang out. "A truly wonderful one."

Johnnie wore a frown and stared at the sand. "Jesus, Cud."

"What's wrong?" He walked toward his towel.

"Look at yourself."

Cud's soaked white boxers were nearly translucent, leaving nothing to the imagination. While nudity on St. John beaches was prohibited, he wasn't technically naked. "Ha! The old twig and berries. There they are! Oh, my, you should see your face."

Johnnie sighed and scratched his collarbone. "Put on your towel. I can't talk to you like this."

Cud heard some laughing. The men with the football snickered in their direction.

"Fine, but God made us all perfect." He wiped his face with the towel and then wrapped it around his waist.

"That's why I'm here. Gertie wants to know if you'd like to go to church with her today. The service is at 9:30 and then after, she's manning a table at the bake sale."

"Is there a dress code?" Cud began walking back to his nest. Stumpy shot out of a nearby bush to follow him.

Johnnie also followed. "I don't know. But probably shirt and shoes required."

Cud laughed and shimmied. "And pants!"

"Do you want to go? I can take you to my place to clean up more. Then you can drive with her to the church."

"Jolly good. Let's get cracking!" Cud smiled, then winced. He was doing it again with the British accent. "Sorry. It comes and goes."

"You know what? You talk however you want. I was just in a bad mood before."

"Thank you for that." Cud combed his wet hair, put on his day clothes and flip flops, a green and a blue one, and grabbed his satchel. He selected a banana fig from his bag, cut it into quarters and threw it to Stumpy. "Okay, let's go." Cudlow walked a few steps and stopped. "No. Wait. I have a gift for Gertie." He rifled through a handful of colorful stones next to his cooler and picked out a pale pink one, the size of silver dollar "Sea glass. For her garden."

Johnnie smiled. "I think she'll like it."

They walked toward the parking lot.

Johnnie said, "Hey, I figured out the password for the stick thing last night."

Cud said, "What? That's fantastic. What did you find?"

"A spreadsheet with a bunch of numbers and letters. Could you look at them before you go out with Gertie?"

"Oh, I'd be honored to."

"I wrote one down." Johnnie fished into his back pocket and pulled out a folded wad of paper. "Here."

Cud inspected the long key code. He instantly knew what it was. At least, he was ninety-eight percent certain. "Were all the numbers the same length?"

"Nah, seemed to be three different lengths. The file name was registration something."

This confirmed his suspicion. These were the sort of numbers that spelled big trouble. Trouble that Johnnie had no concept of.

When they arrived at the scooter, Cud lied. "Looks like license codes for software. Maybe someone kept their software registration info on the drive. Ordinary stuff."

Johnnie hung his head. "Dang. But what if it's a secret code that reveals a message? Like when you substitute one's for the letter A?

Something that explains why Bob was killed?"

"Sorry, man. If it is a secret message, it would take a thousand years to crack, because there are so many digits." This part was mostly true.

"Okay, I had to ask. Let's go."

"How did you figure out the password?"

Johnnie laughed. "The key-chain. I figured if Bob was a Bugs Bunny fan, he might use something from the show as his password."

Cud needed to see the contents of the thumb drive. Because if his instincts were accurate, someone might come looking for this drive. And they would have inordinate reasons not to give up searching.

"What was it? The password?"

"Ha! What Daffy always called Bugs."

"Sorry, I don't believe they showed that cartoon where I grew up."

Johnnie stopped when he got to the scooter. He smiled, which was rare. "Turned out the password was one of my favorite words as a kid."

"Just tell me." Cud grabbed Johnnie's shoulder. "Spit it out, man!"

Johnnie handed his extra helmet to Cud and took a seat on the Pig. He grinned. "You'll see."

* * *

When they arrived at Johnnie's, Cud examined the file with the numbers on Johnnie's laptop. It was what he assumed. He scratched his stubbled chin to think. But he had little time before heading to church with Gertie.

"Johnnie," Cud said, "this looks like nonsense to me. You should just toss it in the trash."

His friend, leaning against the kitchen counter, put down the dish he was cleaning and shook his head. "No. No way. I heard that Mark guy on the phone. He's going to search the safe deposit box tomorrow, if he can bribe the manager. There has to be something important on this thing." He put away the dish and walked over to look at the file over Cud's shoulder.

"Hmm." Cud scratched his scalp. This bit of information was not helping. In fact, if Johnnie pursued his investigation, things could go very wrong.

"Well?"

"I'll tell you what, chap." Cud closed the file and pulled out the thumb drive. "There are a few more things I could check out. Can't promise anything. Can I take this with me and I'll look it over at Gertie's later?"

John walked to his bed and chose a book off the nightstand. "You're not going back to the beach after church?" He fluffed up a couple pillows and reclined in bed.

"If I count myself lucky, and I do, I'm going to finagle an early Sunday supper from Gertie. I must say, I could get used to hot meals again." He pocketed the thumb drive.

"Sure. Sounds good." Johnnie didn't look up from his book.

Cud went to the bathroom and combed his hair until the tangles dispersed. After shaving his face smooth, he washed his armpits with water and soap at the sink. That helped. His once impeccable clothes he wore to the bank were now dirty and the fabric had unraveled along the edges where they had unceremoniously cut off the pants bottoms and shirt sleeves. "Johnnie," Cud called.

"What?"

"Can I borrow a clean shirt?"

"Of course."

He padded out in his mismatched flip-flops and took a polo shirt from Johnnie's pile on the clothes rack. It was emerald green, like his eyes.

"How do I look?"

Johnnie flipped down his book. "Fine."

"Okey-dokey. I'm heading to Gert's. See you when I see you." Cud headed out without waiting for a goodbye. He felt for the thumb drive in his pocket. If anything, he needed to find out what it was worth. Because it might be worthless, meaning all the anxiety he was feeling could be for naught.

He rang Gertie's doorbell.

She came to the door wearing a blue sheath dress with a long necklace of freshwater pearls. Her aura was slightly different. Bluer today. Enlightened souls often, he noticed, matched their outer garments or accessories to their inner feelings. Blue was a color of love, emotions, spirituality. Which made sense for a church day. He hoped it also meant she had feelings for him.

He stepped inside. "Gertie, you make the rainbows weep with envy." He took her hand, kissing the top of it.

She blushed. "I've never heard that compliment before."

"Hmm, I haven't either." He rubbed his newly smooth chin. "But it means you look ravishing."

"You look nice, too. The T-shirt brings out your eyes." She gave him a side smile.

Cud sighed. "I dare say I could look into your soulful eyes all day, but I suppose we must get going."

"Cudlow, I meant to ask, are you free to stay after the service and help me at the bake sale? I know this is last minute." She walked to the counter to pick up a circular plastic Tupperware container covered in plastic wrap.

"My dear, I can't think of a better afternoon."

Gertie beamed, "I was hoping you'd say that."

Cud held his breath as he dared to inquire about dinner. He hoped she still had some pecan pie left. "In fact, you can have me to yourself all day in exchange for supper later." He stepped outside and held the screen door open for her. "I loved your cooking and your company and have thought of little since. Oh, before I forget. I brought you a small something."

As she stood in the doorframe, he handed her the sea glass. "It isn't much, but I wanted to repay your hospitality. Beauty for a beautiful woman."

Gertie balanced the Tupperware on one arm, taking the stone in the other; she held it up to examine it in the daylight. He searched her face. *Did she notice the heart?* He had scratched a heart shape in the center of the pebbly surfaced glass. The heart was faint, small, and misshapen, but the best he could do with his new pocket knife.

She tilted her head and squinted. "Cudlow, are you sweet on me?"

"Gertie, I would never be so forward." He swallowed hard. "But, yes, I would very much like to pursue a courtship. If, by chance, you could develop feelings for someone like me." His face felt red. *Had he gone too far?*

Gertie's wide chestnut eyes met his. She dropped the plastic container on the ground. Baked squares scattered along the grass like odd mushrooms; the circular tub rolled away from the door. She took Cud's face in her hands and planted a kiss.

Rockets went off in Cud's chest. He hadn't been touched, no less kissed, like that in ten years. Not since before his wife's diagnosis of late stage cancer. He placed his hand on the back of her neck and returned her kiss. *Was this really happening?*

After a few seconds, birds descended on the lemon squares, pecking at them in earnest, somehow unconcerned by the proximity of humans.

Gertie broke the kiss and laughed. "See, they aren't going to waste."

Cud looked at the birds. They were diminutive, gray with yellow heads. One of them bounced up and into the house. The rest of the flock perked up, glancing toward the open door, bobbing their heads sideways as if intrigued and getting ready to follow the first one's lead.

She waved excitedly, "Come in, shut the door!"

Cud closed the screen door tight and latched it. Their eyes followed the bird which landed on the counter, then flew to the rafters, then landed on the high ceiling fan, causing it to rotate slowly; the bird held on and stared at them, seeming to enjoy his merry-go-round ride and position of power.

Gertie shuddered, "We need to get him out." She yelled, "Shoo! Go bird!"

As they stood shoulder to shoulder under the fan, the bird dropped a poo on the front of Gertie's dress.

Cud laughed, "He told you off."

"Dang." Gertie unzipped her dress, revealing a light blue satin slip, and walked to the kitchen sink to rinse out the spot. "There's a broom by the back door. See if you can shoo him out. But don't let his friends in."

"I'll try not to hurt him." With the broom he swished it in the air near the fan blades, but couldn't reach. The bird didn't move. Cud found the wall switch, powering the fan on. The bird swooped down and flew in circles around the room. It smacked its head into the picture window.

"Oh, dear. Gertie? I may have killed it." He found it behind the sofa and cradled it in his palm.

She padded over in her bare feet, still in her slip. "Goodness." Gertie brushed a finger over its head. The bird opened its eyes and burst from Cud's hand in a crazed flutter, flying into Gertie's bedroom.

They followed it inside and closed the door. The bird perched on her dresser mirror. Gertie opened the double-hung window facing the backyard. "Go on, shoo!"

The yellow-headed intruder stared at them for a brief second before flying out. Gertie shut the window, closed the roller shade, and collapsed backward onto the bed. Cud took a seat beside her. With the commotion over, he surveyed the room. Her bedroom was feminine, with embroidered pillows, white-washed furniture, and a lamp with a butterfly shade. The room was cool and dark.

Gertie sighed. "Do you believe in omens?"

"How so?" He laid down next to her, on his side, his face several inches from hers.

"My momma used to tell me that a bird entering your house has meaning. If it's white, it means good news. If it's black, it means death."

"But it was gray."

"Yes. So…what does that mean?" She stared at the ceiling.

Cudlow chuckled, "As long as it isn't death, I'll take it as a good sign."

"You're sweet." She touched his face and kissed him.

The kiss continued and grew in intensity.

Her aura was red now and he felt a stir. Cud sat up. "I think we should get going."

"Cudlow, at our age, life is short." She pulled on his shirt, forcing him on his back.

"Yes, but what about church? And the bake sale?"

Gertie wedged her body next to his and brushed his hair off his forehead. "God will understand."

He traced her shoulder with his fingertips. Her eyes sparkled like the moon. Prettier than any star-filled sky he'd ever slept beneath. Caressing her hair, lost in her dark irises, he said, without forethought, "I love you, Gertie."

She whispered, "Show me."

He wrapped his arms around her, every vein in his body desperate for her touch, his mind succumbing to the moment, as if he were bathing in the ocean under the midnight sky.

It wasn't church, but he was in heaven and felt saved.

After Cudlow went to Gertie's, Johnnie read a book for a couple hours, then prepped for his therapy session with Dr. Phillips. He checked his laptop's camera and speaker. All were working. He stacked books on top of his coffee table trunk to get the right camera angle. *Should he greet her with a smile?* "Good afternoon, Doctor Phillips," he practiced, assessing his image. His gummy smile looked dumb.

It was a minute until one o'clock. He entered the online meeting. His therapist was already there, early as usual.

She waved. "Hello, Johnnie. How are things in paradise?" She wore a plain white cotton T-shirt, no make-up and her medium-length wavy blond hair clipped up in a twist.

Doctor Louella Phillips, Lou to nearly everyone, always started their sessions with this greeting. Perhaps it was her way of reminding him how well he had it in life. Or maybe she was a tinge jealous. It wasn't uncommon for main landers to imagine life in the Virgin Islands was always idyllic. Still, he never knew how to answer that.

"I'm fine."

The smile vanished from her face. "Your sister called me Friday. Do you want to tell me what's going on?"

No. No, he didn't. "Last Monday I arrived at work and found a dead guy washed up on the beach. Did my sister mention that?"

"Robin said you had a possibly traumatic discovery. That must have been awful. Can you tell me about your feelings when you found him?"

"I didn't feel anything. I mean, it sucked that he died. But I didn't know him."

"You've seen deceased people before, on deployment, right?"

"Yep. A few."

"Did seeing this person—"

"Bob. Well, not his real name. But that's what I call him."

"Did seeing him remind you of the deaths you'd seen before? Bring back any upsetting memories?"

Johnnie had to think about that one. "No. Bob was all bloated and mushy. The other dead folks I saw were skinny and bloody, and their faces were clear and recognizable."

"Okay, so what happened then?"

"Not much. The next day was my birthday."

"Yes! Right! Happy Birthday. How was that?"

"Good. I went to lunch with Robin. And Gertie made me a nice present." He grinned, "Something besides a bookmark."

"Did you get into any altercations or expressed anger this week?"

He recalled his interaction with Mark and the rude teenage boys. "No. I wanted to. A couple times. A dude got up in my face. But I did all the calming exercises and it worked out."

"If finding a deceased person didn't upset you, why do you think your sister is so concerned?"

"I don't know."

Lou sighed. "I normally don't do sessions on Sundays. I think you're holding back something important and frankly, I thought we were past this nonsense." Lou took off her round tortoiseshell glasses and rubbed the bridge of her nose. A doorbell rang in the background. "Hold on." Lou rolled her wheelchair out of frame. He heard some voices—hers and another woman's—and some rustling noise. After a few seconds, she rolled back in front of the computer. "Sorry, Ann got home from the grocery store and I forgot I left the deadbolt on. Now, Johnnie, why do you think Robin is so concerned?"

"I...I don't know. I don't remember." He felt sweat pour from his pits and his forehead looked shiny on the inset image on the screen. He looked like a liar, which he was, and Lou was a famously good bullshit detector. Maybe he should come clean. But the truth would still seem ridiculous.

"We've talked about this. Lying to me is a one-way road."

A one-way road meaning a one-way ticket to another doctor. Because he had lied to her before. In fact, many times. In her frustration, she dropped him, referring him to another therapist on St. Thomas. That guy was a complete disaster, experimenting on him with combinations of medications that would stun a horse. But in his case, they led to a complete psychotic break, culminating in the ferry incident during his first year on the island. Johnnie begged Lou to take him back. And she did, but with strict conditions.

"It's really a silly misunderstanding." Johnnie rubbed the back of his neck. He recalled his embarrassment at the bank. "I'm not sick, but I don't want to get into more trouble."

"If you are afraid of new medication, I promise I won't push it."

"I know. If I tell you everything, you can't rat me out, right? Doctor-client privilege and all?"

She pursed her lips. "You didn't kill this person, right?"

He flipped his hands in the air and rolled his eyes. "No, come on."

"Then, yes. You can trust me."

He took a deep breath and closed his eyes. His voice seemed disembodied to himself. "I found a safe deposit box key on Bob and tried to access it at the bank, because there is this weird brother guy that isn't like a real brother and I needed to know if the box had anything in it about why Bob was murdered."

She shook her head. "Okay, slow down. One more time, but I need you to breathe normally."

He relayed the story about visiting the bank and the bank manager calling the Chief, who then called Robin. "So, I lied to Robin about having a weird dream and now they all think I'm deranged."

"I see. What do you think? Do you feel deranged?"

"Maybe a little. But more curious than unstable."

"Got it." She leaned her head back and stared at the ceiling as if she was in deep thought.

"Well, aren't you going to say anything else?"

She took a deep breath. "I think you're telling me the truth. Thank you. Let me ask you a few more routine questions."

"Sure."

"Are you having any suicidal thoughts recently?"

"I did once this week. Right after the bank thing. But it left quickly."

Lou leaned closer to the camera. "Tell me about that."

"I was mad at myself. I took a swim and felt better. I didn't try anything."

She appeared to be writing. "Are you sleeping and eating well?"

"Pretty good. Robin got me Mallomars for my birthday. I ate half for dinner the other night and felt foggy in the morning."

"Any sleep-walking, nightmares or night terrors?"

"No."

"Vision, motor skills, energy levels?"

"Vision is the same. Motor skills fine. Energy is good, but I'm still taking mid-day naps sometimes on weekends."

Lou wrote a few notes in a book resting on her lap. "Are you planning—or thinking about—any more stunts like the bank visit?"

"No. I hit a dead end. I mean, sorry. No, I don't have any leads to follow, so that's about it."

She tapped her pen against her chin. "Right. Hmm. As you know, lying to Robin is counterproductive. She's genuinely afraid for you. How are you going to fix this?"

Telling Robin the truth might make her worry more. "I can't tell her the truth about the safe deposit box key."

"Why not?"

"She'd be angry."

"I think she's already upset."

How was he going to fix this? "What if I write her a letter? Explaining?"

"That would be a good start. Honesty is the only way to real health. Alright. I want to talk to you again on Friday to follow-up. Is four-thirty good for you?"

"Yes, Friday. I can make it."

"Great. Keep up your journaling. If you hit any dark patches, call or email me. Before we disconnect, tell me three things that you're grateful for or that made you happy this week."

She always ended sessions this way. Sometimes he couldn't think of positive things when he was in a dark mood. But today, the list rolled off his tongue. "I'm grateful for you, and Cud and my new spearfishing pole."

Lou smiled. "I'm grateful for you, too." In the background, Ann came up behind Lou and wrapped her arm around Lou's shoulders, looking into the camera. Ann had olive skin, short brunette hair and a pin-up tattoo on her upper arm. "Hey, Johnnie, did Lou tell you how she did in the half-marathon yesterday?"

Johnnie winced at forgetting, "No. I forgot you were training for that. How was it?"

Lou shook her head. "Sorry, Ann's always bragging on me. I came in second in the women's pushrim division."

"Congratulations." He recalled Lou won a similar event last year but not the details. When Lou wasn't treating patients, she was in the gym pumping iron.

Ann said, "She's a beast." She wrinkled her nose and made a howling noise, [RA-ROO!], then kissed Lou's head.

Johnnie smiled. "I worry sometimes she's going to get on a plane and whoop my ass." He did a mental check. Yes, that was an actual worry.

Lou said, "Alright, enough you two. Johnnie, always a pleasure. Bye."

And the call was over. Johnnie let out a deep breath and flopped sideways on the sofa, staring at the ceiling. He didn't really want to write a letter to Robin. He understood why he should, but self-reflection led to self-doubt, which led to self-pity and loathing.

Johnnie picked up the paperback he'd been reading, a story about a young woman who was the lone survivor of a space-ship attack. The protagonist was funny and daring but, most importantly, knew who she was and what she wanted in life; in her case, seeking revenge on a band of galactic pirates.

He enjoyed losing himself in that other world for a while.

Writing the letter to Robin could wait.

* * *

Dear Diary,

I talked to Dr. Lou today and it went okay. But the real news is crazy. I knocked on Gertie's door this evening to return her towels and apologize for forgetting about helping with the shutters, and Cud was there, walking to the kitchen in his boxers. I guess they're an item now.

I'm happy for Gertie and Cud, but now I wonder if they'll forget about me. That's what happens. Like when dad left mom and moved away to live with his girlfriend.

I started writing the letter to Robin, but it made me feel like crap, because after everything she's done for me, she deserves better. I may have to tell her everything if I can work up the courage. Maybe she'll laugh. It is a little funny. But then I might have to tell her about Cud and the stick thing, and that would get him in trouble, which would be wrong.

See, Diary, this is why lies never work.

Anyway, I'm going to bed early. I'm having a bad headache.

Love, Johnnie.

Chapter 10

Not again.

Why this beach?

Another body. This time, it was a young woman. It was still very dark out. Just five o'clock. She wasn't water-logged like Bob. She was face down in the sand, with a machete in her back. Her long dark hair floated and then fell with each ebb of the tide.

Johnnie wondered if he should name her as well. But somehow, this death was different. Giving her a random name felt insensitive...wrong. He called the police.

Operator: "What is the nature of your emergency?"

"I'm at Hawksnest Beach. I found a deceased woman."

Operator: "Johnnie, is that you? It's Janice."

"Hey, Janice. Could you tell Tobias?"

"Sure. Did you check the woman's pulse?"

"No, I didn't touch her. Should I check? She has a machete through her torso."

"Oh. Oh, I see. Just wait. An officer will be there shortly."

"Thanks, Janice."

"Bye, Johnnie. Be good now."

He needed to call his boss next.

She answered on the sixth ring. "Good morning, Johnnie." Her voice sounded weak, like maybe he woke her up, but also sad, like she'd been crying.

"Kemper, it happened again." He walked in a small circle, carving a path in the sand, keeping an eye on his boots and the imprint they made.

"Sorry, what happened?"

"I arrived early this morning because I couldn't sleep. I was getting ready to comb the beach and there was a young woman, dead, on the shoreline. Close to where the other one was. The police are on their way."

There was a pause. "Johnnie, I'll be there soon. Don't touch anything."

"Yes, ma'am."

Kemper hung up.

He looked around. He was alone at the beach. The moon was low in the sky, reflecting off the water like twinkling Christmas lights. Serene despite the situation. He looked toward Cud's nest, wondering if Cud would ever come back or if he planned to move in with Gertie.

He sat on the sand cross-legged about fifteen feet from the victim. *Who was she? Who would do that to her? Did she have ID on her?* He resisted urges to check her pockets for information. Because that got him into trouble with Bob. He rocked back and forth, sitting on his hands. *No, he couldn't look for clues. Couldn't.* A Sesame Street song popped into his head. *One of these things is not like the other...not like the other...not like the other.* He hummed along.

After a few of minutes, sirens wailed in the distance.

Should he greet the police in the parking lot? Or keep an eye on the woman? A wave of guilt washed over him, as if he did something wrong that led to the woman's death. He knew it made little sense, but the feeling was strong. But sometimes he felt the cause of all bad things.

Would Tobias look at him — peer into his soul—and make the same conclusion? That he had something to do with this murder?

Johnnie shook his head. He rose to his feet and walked toward the parking lot. Two police vehicles pulled in and parked diagonally across the lot. He approached their headlights.

One officer opened his door, training a gun at Johnnie. "Put your hands in the air!"

Two of the officers from the other vehicle exited, crouched behind their doors, also aiming their guns at him.

He put his hands in the air. "I'm Johnnie Crosswell. I called it in." *Could they not see his uniform?*

The officers kept their stance. The first one said. "Remain as you are."

Another vehicle pulled in. A black SUV with a white emblem. The chief's car.

Officer one walked up to Johnnie. "Get on the ground. Face down."

"Sir, I work for the Park Service." He relaxed his arms to his sides. "Come, I'll show you the victim." He turned his head toward the beach.

Behind him, he heard running. He turned.

The officer unhitched his baton and hit him across the stomach.

Johnnie clutched his mid-section and crumpled to the ground, rolling into a ball. The officer kicked him in the chest.

Johnnie braced his arms around his head. He couldn't take a blow to his cranium. Not with the weak spot. A doctor told him one strike could be a death blow. "Stop! Ow. Motherfu—"

A hulking figure walked up, standing over him.

Johnnie's glasses were missing. He couldn't make out the man's features, but he knew it was Chief Tobias from the stench of cheap aftershave.

"Johnnie Crosswell."

Johnnie remained frozen in a ball. "Sir. Fuck you."

Tobias said to the first officer, "Put him in restraints and take him to the station."

Game over. He heard Robin's voice in his head, 'Don't fight'. Johnnie began counting in his head and laid down on his stomach, his hands behind his back, waiting for the cuffs. A familiar move from his days in Miami.

His mind raced, evaluating the repercussions. If Robin was mad before, she'll be blazingly furious now. He had to clam up. At least that's what Robin would want until she could get him a proper lawyer. *How much was this going to cost him?* A shit-load. In that moment, he despised Tobias. Wanted to spit in his face as they led him to the back of the police car.

Why couldn't it be Tobias in the surf with the machete?

In the back of the police car, he waited. And waited. He touched his skull in the spot with the bone graft. It seemed fine. Months into his recovery, Robin told him the hospital used bone from his pelvis to patch up his busted skull. She teased him affectionately that he was literally a butthead; it became a running joke. Sometimes they joked about brain farts. The thought made him chuckle.

The sun rose. He saw Kemper's truck arrive. Maybe she could talk sense to Tobias.

Sitting in the back of the patrol car felt like he was watching a drive-in movie with a broken speaker, but a strange one where the actors were all talking about him. He couldn't hear much of what they said. From Kemper's body language, she seemed aggravated at Tobias. She waved to Johnnie.

He nodded back.

Through the glass, he heard her muffled voice call out, "I called your sister."

He mouthed, "Thank you."

More waiting. The coroner's vehicle arrived.

A few minutes later, officer one returned to the police car and drove him to the station in Cruz Bay.

He hated jail. If he had a book to read, it wouldn't be so bad. But the chances of them giving him something to read were slim.

With each deep breath to calm himself, his ribs ached. He ran his hands gingerly across the painful spots on his back, feeling for misaligned bones. *Would they let a doctor check him out?* He prayed Robin would be at the station when he arrived.

She would know he was innocent.

Because if she didn't, he was screwed.

Kemper helped Merv put cones outside the parking lot, directing visitors away. Her brain went through the mental gymnastics of trying to understand how there could be two dead bodies in as many weeks. This wouldn't bode well for her monthly operations report. *What was going on?*

A policeman with a nametag 'Roberts' walked up to them. "Ma'am, are there any security cameras on the property?"

Kemper stood, feet apart, and winced. "No, sorry." Given some recent thefts and the pile of bodies, she wondered if she should put cameras in next year's budget.

"Just checking. We'll be out of here shortly. Let you reopen by noon." He tipped his hat at her.

"Thanks, officer." She chewed on a hangnail.

Officer Roberts waved and walked away.

Merv turned to her and whispered, "Do you think he did it? I mean, I know he lost some of his marbles in Afghanistan, but killing a woman? Heck, maybe he misses killing people. Like he developed a taste for bloodshed. Did you ever see Platoon? The quiet ones are always guilty."

Kemper narrowed her eyes. "He's shy. Do you even know what

happened to him?"

"No, explain it to me."

"Before I hired him, I had a long talk with his sister. God, I don't know if I should tell you. John's so private."

"Come on. I work with the guy. I need to know if he's a serial killer! I mean, what if I say something wrong to him and he," Merv made a cutting gesture across his neck, "filets me like a halibut? Geez, the guy has severe anger problems. I see him give the finger to visitors all the time. And the other day? I thought he was going to fight me."

She gave him a stern look. "Merv, I'm glad you could get here on such short notice but I think it's best if we reserve judgement and wait for the facts."

"No. No way. Come on. What's his story?"

Kemper scraped her fingernail across her teeth. *Would it be a betrayal?* Maybe if more people knew the truth it might help?

She waggled her finger at him. "Fine, but you can't tell anyone else."

"Sure, no problem-o." Merv grinned, his arms crossed.

Kemper drew a deep breath, hoping to get the story correct. It had been years since the conversation with Robin.

"He was in a peace-keeping unit. Five years ago, his team was escorting an American congressional delegation through Kandahar when a Taliban vehicle came up behind them, weapons aimed. Including a grenade launcher. The convoy was able to outrun them for a bit, but to help the others escape, John dove out of the rear Humvee. He commandeered a taxi cab and drove it head-on into the enemy vehicle."

Merv's eyes widened. "No shit."

Kemper continued, "He was shot in the head seconds before the vehicle collision. John's a bonafide hero; he literally saved the lives of six people."

"Damn. Really?"

"Robin said it was a miracle he survived. Skull reconstruction, multiple broken bones. She said he flatlined once on the operating table. It took months of rehab in VA hospitals to put him back together." Kemper wrung her hands and nodded. "I really admire him."

"Shit." Merv shook his head. "Maybe I owe the dude an apology."

"No. Again, don't let him know—"

"Whatever you say, boss." Merv waved at another car to keep going down the road to the next beach.

Kemper took off her broad-rimmed flat hat, dusted it off, and re-set it squarely on her head. It was time to get answers. "I'm going to talk with the Chief." As Merv waved at the next car, a flash of gold caught her eye. She cocked her head to the side. "Hey, nice watch."

"Um. Thanks. It's a knock-off. A guy was selling them on the dock."

She wrinkled her brow. "Right. I'll be right back. Are you okay here?"

"I'm good." Merv nodded and turned his attention back to the next car approaching.

Kemper walked down to the water line. Medics were lifting the woman's body, now in a black bag, onto a stretcher. Tobias was busy talking with a detective wearing a white shirt and black dress pants. She waited a few feet away until he was available, trying to make eye-contact, occasionally raising her hand like a school-girl. Quickly hiding her hand again when he continued to ignore her.

The beach was technically *her* jurisdiction as a National Park. *Was Tobias a misogynist or was he a schmuck to everyone?*

She started to understand why Johnnie wanted nothing to do with the Chief.

Clearing her throat made no difference. Kemper couldn't take it any longer. She planted herself in front of Tobias and launched right in with her burning questions. "Chief? I hear your team will be done soon? When can we reopen? Will Johnnie be released today? Are you charging him? I need to make staffing plans."

Tobias crossed his arms. "I plan to hold him and then we'll see. If I were you, I'd make long-term plans that don't include Johnnie Crosswell."

Kemper huffed. "Well, I think you are making a big mistake."

He scowled. "You do your job and I'll do mine. Got it?"

She shook her head and walked away. As she turned toward the parking lot, the marked-out area around the turtle nest caught her eye. *Should she tell Tobias?* No, he didn't deserve the courtesy and, besides, she wanted check it out first.

On the edge of the parking lot, she spotted a pair of glasses. They were unmistakably Johnnie's with the round lenses and flip-up tinted covers. She tucked them in her shirt pocket and fastened the button to secure them. Next, she found Merv. He was moving the traffic cones so the ambulance could depart. "Hey, we should check the predator cam."

Merv's eyes went wide and his jaw dropped. "You think…?"

"Can't hurt to look. But let's wait until things settle down and Tobias leaves, okay?"

Merv snickered. "Sure. Whatever you say, boss."

Chapter 11

Robin was in the shower when her cell phone rang. She rinsed the soap around her eyes, wondering who would call at six in the morning. Grabbing a towel, her hair dripping, she went to her nightstand to check the incoming number. She'd missed the call but recognized the caller. It was Kemper Snow.

She mumbled under her breath, "What the hell did you do now?"

Walking back into her bathroom, she brushed her jet-black wet hair and toweled her body dry. She got dressed in a red blouse and black suit, putting on her most sensible and comfortable dress shoes, because it might be *one of those days*.

Robin took a deep breath and checked the voicemail from Kemper.

> "Robin, it's Kemper, Johnnie's boss. It's now ten til six. Sorry for bad news, but Johnnie was arrested. They're bringing him to the station. He seems okay. Another dead body washed up this morning and he called it in. Thought you should know. I need to handle things on site. Call me when you get a chance."

Robin rubbed her eyes. *Should she call a lawyer or the bail bond's office first?* She'd need to put her condo up as collateral. *What a mess.*

She sat on the edge of her bed and clasped her hands together. "God, if you can hear me, send me strength."

The sun streamed through her window, a bright orange. Not a sign from God, she knew. But she would take any hopeful signs at this point. Maybe she needed to reserve judgement until she had the facts. That was the lawyerly way to handle it. Still, she wanted to hit something, kick something. Smash the walls with her fist until her knuckles bled. *Was this how Johnnie felt during his rages?*

She didn't bother with breakfast and headed out the door to the police building. It was only a two-minute walk. The town was asleep except for two groggy tourists who stopped her near the traffic circle, asking where they could buy a cappuccino.

The two-story stucco police station and the legislature building were next door to each other. On an island this small, she knew everyone at the police station. In fact, her best friend Janice ran the police switch board. Robin entered and walked up to the Desk Officer.

"Good morning, Arturo."

Officer Arturo Bell, sitting behind the plexiglass reception desk, touched his cap. His friendly face, with a wide nose, dimples and flawless ebony skin, was a sight for sore eyes.

"Ah, Good morning Senator, what can I do for you this fine day?"

She leaned on the counter. "You didn't hear?"

"No, ma'am. I just came on shift."

"Is Johnnie here?"

His forehead wrinkled. "Your brother? He's works for the Park Service, correct? Why would he be here?"

She sighed. "I heard he was arrested and coming here. Could you check his ETA?"

"Oh, so sorry, Senator. I'll find out. Take a seat and I'll let you know."

"Thanks, Art."

A large intoxicated man was asleep in a corner chair, leaning his head against the side wall. His stench polluted the air like sour milk.

She needed caffeine. Without it, her head would start pounding and she didn't need to feel any worse. "Arturo?" she called. "I'm going out for a latte. What can I get you?"

From the back, out of view, he said, "Coffee, a little cream."

"Got it."

She pushed the glass door open and headed back up the hill to the closest café. On her way, she saw two police vehicles drive up from the west. She kept going, determined to enjoy some self-care before going into the fray. Whatever Johnnie did could wait five goddamned minutes.

The Java Crescent Café was a local favorite and had the best coffee in her opinion. It was small, with only four small round tables, but most of their business was to-go orders. The place was sheathed in dark wood paneling and the floor was terrazzo. Blown-glass pendant lights in various colors framed the space above the counter. The owner,

Redmond, was in his sixties but was bouncy like a teenager, and he loved to gossip. A television mounted on the wall was always running Spanish soap operas, but in the mornings, was tuned to the public television station showing children's programming. Dora the Explorer was on some type of case.

She got in line behind another customer. The person in front of her, a man she didn't know, was talking with Redmond.

Redmond said, "Did you hear about the dead girl?"

The customer said, "No! What happened?"

"I hear she was murdered. Hacked up with a machete. They said it was gruesome."

"Say what? What kind of madman would do such a thing?" The customer clicked his tongue in disapproval.

"I tell you, it must be a bad element. Enjoy your day now!"

The customer took his order and left.

Robin glared at Redmond.

"Miss Senator, why are you lookin' at me like that now?"

She crossed her arms. "How on earth do you know about this already?" News moved fast on the island, but this was ridiculous.

"What? The murder? Some police came in before. I overheard them talking."

"You know what? I don't have time for this." She got out her money. "I need a latte and a coffee light, both to go. And I'd appreciate it if you could keep the news to yourself."

"Ooh, so testy. Yes, Miss Robin. You need your java. Redmond will fix you up!"

Robin exhaled, a million thoughts running through her brain.

Someone tapped her shoulder. "I'm sorry to disturb you, but did he call you senator?"

Robin regarded the woman. She was petite, pale, with shoulder-length blond hair, wearing a flowered T-shirt and cotton skirt.

"Yes, I represent St. John in the legislature. I'm Robin Crosswell. What can I do for you?"

"I'm Mary Taylor. My husband was found dead last week. But I can't get any answers from the police."

Robin's mouth fell open. "I'm...I'm so sorry for your loss. Um. I'm headed to the police station now. But...um...you know what? I can make some time. I'd like to hear about your husband."

They sat down at one of the bistro tables near the window.

Mary whispered, "Thank you. I'm scared and don't know who to trust."

"Tell me what I can do. You can trust me. Anything you tell me will be kept in strict confidence."

Redmond walked over with two cups, the latte and the coffee, and placed them in front of Robin, and walked away again.

In a whisper, Mary said, "A man came to my home yesterday. He was looking for something. Threatened my life. But I don't have it. I think this is the same man that killed Robert."

"What was he looking for?"

Mary looked around the room. Robin also turned to scan the room.

They were alone except for Redmond and he now had headphones on, bobbing his head to what Robin assumed was music, as he swept the floor behind the counter.

Mary whispered, "A computer file. He said Robert stole it. This guy ransacked our entire house looking. He put a knife to my throat. Said if I mentioned this to anyone, he would kill me in my sleep."

"And you didn't tell Chief Tobias?"

Mary fiddled with her hands on the table. Her eyes conveyed panic. "I've been sitting here, trying to get the courage. But if another person was killed…just like my Robert…I don't know if it's safe. Tobias wasn't very keen on finding Robert's murderer when I met with him last week. Said he didn't have any leads. I almost think he doesn't want to pursue it."

"Do you know what's on this computer file?"

"No idea. I don't know what he got mixed up in. I mean, he was a marine biologist. He did surveys. Boring stuff."

"What was he working on recently?"

"A project for the British Virgin Islands, doing surveys around Great Thatch Island for the last month. But he said he couldn't talk about it. Strange, because he had to sign a non-disclosure agreement."

Robin shook her head. *Biologists signing NDAs?* That didn't sound logical. She opened her handbag and retrieved her business card. "Here's my card. It has my personal cell on it. I know someone in the FBI who might help. But let me dig around a little first. Do you have somewhere safe to stay?"

"I stayed with a friend last night. I could move in for a few days."

"Good. Give me your phone number. I'll call you by the end of the day."

Mary wrote her number on a square white napkin and whispered, "Thank you, Senator."

"Call me Robin. Take care of yourself."

Robin left with both cups, nodding goodbye to Redmond, who waved, still with his headphones on.

Back at the police station, she walked up to Arturo's desk. "Is he here?"

"Johnnie arrived a few minutes ago. He's in processing."

"Your coffee might be a little cold." She handed it through the cutout in the plexi. "I need to see him right now. I'm his lawyer…for now."

"I don't know if you can. Let me check."

Arturo disappeared to the back.

Yes, it was going to be *one of those days*. Waiting and worrying. At least the drunk guy from the corner was gone. The waiting room wouldn't smell so bad now.

Arturo returned. "Chief is still at the scene, so you can see your brother for a few minutes. But be quick."

"Thanks." The side door buzzed and she walked through. Arturo showed her to a door with a sign that said "Int-1" and used a key card to open it.

Johnnie sat at a stainless-steel table in a ten-by-ten windowless room, wearing only his white cotton briefs and tank-style undershirt, his wrists cuffed. He raised his head as she entered. "Hey."

Arturo said, "Three minutes," and closed the door behind her.

She inhaled and jutted her chin at Johnnie. "Where are your clothes?"

"They took them for evidence. Good thing I shaved." He grinned.

"What? Johnnie!"

"I didn't want to argue with them. They won't find anything."

"Fine. Go." She crossed her arms.

"Go? Go where?"

She shook her head. "We don't have much time. Tell me everything."

"Are we being recorded?"

"No. Now go."

"I didn't do anything."

Not this shit again. She pounded her fist on the table. "*Why* were you arrested?"

"Tobias hates me? I don't know. I saw a dead woman. I called 9-1-1 and talked to Janice. The next thing I know, police cars roll up, they hit me, knock me to the ground and arrest me. They didn't ask any questions."

"Where were you last night?"

"Home. Reading. I talked with Dr. Lou by video in the afternoon. Cud stayed over at Gertie's. I gave back her towels around five. Watched a little TV and read a book until nine. Then went to bed with a headache."

Robin took a seat. She studied Johnnie's face. He kept her gaze, which showed he might be telling the truth. "Did you fight back or harm anyone during the arrest?"

He shook his head, "No. You would have been proud. But they hit me with a baton. Kicked me. I should sue Tobias."

"Do you need a doctor?"

"My ribs really hurt. So… yeah, maybe." He pointed to his side.

"Okay." Robin sighed. "I'll talk to Tobias. Anything you need right now?"

"Tell Kemper I'm okay. I lost my glasses. They might be in the parking lot. Let Gertie know where I am in case I don't come home." He cracked a smile. "I could use a book or five to read depending on how long I'll be here."

Robin knew that without his prismatic lenses, Johnnie's misaligned vision gave him headaches and made reading a challenge. She placed her hand on his. "Little brother, I've got you. Behave yourself in here. Don't be a butt head. I'll be back later."

Arturo knocked on the door. "Time's up."

Robin rose from the chair, her eyes narrowed at John. "Do *not* answer anything. Understand? Even if they ask what your favorite color is."

Johnnie nodded. "I'll tell them red, like human blood."

She wrinkled her nose. "Not funny." Straightening her skirt and jacket, she walked out of the room.

Arturo closed the door behind her.

"Thanks, Art."

"Chief is back. You want to see him now?"

"You know it."

"Okay, follow me."

She was going to rip Tobias a new asshole. Her phone read seven o'clock. In an hour, she was due at her office next door. Still, she knew Johnnie needed a different lawyer. One who wasn't a relative. She'd make some calls.

They reached Tobias' office. It was tiny, like all the rooms in the police building. Framed photos of the police force, a letter of appreciation from the little league team, and his picture with the Governor lined the dark wood-paneled wall behind his cluttered desk. He greeted her with a glower.

"Why?" she asked.

Tobias rose from his burgundy leather office chair. In such a small room, he seemed like a giant.

"Your brother is a psycho, that's why."

"Do you even have a case?"

"I can hold him for twenty-four hours without charging him."

"And I can hold your nuts in a vice for the next year if you don't release him. I think I'll zero out your equipment budget for next year. The bill is on my desk right now."

"Crooked like your criminal brother? I'm not surprised."

"I heard you gave up looking for Robert Taylor's murderer. Maybe *you* are the crooked one."

"Well, I think it's obvious your brother is a serial killer. We haven't had a murder in four years and now two dead bodies show up on the same beach, both called in by your brother? What kind of coincidence is that?"

"I want him released now. Unless you charge him…but I know you won't because you don't have a real case. You need to end this bullshit."

Tobias barked, "Fine. But I'm going to talk to him first."

"Not without a lawyer."

"Then you better get him one."

"I will."

"Good.

"Fine." Robin stalked out, wondering if she just did more damage to Johnnie's situation by confronting Tobias. Maybe her brother wasn't the only hot-head in the family. She headed toward the exit, unable to utter words to Arturo when he asked how it went. She just pointed to the door and he buzzed her out.

Her heart raced and her breath came out in huffs through her nose as she walked the eighty feet to the government annex. Storming back into her office, she slammed her handbag against the wall behind her desk; the contents exploding onto the floor. She screamed, "Shit, shit, shit!"

She threw her door closed. [Blam]

Down the hall, her assistant, Dottie called, "Good morning, Robin. Are you okay?"

"Good morning. I'm fine," she yelled through the door. On reflection, she was fine, as in, not in immediate physical danger; but mentally, well, that was a totally different conversation. And Dottie would learn soon enough how 'not fine' things actually were. Robin shook her head, opened her door, and called out, "Get me the number for that criminal lawyer on St. Thomas. Deals in homicide cases. Begins with a G— Grimes or Graves or something. And, no, don't ask."

Dottie said, still out of view, "Yes. I'm on it."

Robin collapsed in her chair. Her schedule was full today. Meetings nearly every hour with colleagues and constituents. An economic proposal she needed to review. And a brother to break out of jail.

So much for island time.

She found a loose cigarette in the back of her desk drawer. She'd quit smoking a couple years ago, but this was an emergency. Robin lit the end with a match and inhaled the sweet nicotine. Her brain received the chemicals with deep appreciation. But her lungs fought back, hacking and coughing.

I picked the wrong decade to give up smoking, she thought. She put the cigarette out and coughed repeatedly, trying to clear her chest.

Dottie rushed into her office. "Are you okay? Because you're cursing and coughing and I don't know what else. You sound like a right banshee giving birth to triplets!"

Robin laughed; her eyes moist from trying to hack up a lung. Dot was the best. She was wearing her signature culottes and gauzy blouse with espadrilles on her feet. Her eyes were alert, like they could pierce steel, with narrow arched brows. She was short, but had a button nose and high cheek bones that any model would envy. But it was Dottie's razor-sharp wit and can-do attitude that Robin envied. Like nothing phased her.

Dot said, "When you get yourself together, Mr. Greaves is on line one." She dashed away again.

The button on her desk phone flashed red.

"Thanks," Robin shouted. She pulled the napkin from her jacket pocket and traced her finger along the ink of Mary Taylor's phone number.

    Tobias was right about one thing. The cases had to be related. And it was time to put the pieces together.

Chapter 12

It was the happiest of days. Cud stretched his legs; a sunbeam warmed his bare torso. He hadn't slept this well in years. He rolled to his side. Gertie was gone.

Cud got out of bed and hunted for his shorts. Pillows and sheets lay in piles on the floor. He smiled as he sorted through the mess, carefully folding the linens and placing them on the bed.

His shorts weren't on the floor. He looked around, finding them dangling from a post on the headboard. He couldn't recall how that happened, but much of yesterday was a blur. A sweet John and Yoko kind of blur. An out-of-body experience.

A sound outside caught his attention. Gertie was singing in the garden out back, like he'd seen her the first time they met. This time it was "Dream a Little Dream of Me". But somehow, now she looked more radiant. More beautiful. The *most* beautiful.

As he zipped his fly, he felt the bulge in his pocket. The thumb drive.

He opened the window and called, "Good morning, my love!"

She waved. "Good morning. I'm going to make breakfast." She wiped her garden gloves together, brushing off the soil. "I'll be right in."

"Um, no, you enjoy yourself. Can I use your laptop and your phone? I want to call my grandson."

Gertie walked up to the window. "What's mine is yours, sweet Cudlow."

He leaned through the opening to kiss her. "Thank you, birdie."

"Birdie? My dad used to call me that. I like it. I'll be in soon. The passcode to my phone is 222."

He grinned as she walked back to the garden.

After continued searching, he located his polo shirt under the bed and went to the living room. Gertie's electronics were on the kitchen counter, plugged in next to a glass vase with two-dozen long-stemmed pink roses. The card read *an admirer*. Jackson had come through after all.

He called his grandson.

"Pawpaw, I'm glad to hear from you again. How are you? How was your project?"

"Jackson, I don't have much time. I need another favor. Again, no questions."

"Really? Again?"

"Yes, will you help me or not?" Cud tapped his fingers on the counter.

"Sure. What is it?"

"I'm sending you a file. I need you to look up these numbers. Give me the total net worth and then delete all record of this communication. Can you do that?"

"Where are you calling from? I don't recognize this number."

"My girlfriend's place. The one you sent the flowers to. But I don't have time. Call me right back on this number and then delete it from your phone log. Understand?"

"Hold on. You have a girlfriend? Paw, I'm so happy—"

"Just do it!"

Jackson sighed. "Okay. Standing by."

Cud ended the call, plugged in the drive and Bob's password, '*despicable*'. He logged into an old email system, an untraceable one, and sent the numbers to Jackson. Encrypting the file would have been wise, but Gertie's computer wasn't set up for that. Then he deleted all the remnants from Gertie's' system—for her own protection.

He stared at the phone, too paralyzed to move, willing Jackson to call him back.

Two minutes later, Gertie walked in carrying a basket of squash and peas. "Do you want some eggs? I make a mean omelet."

He closed her laptop. "That sounds lovely. I...I'm waiting for a call back from Jackson. A good kid. Just graduated from Yale."

"I hope to meet him someday." She walked to him, set down her basket on the blue counter and wrapped her arms around his waist.

"Yes, I'd like that, too." He kissed her cheek.

She left his side to start breakfast.

"Anything I can do?"

"No. Just take a load off." She began breaking eggs into a bowl.

The phone rang. Cud grabbed it from the counter. "Um, it's Jackson. I'm going to take this outside." He walked to the front door. There were fewer remnants of the lemon squares on the ground, indicating birds or other critters had continued noshing on them during the night. The Tupperware container was gone.

He accepted the call. "Jackson? Bottom line?"

"Thirty million. Give or take. Is this yours? Have you been investing again?"

"Aaaagh." He dropped the phone on the ground.

Jackson's voice rose from the device below, "Are you still there?"

He picked up the phone, wiping off blades of damp grass. "Delete it. Everything. All traces. We never talked. Do not call this number again. Bye." He hung up, then deleted her call history, incoming and outgoing. Not that it would matter much. There would be records elsewhere. *Bollocks.*

Cud walked back inside. Gertie was still occupied with cooking. He took the thumb drive out of his pocket and clenched it in his fist. He scanned the room. *How to hide it?*

A few minutes later, breakfast was ready. The eggs were delicious. They talked about going for a walk and then the grocery store. Later, as Cud washed the dishes, Gertie gave him a look and ran her hand along his backside. Her aura was rose pink. And he was feeling the same. But first, they took a shower together.

Life did not get much better than this.

Yes, he decided, despite the bad news about the blasted thumb drive, it was the happiest of days.

* * *

Johnnie's thoughts turned to those first days in the hospital. When he couldn't speak. Intubated. His hands tied down. Pleading with his eyes to the nurses, "Please kill me," but no one listened. Not sure of where he was or even who he was. Only wanting out.

He pulled on his cuffs, bruising his skin. Doctor Lou was in his head, saying this was temporary. *Be strong. Do the work. Use your choices.*

Staying calm was easier said than done. There was nothing in the room to distract him. No windows. Nothing on the walls. He counted the vinyl tiles on the floor. A hundred and twenty-one, not counting the partial ones. In that first month of rehab, he could watch television as a reward for completing his physical therapy. There was something about the cartoons that put him at ease, made him not worry about all the things he couldn't do or couldn't remember. Rare times he felt contented.

A song popped in his head from the Rabbit of Seville, *"What would you want with a waaa-bit? Can't you see that I'm much sweeter. I'm your little señorita..."* His head bopped to the tune.

Arturo walked in.

Johnnie shook his head. *Had he been singing aloud?* He clammed up.

Arturo waved and handed him a pamphlet about safe driving in the USVI. "Sorry, it's all I could find. Robin said to give you something to read. I'll see if I can get something better."

Johnnie nodded. "Thanks, appreciate it."

Arturo nodded and left.

Singing Looney Tunes songs aloud might be advantageous. It would get Tobias's attention, reducing time waiting around for him. But might help in an insanity defense if things went badly, and that was always a possibility.

He began shouting, "Kill da waabit, kill da waabit..." It was kind of fun. Robin wouldn't approve, but she wasn't here. He recited the whole opera, changing voices. Pleased with himself that he remembered so many lines, but also improvising ones he wasn't sure of. After five minutes, his throat hurt. Yelling was not sustainable. His ears began to ring.

The door opened. The lumbering figure of Tobias entered the room, shouting, "Shut up!"

He quieted but grinned, "Don't kill da wabbit?"

"This is *not* funny, you friggin' psycho." Tobias closed the door behind him and stood with his feet far apart, in typical alpha-dick style, with his gorilla hands on his wide hips. "We're going to have a little talk."

Johnnie sighed. *Not another talk.* "Is my lawyer here?"

"No, he called. Arriving soon." Tobias took out a notepad from his shirt pocket and began reading to himself. "What were you doing at the bank the other day?"

"I had a weird dream. I got confused. You know I have a brain injury." He left out the part about Oprah.

"We received an anonymous tip last night. Mr. Taylor rented a safe deposit box at that bank branch. So, what was so important that you killed him to access it?"

"Who?"

"Robert Taylor. The first victim."

Johnnie's eyes widened and he shook his head. "His name was Robert? Wow. What are the chances?"

"You told the bank manager you had a key."

He closed his eyes. *Not supposed to talk, idiot. Not without a lawyer.* "I'm invoking my right to plead the fifth." He'd watched Bart Simpson say that in an episode the night before. But then, Bart also responded to questioning with, "Eat my butt." So tempting…

"Really? That's what murderers do. I guess I was right. But *why* did you do it? For money? Was it self-defense? If you were only protecting yourself, I would understand. Surely, *any* jury would understand."

Johnnie stifled a laugh. If Tobias thought this bull-shit 'understanding' approach was going to get him to talk, he was delusional. Even a brain-damaged person could see through this nonsense. He shook his head, staring at the vinyl floor tiles. One of them had an old bloodstain. Or maybe it was diet soda. He wondered how it got there and if bleach would remove it.

Tobias sat in the chair across from him and took a calmer tone. "Look, Johnnie, I know you've been through a lot. A war hero. I can't imagine what it was like there. Lots of guys have PTSD or anger issues after something like that. If you cooperate, I can send you back to your sister tonight. I can make this easy on you. Just tell me *why* you did it."

Don't say a word. Staring at the floor wasn't holding its original appeal. A melody popped into Johnnie's head. Pirates of Penzance. He'd been an extra in his high school production. He surprised himself by recalling it. But his memory worked that way. Sometimes odd bits from decades ago would come back in full; and other times, he'd come to a dead stop completely forgetting where he was going. He started humming with his eyes closed to concentrate; then sang in a whisper, trying to get the words in the correct order. "For I am a Pirate King. And it is, it is, it is…" He had to think of the next line.

Tobias frowned. "What's that? Speak up."

"…A glorious thing to be!" Johnnie sang the next part loudly, "To be a Pirate King! Hurrah for our Pirate King!" He swayed in his chair, shouting at the ceiling. "With a pirate head and a pirate heart, away to the cheating world go you!"

Tobias stood and walked to the door. He yelled into the corridor,

"Take this psycho to his cell. Now!" and exited swiftly. The heavy door shut with a resounding clang.

Johnnie stopped shouting and grinned. This singing stuff was as good as insect repellent. He wondered what would have happened if he took singing lessons instead of joining the Marines. But his dad had called theater sissy stuff. Or was that an episode of Glee? The night nurse at the Miami VA hospital loved that show and played reruns on her phone.

A couple minutes later, Officer Arturo escorted him to a cell at the back of the building. There were two eight-by-eight-foot cells with iron-bars. One cell held a dark-skinned drunk guy wearing a flowered shirt, sleeping in the corner. The other held a younger man, white with a grotesque spray-on tan and a crew cut, wearing a cut-off T-shirt revealing massive muscles and a thick gold chain. Johnnie decided to call them Flower Man and Chain Boy. Arturo put him in with Chain Boy.

Arturo said, "Your sister will be back when your lawyer arrives. Tobias won't let a doctor come in, sorry. I can bring you a book tomorrow."

Tomorrow? How many days would he be there? "Thanks, Art." He sat on the wood bench furthest from the other guy.

Arturo whispered, "Johnnie, your sister Robin? Is she single?"

Johnnie smiled. "Art, are you thinking of asking her out?"

Art looked sheepish. "Yes."

"Hey, go for it, man."

Arturo smiled and exited, locking the cell door.

Chain Boy sat forward, leaning his elbows on his knees, and nodded. "Yo, man. What you in for?"

He wasn't in the mood to chat but found himself answering, "Murder. And you?"

"Duuuude! What? Who did you murder?"

Chain Boy seemed impressed. In a stony voice, he replied, "I didn't kill anyone. It's a misunderstanding." Johnnie stared at the ceiling. There was a crack in the concrete about two feet long. He wondered if the ceiling would cave in. With his luck, it wouldn't surprise him.

Chain Boy chuckled. "Riiiiight." He tapped his nose. "I got you."

"No. Really. I'm innocent."

His cell mate grinned, "Yeah, and I didn't 'assault' that cute bartender last night either."

Johnnie grew still, unable to breathe, but his cheek twitched. "*What bartender?*"

"At the Yellow Bird place."

His nostrils flared. "Yellow Parrot? Mandy?"

"Yeah, dude. Parrot. Mandy, Sandy... I don't know. Long braids. Juicy ass."

Johnnie slowly exhaled, his muscles tense, his brain on fire, eyes blinking. He sprang towards Chain Boy, his hand around his throat, squeezing, wanting to rip out his larynx. "You piece of scum!"

Chain Boy swatted at Johnnie with his fat, stubby hands. "Dude, get off!" He wiggled off the bench. Johnnie lost his grasp. His opponent pulled him to the floor, climbing on top, punching him in his already damaged ribs. He grabbed the man's wrist, twisting it in a way he learned in the Marines, or so he assumed. With a few strategic moves, Chain Boy was face down on the concrete floor, Johnnie straddled him, holding the man's arm at an unnatural angle.

Johnnie yelled, "Motherfucker. I should break your arm." Just a little more pressure would do so...

Arturo ran up and unlocked the door. "Crosswell! Let him go."

Johnnie looked up. Arturo strode toward him with a taser. The barbs hit his shoulder blade and electricity shot through his brain. He rolled to the side, convulsing. Through half-lidded eyes, he saw Arturo drag a jittery Chain Boy to the other cell.

Before he passed out from the pain, he had only two thoughts.

I should have broken it in three places, and *Robin can't find out.*

✻ ✻ ✻

~*Eight hours earlier*~

The bank manager was such a sissy. Crying like a baby when he held his hand over the stovetop's flame. Thomas expected the task to be harder. But the manager acquiesced quickly, driving them to the bank, disabling the alarm, opening Mr. Taylor's box.

Thomas Smith rifled through the contents. *Garbage.* No thumb drive.

He turned to the manager, whipping out his knife and holding it to his throat. "Where is it?"

The man trembled. "What? What are you talking about?" More tears streamed down his nose.

"Stop blubbering, ya wimp. There should be a thumb drive. Did anyone else access this box last week? His wife? Any reporters or investigators?"

"No…not that I can think of.

"Do you keep a log of people who come in?"

"Um. Well, there were a couple strange visits last week."

"Strange? What do you mean? Who?"

"Um. I…let me think. There was a billionaire from the Bahamas. He talked to his dead mother. Eccentric, but I don't think he would steal anything. And the park maintenance guy. Croissant? Cross…something."

Smith removed the blade from the man's neck, scratching his head with his free hand. "Crosswell? John Crosswell?"

"Yes!" The man sighed with relief. "That's the one. He didn't go into the vault, but he said he had a safe deposit key. Acted weird. I reported it to the police. Maybe someone else in the bank let him in?"

He grabbed the man by his shirt collar. "What kind of bank is this? What about security footage?"

"Oh, um, yes. We have footage of the main floor. Come, I'll show you."

Thom hissed, "I don't have time for this crap. It's got to be Crosswell. Wait, has the camera been recording? Yes, show me."

They went to a small back room with three security screens and a disc recorder. Thom opened all the drives, broke the discs with his bare hands and picked up the pieces, shoving them in his jacket pocket. He turned to the manager. "I was never here. You will not say a word. Otherwise, your daughter could go missing, if you get my meaning."

The manager wrung his hands and nodded.

"Good. I'll let myself out. Count to a thousand and then you can leave."

Smith walked out the back door, whose alarm was disabled earlier. The alley in the back was dark and his black clothing blended perfectly. He wondered if he should have killed Samuel. Leaving loose ends was sloppy. But leaving stacks of dead bodies around the tiny island would bring more unwanted attention, making his boss unhappy. It was bad enough he had to kill that reporter. But she was young, idealistic, and refused to be bought. That was the trouble with twenty-year-olds. Always so aspirational.

Now that he had his answer, he needed to track down Crosswell, the park janitor, which would be easy. The man seemed like a moron and a pacifist. But first, he needed to apply pressure and have a bit of fun.

He climbed into his SUV and headed to the beach. Multi-tasking was his favorite thing. Why run here and there putting out fires like most fixers when you could simplify your work? Sure, Ray Donovan was fun television but no one could sustain that level of sheer chaos and family drama. Others in his line of business usually burned out in six months. He was in his fourteenth year and still going strong. With his innate efficiency and rule book, he put in fewer hours making more per job and had time to decompress for days at a time. It was a shame they didn't give out lifetime achievement awards for corporate fixers.

At the beach, he parked, changed his shoes to a size fifteen, three sizes larger, and made other adjustments to his appearance, like donning a ski mask. He scouted for prying eyes. The place was deserted. It was two o'clock and the moon was obscured behind clouds. *Perfect.*

He opened the back hatch of the SUV and threw the girl's body—covered in bubble wrap—over his shoulder. At the beach line, he rolled her out, reinserting the machete back into its original slot in her back. He pushed it in with a little hop to apply more force. Smith stood back to review his handiwork and scanned the beach one more time.

Back at his car, he put on his dome light and wrote some notes in the small lined pad. His how-to book was coming along. The chapter on multi-tasking and using the police as an asset would get the reader's attention. It all came down to using a systems approach and delegating to others without them knowing. And never working in teams. That was a killer. Maybe when this assignment concluded and all the politicians fell in line, he would spend afternoons at cafes, completing his manuscript.

Smiling at his accomplishments, Smith drove back to town. Under the largest cell phone tower, he left an anonymous tip on the police hotline.

With that out of the way, he could get some well-deserved sleep, have a late breakfast, and ransack the idiot's apartment—all before noon—and maybe go snorkeling later, knowing that the Crosswell guy wasn't going anywhere.

The app on his phone predicted a wonderful sunny day.

Yes, he should get an award.

Soon enough, he'd have the thumb drive and the codes for the bribe money back.

Chapter 13

Robin squirmed at her desk, trying to concentrate on the papers before her. A vote was coming up next month on a new zoning plan. After the hurricanes, investors sought to change zoning to consolidate tracts of condemned residential properties to build big resorts. The legislature would not turn its back on residents. These proposals were likely DOA.

Dottie burst through her door. "Urgent call. Judge Montrose. Can I put him through?"

She put down the proposal. "Is it about Johnnie?"

"He didn't say."

"Yes, put it through." A couple seconds later, Robin answered on the first ring. "Your honor, nice to speak with you again. What can I do for you?"

"Robin, I have a search warrant on my desk for your brother's place. As a courtesy, I wanted you to know I'll be signing it within the next half-hour."

The air went out of her lungs. "Oh. Yes, thank you for letting me know. If there is anything I can do for you in the future, please don't hesitate..."

"Goodbye." The line went dead.

Shit. *The diary.* She looked through her calendar. A meeting with the Economic Council began in fifteen minutes. She screamed, "DOTTIE!"

Dot reappeared, "Yes, ma'am? What can I do?"

Dottie was always listening in. A few years older, she was a fixture in the building. Her superpowers were knowing every soul on the island, and spreading gossip faster than a peregrine falcon in a race against a Lamborghini. Which was exceptionally fast. "Did you hear that?"

Dot blushed. "I, um. Yes."

"Take my phone. In my contacts, find Gertrude Brown. Tell her to retrieve John's diary. It should have a black leather cover, about the size

107

of a steno pad. Tell her to keep it, hide it, until he gets back. She has to get it right now."

"Yes, ma'am." Dottie took the phone and jogged out.

Robin rested her head on her desk, moaning slightly. Maybe she should have asked Gertie to burn the damned diary. Who knew what kinds of insane rantings were in it? Even Johnnie's most benign innermost thoughts could trouble a jury, leading to a conviction. Dr. Phillips insisted a daily journal was part of the healing and mood management process. But most patients didn't get into the trouble Johnnie did. The diary could put him away for life, guilty or not.

Three minutes later, Dot came back, returning the cell phone. "Gertie understands and will get it right away."

Robin eased her head off the desk. "Thanks, Dot." She noticed the time on her phone and bolted up. "My ten o'clock economic committee meeting is starting soon. Come get me the second Mr. Greaves arrives."

Dot nodded. "Can I get you some coffee?"

She straightened her jacket and began gathering materials for the meeting, stacking papers. "Yes. With a dash of secret sauce."

Drinking on the job was not something she was proud of, but she needed relief. A couple dashes of rum wouldn't hurt.

But if this kept up, she might need to refill her Xanax prescription, and she hadn't touched the stuff since her divorce. That was a dark time she didn't want to revisit. If a jury found Johnnie guilty, she'd likely lose re-election next year. It could all culminate with no job, incredible legal bills, a murderer brother, with no other family to lean on. What would become of her? Maybe she could live off the land like Cudlow. Or drown herself.

She couldn't think about this now.

On the way to the stairs, she picked up the coffee from Dot, taking a sip. The warm liquid radiated down her throat. "Thanks, Dottie. I needed this."

Dot smiled. "Go. I'll hold down the fort."

Robin smiled back. "I know." Her eyes teared up. She straightened her back and blinked. "See you in an hour."

"It will all be fine. You watch."

Robin took a deep breath and headed to the stairs. She clutched her folders in one arm, and held the coffee with the other, taking each step carefully, unable to hold the handrail. Five steps from the bottom, her foot slipped. She fell backwards, her folders flying off in front of her down the stairs in a spray, her coffee now spilled across her blouse. The mug danced down the stairs and fractured on the floor below. Heat seared her skin and she flicked the liquid downward with sweeps of her hand.

Donald, the island's treasurer, walked up. "Robin, are you alright?" He extended his hand to help her up.

She righted herself, her back in pain from the impact. She exhaled. "I'm nowhere near all right." Taking his hand, she descended the stairs. "Are you going to the ten o'clock video conference?"

Donald said, "Yes. But if you aren't up for it, I'd be happy to take notes for you." He bent down to gather her folders.

She joined him on the floor, scooping up the paper, contemplating the offer. A janitor walked up and handed her a wad of paper towels to dry herself. He began gathering shards of ceramic off the ground.

Robin blotted the wet areas of her blouse. Holding her sleeve to her nose, the smell of rum was unmistakable, like a goddamned distillery. *Great.*

When everything was back in order, she said, "No, I want to get this mo-fo over with."

Donald smiled. "Couldn't agree with you more."

✳ ✳ ✳

Gertie's phone rang. Cud wasn't sure if he should answer it. But he checked the incoming number in case it was his grandson. It came up as 'Robin'. *Was that Johnnie's sister?* He accepted the call. In a formal British accent, he said, "Madam Brown's residence."

"Hello? This is Dot McPherson, Senator Crosswell's assistant. Is Gertie there?"

"Um. She's indisposed right now. Can she call you back?"

"Who am I speaking with?"

"My name is Cud. I'm...a friend."

"Oh, right. Can you give her a message? It's *very* urgent."

Cud sensed some panic in her voice. He wanted to ask what she meant by, '*oh right*'. Had Gertie told others of their new relationship? "Yes, what is it?"

"A search warrant will be issued any minute for John's apartment.

Robin needs Gertie to retrieve John's diary and keep it safe. Right away."

"Wait. What?"

Gertie came out of the bathroom, wearing her bathrobe. Her hair was damp—now a dark cobalt blue shade—and a yellow towel wrapped around her shoulders. "Cudlow, who's on the phone?"

"Johnnie's sister's assistant."

"I'll take it." Gertie took the phone. "Dot? What's going on?"

After a few okays, yeses and long pauses, Gertie said, "Thanks, Dottie. I'll get it right away. Tell Robin not to worry."

Cud sat on the edge of the bed, mouth open. "What's going on?"

Gertie took a seat beside him. "Johnnie was arrested. The police plan to search his place and I need to get his diary out of there."

"Arrested? For what?"

"Murder. Another person washed up on the beach this morning and he called it in."

"No."

"Yes. That's what she said."

Someone pounded on Gertie's front door. They stared at each other as the battering continued without pause.

Cud whispered, "Good graces, what if it's the police? You keep them occupied here and I'll slip out the back and get the diary."

Gertie kissed him. "Go, my sweet." She hurried out of the bedroom. From the living room, he heard her call out toward the front door, "Hold on! I need to get dressed."

He ran through the kitchen to the back door. Cud peeked around the corner of the house, no police car. Only a black SUV with dark tinted windows and no markings. He snuck behind the vegetable garden, crawling on his belly to avoid being seen. He dashed the two yards out in the open to the rear of Johnnie's garage apartment. There was no way to go through Johnnie's front door covertly.

The easiest way inside would be through the large window next to Johnnie's bed, that faced the trees on the left side of the property and was hidden from the driveway. He tried to budge it. Locked. *The bathroom window!* It faced the rear of the property and was never closed, at least during his stays. It was a high awning window. Not the best for breaking in, but he had no choice. His thin physique would come in handy, if he could scale the height. Scanning the yard behind him, a blue rain barrel caught his attention. It could work.

He rolled it under the window, climbed on top and pulled the window open as wide as the hinges would allow. Cud pressed his upper body through, bouncing his toes against the barrel top for momentum. The plastic barrel buckled under his weight and he dangled, half inside the room. He grasped the towel rack, tugging on it to help propel him forward. The towel bar snapped and he tumbled, landing head-first in the ceramic sink. He muttered, "Fudge ripple!" It hurt and he'd likely have a lump on his head soon, but he was in.

After righting himself, he dashed toward Johnnie's nightstand; the notebook was there as he expected it to be. Cud shoved it under his waistband. He heard voices at the front door. The knob jiggled.

Trapped.

He ran back into the bathroom, closing the door. Climbing on the sink, he threw the diary out first; it landed in some tall grass. He shoved his body out the window again, this time without concern for pain or caution, his arms aimed at the barrel. He ricocheted off the plastic and somersaulted onto the ground in a heap and saw stars.

Cud heard the front door open and close and voices inside the apartment. Reaching up, he closed the window as best he could and then rolled the barrel a few feet away.

But where to hide the diary?

He spotted the answer at the vegetable garden. The large garden gnome in the center was hollow and he stuffed the book up inside, then pretended to pull weeds in case anyone was watching.

Just in time. A police car swerved into the compacted dirt and stone driveway, spewing dust. It parked beside the black SUV, but the officer waited in his vehicle.

Gertie exited Johnnie's apartment, closing the door behind her. She wore a loose-fitting, geometric print, orange maxi-dress, her damp, now blue-tinged hair tucked under a white bandana. As she walked up to the police car, a gust of wind billowed her dress like a cloud.

Cudlow thought she looked like Venus, the goddess of love. Or at least how he envisioned she would look. Like the purest sunshine, more radiant than rays reflecting across a calm sea. His breath caught in his throat as he gazed at her, almost forgetting their current predicament. Shaking himself from his delight, he left the garden so they could talk with the officer together.

"Good morning, Officer. What can I do for you?" Gertie said.

"Ma'am, do you have a key to John Crosswell's apartment?"

"Yes, I'm his landlady. But it's open now. His lawyer is in there."

Cudlow scratched his head. *Lawyer?* Who makes house calls while their client is in jail?

The officer, opened his car door. "What? He can't be in there." He stalked to Johnnie's door and turned the knob. It was unlocked.

The officer's voice rang out gruffly, "Hello? Sir? I need to ask you to not touch anything and leave." He went inside, his hand resting on his gun holster, leaving the door wide open. He scanned around, then went out of view.

Gertie and Cud hovered just outside John's door. She whispered to Cud, "Did you...?"

He nodded.

Gertie forehead visibly relaxed and put her arm around Cud's waist. "I swear, trouble follows that boy."

The officer returned. "Miss Brown, there's no one in there. Where did his lawyer go?"

Gertie pointed, "I don't know, but that's his vehicle."

The three turned to face the driveway.

Almost silently, the black SUV rolled backwards onto the road; the driver unrecognizable behind the dark windows. The officer took out a notepad. "What did he say his name was?"

Gertie shook her head. "Actually...I don't think he said."

"Did he say what he wanted?"

"Said he was going to get John a change of clothes for his court hearing."

"Did he take anything?"

"Um. I don't think so. But I can check."

The officer shook his pen. "Have you ever seen him before?"

Gertie furrowed her brow. "No, Officer. Not that I can think of."

The officer closed his notepad. "I guess I'll run the plate. You two, wait in your house."

They nodded. Another police vehicle, a tan sedan with a forensics emblem arrived and two plain clothes officers got out.

Gertie and Cud went back inside the house.

She sighed. "I think John's in a heap this time."

Cud hugged Gertie, his mind racing. That man was no lawyer. And while he didn't see the guy, he had a hunch it was that fellow with the black aura.

This Mark person was obviously on a mission.

And the next time, they could all be in danger.

* * *

~Fifteen minutes earlier~

Thomas drove up the narrow winding road. He scanned the mailboxes and turned at the one with the painted flowers, number 123 and the name 'G. Brown'. Pulling up the bumpy driveway, he cut the engine, put on the parking brake and turned off his police scanner. The Crosswell guy was in prison and he could search the moron's apartment. There were lights on in the main house, meaning someone was home. He walked up to the house and knocked on the front door.

A woman's voice called out, "Hold on, I'm getting dressed."

He looked at his watch. It was ten o'clock. This person must be a late sleeper.

When the woman opened the door, she gave a look of surprise. "I thought you were the police."

She knew he was arrested...perfect.

He smoothed his blue striped tie and gave his most winning smile. "Yes, sorry to trouble you. I'm Mr. Crosswell's lawyer. He has an arraignment this afternoon, and I need to pick up a change of clothes. He can't show up in his park uniform. Service regulations and all. Are you Miss Brown, his landlord? I was hoping you could you let me into his place?"

"Oh. Yes. Of course. Let me get my keys." She retreated into the house and he watched her through the screen door. She seemed to take her time, when he could clearly see her key chain on the blue counter. It was like she was walking in molasses. Finally, she escorted him toward the converted garage.

"I don't think he owns a suit," she said. "But he might have some clean slacks and a button-down shirt."

He smiled again, watching her slip the key into the lock on the raised-panel white door. "That should be more than sufficient. Sorry for coming unannounced. His phone was confiscated and he didn't remember your number."

"Oh, yes, that sounds like him." She smiled and pushed the door open. "We got word of a search warrant. Honestly, this is so ridiculous. Tell him we got the thing and please send him my love."

He stopped. "Thing?"

The woman looked at him quizzically.

Oops. "Yes, right, *the thing*." He added with a smile and a wink. "Thank you. Yes, I'll let him know."

Her smile returned. "Well, he keeps all his clothes here at the rack. I'd be happy to pick something out."

"Oh. Um. No. He asked me to check on something else…before the police arrive. I'm not allowed to say." *Why wouldn't she go away?*

"Not allowed? That's odd." She put her hands on her hips.

"Well, John is a bit odd, you know how he is." He was shooting in the dark. Nosey landladies were the worse. He could write a whole chapter in his upcoming book on them.

She shook her head. "That boy…just let me know when you're done." She exited and closed the door behind her.

Alone, finally.

Thomas surveyed the dark space and flipped the switch just inside the door. In a room so sparsely furnished, it should be easy to locate the drive. The kitchen drawers were first. Inside the cutlery drawer, only three forks, three spoons and three butter knives. The refrigerator had mostly beverages, a dozen eggs, yogurt, and a bag of Mallomars. He snagged a cookie and popped it in his mouth. The freezer was stocked with frozen dinners. He shook the boxes. People always hid stuff in freezers on television. Lobotomy Boy might try it. *Nothing.*

In the living room, he checked under the couch cushions. On the end table, a pink-glazed, lumpy ceramic thing resembling a deep ashtray or a shallow mug caught his attention. He picked it up. Carved into the bottom, the name *John* in nursery school penmanship. The year, also scrawled, was merely five years prior. *Maybe this Crosswell guy was literally a mental patient after all.*

Inside the trunk: a laptop and more books. The nightstand had a picture of Johnnie with a woman, both in sunglasses, drinking tall tropical beverages at a bar. The inside drawer had Chapstick, a cellphone charger and a prescription pill bottle.

He heard a vehicle's tires crunch against the stone driveway. Through the narrow openings in the kitchen blinds, he saw a police vehicle.

Thomas twisted the rod to close the blinds completely. He had to escape. If it were Tobias, he'd be recognized immediately. The only other window was next to the headboard. It faced away from the driveway. He unlocked the latch of the double-hung window and drew up the bottom half.

Thomas climbed outside, then peered around the cinderblock corner. In muffled voices, the woman was telling the officer something, pointing to the apartment. *Could he escape into the low trees, climb up the hill in his suit and dress shoes, and come back for his vehicle later?* Too messy. Or if he timed it just right…

When the trio moved out of view, he sprang, racing to his vehicle, opening and shutting the driver's door gingerly. Taking advantage of the incline, he rolled his vehicle slowly back to the road without turning on the engine, and slid away.

The police officer, landlady and old man came around the corner from the apartment and stared directly at his SUV. But he knew, while he could see *them*, they couldn't see *him*.

His trip wasn't a total loss, because now he knew three things:

One, where Crosswell lived and how to break in.

Two, the landlady could be a good pressure point.

And three, that John Crosswell was clearly no match for him.

Chapter 14

Richard Greaves was a short stocky man, with a bulbous nose, bald-headed with abundantly hairy arms. Robin had heard wonderful things about Greaves' courtroom abilities, and his track record was the best in the territory. His reputation came at a high price; five-hundred an hour with a retainer of fifteen thousand for criminal cases. Yet, sizing him up in person, he didn't exude the level of professionalism she'd imagined.

Still, here he was, sitting in her office just before eleven in the morning, cleaning the inside of his ear with the cap of a fountain pen.

"Mr. Greaves, thank you for getting here so quickly." She took a seat at her desk and clasped her hands together.

"That's fifteen grand." He wiped a nodule of orange wax off the pen cap onto his shirt cuff.

Robin frowned. "Yes, we'll get to that. But I'd like to discuss your strategy for handling these kinds of cases first."

Greaves shook his head. "Oh. What? You think you can do better? Just try. I got the Red Hook Strangler off two years back, remember that? On a technicality, but that's my specialty. All about procedure. Now, I hear this brother of yours is, how you say, cray-cray?" Greaves spun his finger in a circle near his temple.

Robin chose her words carefully. "He's not crazy. Johnnie has challenges, that's true."

"Well, that could work in his favor, you know?" Greaves leaned back in the chair, tapping his fingers together like a movie villain. "I heard he has a record. That's not so bueno. He might have to spend a few years in an institution, but there's a sweet one in Montana. Has an Olympic swimming pool and first-run movies. Plus, a sweet nine-hole golf course. If we play our cards right…"

She couldn't take it. Robin smashed her palm on the desk. "He *didn't* do it."

"Ha!" He began picking at his opposite ear. "Look, I don't have time to pull punches here. I brought the representation agreement. Just sign and cut me a check and we're off to the races."

"Don't you want to know anything about the case first?"

"You think I don't know? Since you called three hours ago, I got the whole 4-1-1. Rookie reporter, name of Marie Swift Bascome, originally from Frederick, Maryland, was over here investigating some crooked real estate deal and the murder of Robert Taylor. Then goes missing two days ago. Washes up here."

With a two-finger air quote, he said, "Your boy *finds* her with his machete." He stopped digging in his ear, but began squeezing at a zit under his chin. "Open and shut if you ask me."

"Hold on. Crooked deal?"

"Yeah, my paralegals spent the last two hours calling around. The girl was working on some story about pay-offs to grease some international development deal. Not important. The key is, if she was investigating Taylor's murder, that gives Johnnie-Boy motive."

Dottie appeared in the doorway. "Robin, line one. Johnnie's boss. Urgent."

Greaves whispered to Dottie, "Sweetie, could you get me a soda pop? I'm parched from the ferry." He pulled out a handkerchief, yellow with sweat stains, and mopped his glistening brow.

Robin took the call. Johnnie's boss seemed excited. And Robin began to feel all was not lost. "No. Really? Wow. That's amazing…yes, could you bring it over to my office?"

Greaves waved his hands at her. "Hello? I'm waiting here."

Robin, trying to hear Kemper, shook her head and turned to face the wall. "Yes, thank you so much. See you soon." The call was over.

He retrieved a blue leather folder with gold lettering from his briefcase and tossed it with spinning precision on her desk in front of her. "Like I said, just sign."

She crossed her arms and grinned for the first time all day. "I just received a bit of exciting news."

"Oh, yeah. What's that?"

Robin pushed her shoulders back with confidence. *Maybe she could cut this grimy self-important jackass loose after all…getting him out of her office before she needed to call in a de-con crew to bathe every surface in bleach.* "We're just going to wait and see."

✷ ✷ ✷

Park Superintendent Kemper Snow arrived promptly at 11:30, right before lunch. Or what normally would be lunch. Robin wasn't hungry. Maybe it was all the coffee she drank to calm her nerves, only causing her to shake and tense her jaw.

Johnnie's tall, skinny boss had straight light brown hair and an upturned nose most people would consider unflattering, but she had a smile that made Robin feel instantly at ease.

"Please, tell me it's true," Robin said, gesturing Kemper to sit in the visitor chair next to Greaves.

Kemper said, "I think this will clear him. It's grainy and dark, but you'll see." She took a SD-card, the size of a postage stamp, from her chest pocket. "Does your laptop take this?" She handed it to Robin.

Robin inserted the card, located the video file in the directory. "How do I play this?"

"You have Windows, right? The media player should work."

After some finagling, the video played. Robin kept the screen in front of her, away from Greaves. She needed to see for herself first.

Greaves shook his head. "Look, the meter is running here. Do I get to see this or not?"

Robin raised a finger. "You'll see it after I do. If I want you to." The video played. Not much to see, just a dark image of sand and the occasional fleck of light reflecting off a wave or a distant boat. "Kemper, what am I looking for?"

"Skip ahead to 2:10 AM."

She watched. "Holy…"

"Wait for it. He has a tattoo."

She skipped ahead thirty seconds. "Oh my…Yes! That's called a tribal tattoo, right? And that man's arms are much hairier than Johnnies'. Oh…what? Ewww. I can't believe he did that."

Greaves tapped his fingers on the arm of his chair. "What? What did he do?"

"The machete. You can't see the woman's face, but that made my skin crawl."

Greaves shook his head. "So, you have the actual murderer on film? And it ain't your brother? Let me see already."

Robin asked, "Kemper, I assume you made an extra copy?"

"I have one. Wait." Kemper walked behind Robin, moved the mouse, and clicked some keys. "There. I placed a copy on your desktop." She looked at Robin. "I should walk next door and give the original to Tobias. Just wanted you to know first."

"Thanks. I appreciate that." Robin clucked her tongue. "No, wait. I want that massive cockhead to come over here to watch it." She turned to Greaves, giddy now, and flipped her computer screen around to face him. "You can watch this now. I'm going to get Tobias. Superintendent Snow, can you stay for a few more minutes?"

Kemper nodded. "Absolutely."

"Thanks." She brushed the hair from her face and left the office. In a matter of seconds, she was outside the building, feeling the warm sun on her face, bursting with happiness like a five-year-old on Christmas morning, holding back whoops of joy. Looking up at the heavens, she said, "Thank you, thank you, thank you."

A few feet ahead of her, Officer Arturo exited the police building, heading up the hill. Without thinking, she hurried towards him, catching up to him, tapping him on the shoulder, breathing heavy. "Arturo, how's Johnnie?"

He whipped his head around, "Senator, nice to see you again." He looked side to side and scratched the back of his neck. "I tried to get a doctor in to see him, but Tobias said no. And your brother got into a fight with another inmate. I didn't want to—honestly—but I had to... tase him."

Robin's smile vanished. "He got into a fight? Did he start it? Shit."

"No...I...you shouldn't be mad. The guy had it coming. I would have liked to beat his ass myself. Excuse my language."

"Johnnie knows better." She closed her eyes. "Has he calmed down now?"

"Yes. I put him in a cell by himself. Oh, and I asked around the precinct and no one had a book, so I gave him some paper to write on. I'm on my lunch break, so I thought I'd stop up at the library. What does he like to read?"

The library was only blocks away, but was small and not open on the weekends. Her brother knew it well, although he often forgot to return books, racking up late fees. It became a problem. "Oh, Arturo. That's so sweet. But that won't be necessary. Johnnie will be going home soon."

"Really? Did Tobias tell you that?"

"No. But Superintendent Snow has video footage. It's plain as day that Johnnie didn't kill that woman."

"Wow. That's great. You must be relieved." He gestured toward the sidewalk. "I'm going to get lunch. A sandwich at the Crescent. Would you like to join me?" He gave a shy smile and glanced down at the ground, like he was inspecting his shoes.

What was it that Janice said? Something about an officer at the station having a crush on her. She imagined Janice had just made that up, being a trouble-maker as usual. Because at forty-seven, men never gave her a second look. She'd known Arturo for years, seeing him around town many times. Last month, at the grocery store, they ran into each other and chatted about something silly—like what their favorite cereal was when they were kids—and, later in the checkout line, he joked about a tabloid headline. Something about aliens in the Bermuda Triangle. Normal friendly innocuous conversation. *Was Arturo asking her out? Like on a date?*

It was too much to process given how fraught her morning was. "Arturo, that sounds lovely, it really does. But can I get a raincheck?"

"Ma'am, no worries. You're busy. Sorry to take up your time. I'll be going..." He spun.

And there it was. She'd done it. Made him feel foolish and humiliated when obviously he felt so shy around her. "No, wait." She put her hand on his arm. "Arturo, I'm interested, truly. But I'm slammed right now. How about dinner Friday?"

His jaw dropped and his face brightened, showing off his dimples. "Senator..."

"Please, call me Robin."

"Robin, yes, Friday. We can go anywhere you want." He looked happy but seemed to hold his breath.

"Good. Call me tomorrow and we'll make plans. I have to go see Tobias now..."

"Yes, yes...I'll call you." He backed away, grinning, stumbling on a patch of broken concrete, re-setting himself, waving.

She stood for a moment, taking in his form as he turned and walked away from her—appreciating his wide shoulders, narrow hips, and long legs. She chuckled—silently wishing Johnnie had gotten arrested sooner.

* * *

Tobias followed Robin into her office and barked, "This video better be all you said to interrupt my lunch."

Greaves lifted his head from his newspaper. "You bet your sweet bippee." He snapped his fingers in the air.

Tobias pointed. "Who's this bald twerp?"

Greaves shot up and tossed his newspaper to the floor. "I'm the twerp that is going to show the entire V-I what an incompetent ass you are." He stepped up to Police Chief, his eyes mere inches from Tobias' chin.

Kemper, seated in the other visitor chair, nodded, "Good afternoon, Chief Tobias."

"You too? What is this, some kind of lame-ass Johnnie Crosswell fan club?"

As enjoyable as it could have been to see Tobias' reaction to the video, Robin needed the Chief to listen, to back down from his preconceptions, and not lose face. "Greaves, come with me. Kemper, please show our esteemed Police Chief the footage. We'll wait outside."

Greaves scowled at Tobias before following her into the hallway. Robin closed the door behind them.

The lawyer leaned against the wall. "So now what? There's still the issue of the contract and the check. I'm a busy man." He picked at his teeth.

"Slow your roll. Let's wait to see what the Chief says. Allegedly, Johnnie assaulted another inmate. Even if the murder charges are dropped, there may be other legal problems."

"Fine. I'm hungry. Where can a person get a half decent pastrami sandwich around here?"

"The Yellow Parrot isn't bad. You probably passed it coming off the ferry."

He shook his head. "You have my number. Call me when you're ready to sign." Greaves took off his suit jacket and threw it over his shoulder—not noticing a wadded brown greasy napkin fell out of the jacket pocket onto the floor. He stalked away, disappearing at the stairs.

Robin listened outside her office door. No voices for a spell until Tobias asked in a frustrated tone, "How do you rewind this thing?"

After some garbled conversation, Tobias whipped open the door. "Superintendent, thank you for bringing this to my attention." He set his gaze on Robin and held up the S-D card like it was a razor blade and he wanted to cut her face with it. "You win. Come get your deranged sibling. I want him out of my sights." He brushed past her, not waiting for a response.

She lunged for her handbag, grabbed it off her desk, and jogged to catch up with Tobias.

Behind his back, she grinned; her happiness exploding in her chest like fireworks. The reasonable part of her brain chided, "*Not a word.*

Not a bloody word.

Get in, get Johnnie, and get out.

Chapter 15

Dear Diary,

It isn't even lunch time yet. Jail is boring as hell, and I'm getting cold. They keep the air conditioning on blast. But Arturo gave me some paper and a green crayon to keep me busy. I'm not good at drawing and I can't see great without my glasses. I'll probably rip this up later, because Tobias will probably think I'm writing a confession, which I'm not because I didn't do anything.

As jails go, this one is better than Miami. But I already got into a fight, and the guy had it coming. Arturo was cool and said he wouldn't tell Tobias. In fact, he apologized for tasing me. If Lou were here, she'd say I shouldn't have snapped like that. But sometimes pieces of shit need to be beat, and that's just that. I'm not sorry.

My lawyer still hasn't shown up, so I might not go home tonight.

I don't know what to write about. Robin says I should start writing stories because I read so much and it would give me a creative outlet. I'm not a writer—except for you diary—and almost flunked English in high school. But it would be okay because no one will ever see it but me. If I wrote a story, it would be an adventure about a pirate that steals and gives to the poor, like Robin Hood. And he would have a beautiful *mermaid girlfriend that helps him retrieve gold doubloons and other booty from sunken ships. But they could never be together because she loves the water more than him. And maybe the pirate would have a pet iguana instead of a stinky, annoying parrot. I know it sounds dumb and no one would—*

Thunderous footsteps echo in the hall, waking him from his daydream about the pirate king. He threw the crayon away and stuffed the lined paper up the back of his thin undershirt.

"Crosswell," Tobias barked. "Time to move."

"What's going on? Did Robin post bail?"

Tobias unlocked the cell, his eyes like daggers. "Just shut up and move."

He walked out of the cell, pulling up on the waist of his underwear, "Where to?"

The Chief stormed towards the front of the station down the narrow hall. Johnnie followed. They stopped at the bailiff's desk. Tobias handed him a tall paper grocery bag. "Take your belongings and leave. Get your ugly face out of my sights."

Ugly? He'd been called worse things, but never ugly. Not that he had movie star looks, but he wasn't deformed or anything. Johnnie pawed through the bag's contents. In all his life, he was never so glad to see his pants. The bag contained his uniform and boots. He whipped the pants in the air to unfurl the legs and stuffed his cold legs into the openings. As he began winding his belt back through the loops, Tobias shook his head and pushed him toward the front door.

"I said, go."

Johnnie stumbled forward, padding the rest of the way in his mid-calf brown socks toward the exit. The stares of all the station personnel bored into him as he reached for the push bar. He took a deep breath and walked out, wondering if they would change their mind and tase him again.

The first person to greet him was Robin, standing on the sidewalk, with his boss Kemper next to her. The outside warmth felt welcome on his numb skin. Robin stretched her arms outward and drew him in for a long hug.

He dropped the bag on the sidewalk. "Ow, Sis, not so hard. My ribs and muscles are still sore."

She released him, took a step back, and looked him up and down. "Are you okay? I can take you to the hospital."

"I'm alright. I think my back is just bruised. I just want to go home."

Kemper stepped towards him. "Glad to have you back." She handed him his glasses.

Johnnie scratched the side of his head near his scar, "What happened? Why did Tobias let me go? Did his heart grow six sizes?" He fiddled with the glasses, checking the hinges. There was a slight scratch on the outer tinted lens, but otherwise, they seemed fine.

Robin rested her hand on Kemper's shoulder. "Your brilliant boss had video showing the actual killer."

"Really? That's incredible."

Kemper shrugged. "The turtle nest cam came to your rescue. Now, don't take this the wrong way, but I'm putting you on a different assignment for the next two weeks." She chewed on her thumbnail. "It's not a punishment. But word got out about your arrest. Merv told me some tourists are coming to Hawksnest asking to meet the 'St. Johnnie Killer'. It would be best for you to lie low for a few days."

"Shit. I have a serial killer name already?" He donned his glasses, instantly feeling relief from the sun's glare off the white sidewalk.

Kemper chuckled, "Looks that way. Now, I want you to relax the rest of the day and I'll text you your assignment for tomorrow."

He asked Kemper, "Hey, can I see the video?"

Robin grabbed his ear and pulled down on it sharply, putting an index finger in his face. "I love you, but I will kill you myself if you go anywhere near this murder case. You hear, butthead?"

"Okay, okay!"

She released him. His ear throbbed.

Robin said, "Good. By the way, I met Bob Taylor's widow this morning. I'm going to help her get answers."

Johnnie's eyes went wide. "Really? What are you going to do?"

"I don't know yet, but whatever it is, it's not your concern." She pulled on her suit jacket and fiddled with the collar on her blouse. "This is what's going to happen. Kemper is going to drive you back to your scooter. You are going home and staying there the rest of the day. I'm going to try to get some real work done over the next two hours, go home early, and drink myself to sleep. Understand?"

Johnnie hung his head, avoiding her intense gaze. "I know this is all my fault, and I'm grateful for everything, but you always told me that drinking never solved anything."

Robin put her hands on her hips. "Oh, so now you're going to lecture me about drinking? Mister I-Got-Hurt-In-The-War and Drank-Myself-Nearly-To-Death? Huh. Fuck you, little brother."

He raised his hands defensively. "That's not what I meant. I just don't want you to fall off the wagon again."

Robin shook her head and stalked off. From twenty-feet away, she turned and gave him two upward fingers, then continued on, walking toward her office building and was soon out of sight.

Kemper tugged on a lock of her brown hair and dragged her foot in a circle, her chin low, "Family, right?" She smiled.

Johnnie's eyes clouded up. Robin had every right to be angry. He shouldn't have said that in front of Kemper. But after Robin's marriage ended, she spent a year downing pills and bourbon. That was over a decade ago, even before his accident and her move to St. John, though he still worried about her. If his mistakes sent her down that road again, he couldn't forgive himself. "I had that coming. If you only knew…"

Kemper clapped him on the arm. "Let's get out of here. Hey, you hungry? We could go to the Yellow Parrot."

Images of the fight with Chain Boy flooded his thoughts. He desperately wanted to know if Mandy was okay. He should have asked Arturo earlier. "Hey, I could use a favor. Do you know Mandy James?"

"Sort of. She's the bartender at the Parrot, right?"

He explained the story to her. "Could we stop by and maybe you could ask how she is?"

"Johnnie, I know your heart is in the right place, but I don't think it's a good idea. It would be an invasion of her privacy."

"Yeah, I guess you're right." He looked down at himself, still in his undershirt and socks. Kemper was right; he shouldn't pry. "In that case, I think I'll go straight home."

"Right. Let's go."

Kemper's pickup truck was parked down the hill. Before getting in the vehicle, he opened the paper bag and pulled out his uniform dress shirt, ballcap and boots. He sat on the edge of the truck's front bench and bent to put on his boots; his ribs screamed. "Ow! Fuck."

"Are you okay?" Kemper sat behind the steering wheel; her eyes wide with concern.

"I don't know. They hit me pretty hard earlier." He stood and lifted his white undershirt and turned in a circle. "How's my back?"

Kemper whipped open the driver's door and jogged around the truck. "Oh, God! Johnnie." She gingerly touched his back with her index finger. In a soft voice, she asked, "Does that hurt?"

"A little. How does it look?" He twisted his head but couldn't see.

Her face appeared stricken and her blue eyes were moist. "Bad. Worse than bad. Who did this?"

"The cops. Before you arrived this morning."

She sighed and clucked her tongue. "You need a doctor. I'm taking you to the walk-in medical clinic. You should get an x-ray."

He pulled down his undershirt and tossed his boots in the foot-well. "No, it's probably nothing."

"I insist." She jogged back around and took a seat behind the steering wheel.

He pulled his door closed. Reaching for the seat belt involved twisting. Pain shot through his back. "Ow. Fuck." He reached again, slower this time, and fastened the clip. "I don't want to take up any more of your time. I mean, you really saved me today. I don't want to be a bother."

Kemper's eyes were stern. And she was never stern. "Shush. No arguing."

They went to the clinic. In the waiting room, Kemper read a National Geographic and he read Better Homes and Gardens. But he only had to wait fifteen minutes. The x-rays showed nothing broken. Still, the doctor told him to rest for a few days. Advice he planned to ignore. Because being idle and lying in bed reminded him of the VA hospital, and that was worse than some discomfort he might feel at work.

A calendar appointment pinged on Johnnie's phone as they exited the clinic. *His library book!* He had to return it by closing time—five o'clock—or incur the wrath of the head librarian, Ms. Teller. The last time he was there, she stared at him over her reading glasses with a scowl that could take the paint off a barn.

"Hey, I need to get back to my scooter." The time was 4:32. His throat tightened and panic froze his brain. Johnnie concentrated on his breathing. *In…out…in…*

Kemper gave him a serious look. "Let me drive you *home*."

He wrung his hands. "No, I have to get to the library. Now."

"What? No, you need to rest." They got in the truck and she started the engine.

"Please. You have no idea. The librarian? Ms. Teller? She fucking hates my guts. I'm on probation. If I'm late again, she'll put me on the no-lending list permanently. The book is in the seat compartment of my scooter." Johnnie rubbed his face with his hands and groaned.

Kemper pulled out of the parking lot. "Okay. Calm down. Tell you what, *I'll* return it for you. You just get yourself home to rest. Deal?"

"Really? You'd do that?"

"Absolutely."

Johnnie nodded. "Thanks, Kemper." Still, his heart raced with panic. "Text me after, okay?"

"Sure. Just relax." She gave him a quick smile.

They continued the drive to Hawksnest Beach in silence for a couple minutes, until Kemper asked in a soft voice, "It's a funny thing. I've been getting calls about missing wallets and jewelry at Hawksnest. More so than other beaches. Usually on the weekends." She took her eyes off the road briefly to meet his, "During the weekdays, when you're over there, have you noticed any bad characters lurking around?" She hunched her shoulders, chin jutting, miming a lurker.

"No, I mean, sometimes there are teenagers acting like dicks. The signs say to lock valuables. But people are dumb and think they can hide stuff under their beach towels."

"What about that homeless guy? Do you know him?"

"Cud? He wouldn't steal. I mean, if people leave useful shit behind, he might *recycle* them. But like towels and flip-flops. Not anything valuable."

"Hmmm." She wiggled her nose like she was thinking and kept her focus on the road.

Johnnie waited for her to say something more, but she seemed preoccupied with her thoughts.

As they approached the Hawksnest Beach parking lot, Merv moved two traffic cones to let them in. The parked news van, with its portable antenna raised, was an unwelcome sight. Thankfully, the news crew seemed to be taking some shots of the beach. While they were distracted, Johnnie jogged to his scooter, and gave Kemper the book. With adrenaline pumping, he straddled the Pig, gunned the small engine, and drove off before anyone recognized him.

On the ride home, he envisioned his mug shot on the news with the headline "St. Johnnie Killer now on the loose". St. John was a small island. Any kind of infamy stuck like tar, guilty or not.

As his scooter climbed the winding narrow dirt road to Gertie's, he made a mental plan to cook some spaghetti and take a nap. When he arrived, Cud was sitting on a wood bench by the driveway, waving to him.

Cud was still at Gerties? Did he move in with her? Johnnie wondered if he'd need a new place to live to give them some space. The National Park Service lodging at Caneel Bay might be available, but he recalled how he hated it. Living with all those cheerful people playing hacky-sack every evening, and group sing-a-longs to acoustic guitar. One guy played jazz flute. It was like a grownup hippie version of sleep-away camp. He couldn't stomach it.

Cud jogged up. "Johnnie, we were so worried. Robin told us everything."

He took off his helmet. "Yeah. Robin and Kemper saved my life. I'm really tired."

"Johnnie boy, we have a problem."

He walked towards his apartment door, "I can't take any more problems."

"Listen." Cud waved a hand in his face. "That man with the black aura? What's his name?"

"Mark, I think. What about him?" He let out a prolonged yawn. *Time for some sleep.* He put his key in the door lock, but strangely, the door was unlocked already.

Cud gritted his teeth, grabbed both Johnnie's shoulders, his eyes wide and boring into his. "I know you are rightfully knackered after your ordeal, but I need you to listen."

Johnnie winced. Cud's hand landed where Arturo had tased him in the shoulder. "Ow. Yes. Spit it out!"

"Mark's coming for you, son. And we need to set a plan."

✻ ✻ ✻

Mary Taylor arrived at the funeral home west of Charlotte Amalie at five, an hour before the six o'clock service. It had to be a closed casket for obvious reasons. Robert wasn't a religious man and he wouldn't have wanted an elaborate service. Still, when his brother, Gus, asked to do a bible reading, she couldn't refuse.

She sat in the empty space. No pictures. No flowers. Organizing a secret memorial on a different island, while dodging a madman seemed insane. And the last-minute change of venue complicated everything. She spent most of the afternoon texting relatives the new location.

Robert was found dead eight days ago, and his body released by the police only two days ago. What was the point of this service? Most of their relatives couldn't attend, because getting flights during the Easter rush was nearly impossible.

The funeral director came in, short, tubby and wearing a dark suit. "Do you know how many will be attending today?"

Mary did a mental count. "About ten. My daughter's flight just arrived. Roberta is on Spring Break, coming in from Texas. Some local friends. His brother from Georgia."

He took her hand. "How are you holding up?"

She had to think. *Holding up? I'm ready to scream...*

"Ow." The director pulled away.

Had she dug her nails into his skin? "Oh, no. I'm sorry." She let his hand go. Mary stared straight ahead at the casket. "How am I? I don't really know. It isn't right. I cry myself to sleep every night. Then I have nightmares and wake in cold sweats. And poor Robert. All he ever did was care about the earth and protecting the oceans. A good person who never hurt anyone. Why did he have to die?" She realized she was raving and began to cry. In her purse, she dug for a tissue. "I'm mad and I want to hit something."

"I understand." He clasped his hands in front of him. "Can I do anything to help?"

She wiped her eyes and cleared her throat. "No. Is the security person here?"

"Yes, outside. Anyone fitting the man's description will be turned away and he'll call the police."

"Thanks. I appreciate all your help."

The director gave a nod and left.

Her friend Faye walked in. "Are you sure you're up for this?"

Mary said, "No." She stood and greeted Faye with a hug. "Thanks for coming. I don't know how I'm going to make it..."

"You're doing fine."

They sat down at the first row of chairs. Mary said, "I'll be out of your hair soon. I promise. Can you believe Senator Crosswell hasn't called me back yet? I can't live this way." She curled her hands into tight fists.

"Look, your daughter will be here soon. It will get better."

"Maybe I should move permanently. Rent a small place near Robbie's college." Her eyes went wide. "I forgot to tell you. I got an email from the insurance company. Robert had a policy for two million." She shook her head. "Maybe he knew..."

Faye patted her hands "Don't decide now. Let the shock wear off. Take some time."

"Yes, I know. I know. I just hate feeling like I have no control."

A man strode toward them. Her brother-in-law Gus resembled Bob, with his brown hair, bushy eyebrows and hooked nose, but taller and thinner. "Mary, I'm so sorry." He gave her a hug.

"Thanks for coming. Gus, this is my friend Faye. I'm staying with her for the next few days."

They shook hands.

Mary started with the pleasantries. *That's what you do, right?* Better than talking about their loss. "How was your flight?"

"Mary, I don't know how to say this." Gus clasped his hands tightly and avoided her eyes.

He seemed upset, but what could be worse than this? "What? What's wrong?"

Gus blurted, "I just got an email from Robert."

Her hands flew to her mouth. "What? How?"

"When I turned on my phone after touch-down, it showed up. But it was from a Gmail account I didn't recognize. I almost deleted it."

Why would Robert send something to Gus and not her? "Let me see." He handed his phone to her. She read the message.

> Gus, if you receive this, then I may be gone. Which means, you'll want to know why I'm dead. It's a long story, but a client asked me to falsify information on the biological impact study. When I went to confront the project manager, I overheard a conversation about bribing officials. Now the company's fixer is after me because I stole the bribe money.
>
> Once the newspaper article hits the national news, I'll

> be safe. But in case I don't make it, I put you down as a co-owner on the safe deposit box at the Carib Bank. Contact Ms. Marie Bascome at the Washington Times or her boss and give them the evidence if I go missing. Mary knows my favorite password. Tell Mary and Robbie I love them and I'm sorry.

Mary gave Gus back his phone and had to sit. The news identified the dead woman as Ms. Bascome. And the man who came to her house and held a knife to her throat was not bluffing when he threatened her life.

She shuddered and held her head. "Gus, don't tell Robbie. Don't tell anyone. We'll talk afterward, okay?"

Gus put his phone in his jacket pocket. "Mary, I don't understand. We need to tell the authorities…"

Her face felt warm. The authorities were no help so far. *Gus had no idea.* In a biting tone, she said, "It isn't safe." She looked up, pleading to him with her eyes. "Promise me. You have to promise."

Gus held his hands up in surrender. "Yes, whatever you say."

Anxiety raged through every cell in her being. The last thing she needed was a panic attack or a complete melt down. She excused herself and went to the ladies' room to collect herself.

The bathroom was grossly ornate, with a pink tufted sofa, gold faucets, and marble floors. Running the tap at the sink, she splashed cold water on her face, causing her mascara to run. *Which was worse, the dark baggy circles under her eyes or the black mascara streaks?* It didn't matter. Nothing mattered.

The image at the coroner's office of Robert's purple and white skin and staring eyes haunted her. Like he was a ghoul in a low-budget Hollywood movie. Not the loving, sweet, silly man she'd lived with for the last thirty years. The man with the ruddy cheeks and hearty laugh who loved watching basketball and hiking and making pasta from scratch. Who volunteered regularly at local schools to teach kids about sea life. The man who wrote her love notes before every long business trip and crafted personal anniversary cards each year. The man who washed the dishes without being asked and rubbed her feet when they were sore. Her Robert was not that same man on the cold steel table.

With some paper towels, she scrubbed her face.

Mary slammed her hand on the towel dispenser. Under her breath, she muttered, "Robert, you stubborn, stubborn fool."

* * *

Dear Diary,

It was a quiet day. KIDDING! Got arrested, beat up a pervert, got freed, and Mark—the ninja, black-aura dude—is after me. And it's only Monday. Beating up chain boy was bad, but I hope Lou would say it was justified anger. There will be lots to tell her on Friday. Robin is so pissed. I should call her to apologize but I'll give her a couple nights to calm down.

Kemper is reassigning me to give small guided nature hikes to avoid reporters. Which is maybe worse than jail because these privileged Easter vacation looky-loos never wear the right shoes, bring their obnoxious private-school kids and complain the whole time. But hopefully they won't know I'm the killer on the news.

Cud told me he'd charter a plane to take me to the Bahamas to stay with his grandson. But I'm not scared of Mark and his stupid black outfits. I've seen his type in the military a thousand times. All show and no common sense or actual skills. Mark can eat my butt.

And Cud said he threw away the thumb drive, so there is nothing to give Mark.

In other news, I may start writing a short story about the altruistic pirate king. Not that I can write, but no one will ever see it but me.

But this is the BIGGEST news. Cud said he might ask Gertie to marry him. That was fast. But Gertie said once she'll never remarry. Not sure if I should tell Cud. Probably won't.

Good night Diary. Wish me strength for tomorrow, Johnnie.

Chapter 16

It was nine o'clock on Tuesday morning. Robin opened her Outlook calendar. Dottie said something about an early meeting with the Tourism Minister of the British Virgin Islands. A discussion related to the proposal she was supposed to have read yesterday. But that never happened.

Ten minutes later, Dottie escorted two men into her office. Dottie said, "Robin, Minister Jacque Lords and his colleague Thomas Smith are here to see you."

She finished her sip of coffee and shut off her computer monitor. "Yes, please come in."

The pair in front of her didn't seem right. The first man was in a light gray windowpane suit, tailored to perfection, with a light purple paisley ascot and tan leather dress shoes so pristine you could eat off of them. The second was burly, smelled of too much aftershave, and wore a black T-shirt, black jeans and an ill-fitting tan linen Miami-Vice sort of blazer, with black lace-up boots.

She extended her hand, "Gentlemen, nice to meet you both."

"Senator Crosswell, so nice to meet you, finally," Minister Lords said with a titter.

The other man shook her hand, his gaze intense, and said simply, "Hello."

"Please, sit. Call me Robin. I'm sorry, but I had a bit of a family emergency yesterday. I didn't have time to look over the proposal." She rested her hand on the binder as she took her chair. "Perhaps you could give me a quick run-down?"

Smith, who she named in her head 'Miami', took his chair, giving her a black look, as though she said something terribly upsetting.

The well-dressed man said, "Well, Robin, please call me Jacque. You know, my parents named me after Cousteau. They were close friends with him. Rest his soul. They don't make men like him anymore."

Robin smiled. "No, they don't."

"Anyway," Jacque waved his hand, "darling, if you flip to page ten of the proposal, there is a sketch of what we have in mind."

Robin put on her reading glasses and located the page; it depicted a map of St. John and Tortola. She froze, her jaw slack. "Um, Jacque, am I seeing this right? You want to build a bridge between our islands?"

Jacque smiled, extending his fingers like jazz hands. "Bingo!"

"And connect them through Great Thatch Island?" Alarm bells went off in Robin's head. Mary Taylor's husband was doing marine life surveys there. *Was this the project he couldn't talk about?*

"Yes! But it is so much more than a connection. Great Thatch Island would be transformed into an international port of customs, including an airport with an eight-thousand-foot runway, desperately needed for modern commercial aircraft, and a cruise-line terminal to boot. A receiving point for goods and tourism that can serve both our island territories. It makes perfect sense. After Irmaria devastated everything, we knew we needed additional transit hubs to bring in emergency supplies, construction materials…really the whole gambit. And think of the cross-promotional tourism possibilities!" Jacque wiggled his shoulders with a smile big enough to drive a Volkswagen into. Robin expected him to break into song, like a Broadway musical like Cats, but somehow more flamboyant.

He continued, "Visitors could drive between the islands for day trips, expanding commerce exponentially. Picture it! Tourists would get two great destinations for the price of one. A game changer. The two segments of bridge would only need to span a mile. Honestly, I don't know why this hasn't been considered before." Jacque clucked his tongue, "Like, duh!"

Thomas Smith added, his face stony, "You'll find the economic analysis in Section Two. It means a net eighty million a year in tax revenue for your constituents. Better infrastructure will reduce the costs of recovery from future storms. With the state of the Territory's debt and lost revenue, you'd be *wise* to back this."

The way he said wise felt like a threat. Like she was in an episode of the Sopranos.

Smith bared his teeth as he talked. "We're meeting with the Governor tomorrow. We've been assured he endorses the project."

Robin took off her glasses and rubbed the bridge of her nose. She ignored Smith. "Jacque, you know there's a reason St. John doesn't have a port deep enough for cruise ships, right? And the route for your bridge goes directly through waters with a protected reef system, designated part of the National Park by Federal statute. This is ludicrous."

Mr. Smith leaned forward, his chin jutting out, "Senator, with all due respect, if you read the goddamned proposal…"

Jacque rested his hand on Smith's shoulder, "Please, Thomas, let me."

Smith gritted his teeth and sat back in the chair, crossing his legs. "Fine."

Jacque smiled, "Robin, believe me, when I first heard about this concept, I had a similar reaction. But quite a lot has changed since Irmaria. Reports show the hurricanes did more than destroy our buildings, it changed the ecology drastically. The coral reefs we once treasured are gone, wiped out. In Section Five of your binder, you'll see the ecologist's report. A team of renowned marine biologists, from around the world, evaluated the area. Sadly, the reefs are not expected to recover for at least fifty years."

Robin turned pages until she got to Section Five. An executive summary, followed by color photographs of the reef damage. Scientific study references outlining the assumptions and data. It seemed legitimate. "Hold on. Even if the corals are damaged, adding this kind of infrastructure and development would surely slow the reef's recovery, wouldn't it? I mean, all the industrial and airport runoff, the extra sewage from the visitors, it would only exacerbate the problem. The corals might never recover."

"All great points. And the consortium has considered all those aspects and a mitigation plan is outlined in Section Six. In fact, the bridge design will include state-of-the-art technology for micro-plastics removal and create artificial beds to seed new corals. This project will be a model for ocean restoration. The proposal includes a ten-year study of the ecosystem to assess changes."

"And when do they want to do this?"

Smith chimed up, "As soon as possible. All the other players in the BVI are on-board. The House of Commons won't pursue it unless it's a joint effort with the States. Congress needs your buy-in to advance the bill in the House. Senator Soria already wrote a letter of endorsement."

Robin propped her cheek on her palm, staring at Smith with her head cocked. "I'm sorry, Mr. Smith, what is your role in this proposal again?"

Smith puffed up his chest and cocked his head to match hers. "I represent the private entity of this public-private partnership. The company I represent will put up a third of the construction costs for a third of the annual revenue over the next fifty years."

Robin returned his stare. "What company was that again?"

Jacque quaked, "Senator, the terms of the partnership are described in Section Ten. There are hosts of other partners. NGO's like Sea Turtles in Motion and Strong Marine Life Habitat."

"Jacque, I appreciate you coming all this way. But, unfortunately, I need more time to take a closer look at this."

Smith uncrossed his legs. "Crosswell. That sounds familiar. You mentioned a family emergency. Do you have relatives here?"

Robin's eyes bulged. With the news of Johnnie's arrest yesterday, the name Crosswell was in the local news everywhere today. But this was none of Miami's business. "No, just me."

"Hmmm. Who's that in the picture over there?" Smith pointed to a 5 x 7 picture frame on the credenza behind her desk of her and Johnnie, both wearing black rimmed sunglasses, sitting at the Skinny Knees bar with umbrella drinks.

She lied, "My friend, Olaf."

Smith chuckled, "Olaf, eh?" He turned to Jacque, "We shouldn't take any more of the Senator's time." He added gruffly, "Senator Crosswell has some reading to do."

Jacque gave a weak smile. "Yes, yes. We should go. Robin, fantastic meeting you. We appreciate your time to the utmost. If amenable, I'll ring you next Monday to get your impressions of the plan?"

Robin nodded. "That would be fine."

Smith rose from his chair, grabbing Jacque by the upper arm and steering him to the door like he was taking a prisoner to a cell. He gave a look to Robin, his irises black. "Have a nice day, Senator Crosswell. We'll be in touch."

Somehow, Robin felt being 'in touch' was more of a threat than a cordial parting phrase. She rose to shake their hands, but Smith shoved Jacque ahead—apparently not interested in exchanging the usual pleasantries.

Halfway through the door, Jacque turned his head and added a quick, "Toodles," before Smith herded him out of sight.

What an odd pair.

She sat back in her chair, wondering why Mr. Smith was acting like such a belligerent goon. Robin called out, "Dottie!"

Dot poked her head in. "Yes?"

"Clear my calendar for the rest of the day. Something strange is going on and I need to figure this out."

"Yes, consider it done. Anything I can do to help?"

"I need a private detective. Someone local."

"Oh. Really? Well, I know someone who is available and works for free."

"Huh? Who?"

Dot pointed both thumbs at herself.

"Ha!" Robin shook her head. "You're a detective? What have you detected before?"

"Remember when someone was stealing lunch bags from the kitchen? I was the one who figured out it was Milton. And the time my car was stolen? I tracked down the culprit before Tobias."

"Dottie, I think this one's different. That Thomas Smith guy seems dangerous. I mean, it wasn't anything he said exactly, but if you saw the evil looks he gave me..."

With a grin, Dot polished her light blue nails across her blouse and blew on them. "Which means I'm the *perfect* person."

"How so?"

"Bad guys never see me coming."

* * *

The Merv-man whistled.

Stumpy looked around. He ran across the sand toward the pavilion. Meal time!

Sure enough, the man with the jingly pockets and long face greeted him with some unfamiliar words. He didn't know many words except for the important ones that involved treats. Those weeks of playing with the man, learning which items to take—which were good and which weren't—helped him understand. The man didn't want leaves or shells or bottle caps or shards of glass. No reward for those.

But first, Stumpy wanted to see what today's prize was.

The man held out chunks of dried apricot, sweet, delicious. The man said, "Get."

Stumpy blinked and dashed off.

It was never clear what the man wanted with all the sparkly bits and leather squares. Although with sugary fruit at stake—scrumptious, crunchy—he would pick out the biggest sparkle in his cache. But he couldn't let the man see where he went or he might steal it all, leaving nothing for future exchange.

He darted through the grass and low bushes, weaving, waiting, darting again, making his way to the treasure he buried. Scratching at the sand in the right spot where he stored the gleaming pieces for safe-keeping, Stumpy located the looped metal with the stone thingies, clutching it in his jaw. He reburied the rest with waves of his shortened tail, scurrying his way back to the pavilion, saliva dripping around the prize, hoping, longing...

He dropped the item at the man's feet and cocked his head to the side, studying his reaction.

It was a good reaction. Some verbal praise, saying his name. The man picked up the object, dusting off the sand.

The food! Don't forget the food!

Stumpy placed his foot on the man's boot. Don't climb... he doesn't like that. No food if you use your claws... Feed me! Now! I'm right here!

The man chucked the apricots across the pavilion, into a nearby clump of bushes.

He raced toward it, hoping his rival, Green-tail, wouldn't get there first. Because that would be unfair. But he could fight, even without his tail. Fight and bite and claw and run.

The sugary fruit chunks were there, untouched, untaken. He chomped down on the irregular disks, his teeth gnashing, ripping off smaller pieces. His mind went blank with ecstasy, ribbons of sweetness down his gullet, holding down corners of larger pieces with two toes for better purchase. In almost no time, the reward was gone.

He needed more!

Stumpy scampered back to the pavilion, but the man was gone. He swiveled his neck, looking, twitching. The man was at the wood structure with a door. He scurried over.

The tall-faced one looked down at him. "No"—something.

He also understood the word 'no'. It meant he'd have to wait until the next time.

But where was the cheesy-man? He never wanted shiny things for trade. And it had been several days... when would he return? Puffs were crunchy, cheddary, the best. And the round-eyed man talked to him nicely and smiled. Sometimes they would watch the sunrise together. It was special.

Plus, the long-haired, wrinkly man who gave fresh fruit was also gone.

Why did they leave him? Did they forget about him?

Humans were so fickle. So unreliable.

Stumpy heard a certain vehicle, his nemesis. The taker of tails, the metal beast of all evils.

He ambled toward the pavement, toward the sound that haunted him. He recognized the knobby tires, the whine of the engine. Placing his body in front of the devil, he hissed, refusing to move as the gigantic cube of metal inched forward.

"Go somewhere else, Oh, Can of Pain! This is my beach! I demand your departure!"

The cube stopped. Still, he wanted to bite it. Tear off rubber. Maybe the wiper blades...

His foe retreated, moving in reverse, pulling into a vacant area. The engine noise ceased. Doors opened. Two humans got out, laughing.

Were they mocking his pain? His short tail? These were not good people. He could bite them, claw them.

A commotion behind him. Near the curb, Green-Tail was chewing on a sumptuous red apple.

This could not stand. Not within his territory. Not in his presence.

Stumpy dashed toward the red orb. It would be his.

And Green-tail would learn— through slashes and bites and ripped dorsal crests—that he, Stumpy, was the one and only—the true—Iguana King.

Chapter 17

The forest hike was going as badly as he expected.

"Mister Ranger? Why do you wear those weird glasses? Did you know some sharks have fifteen rows of teeth? I can curl my tongue. Can you?" Chase, the six-year-old, looked up at him, matching Johnnie's stride by moving his legs faster. Over the last half-hour, this kid wouldn't stop talking and reciting dumb riddles. "Mister Ranger, do you know what the cow says when it's tired of walking?"

He'd told the group several times he was a park guide, at least for today, and not a ranger. Real rangers were law enforcement, like Merv, or interpretive. There was literally no way he could have qualified to become an enforcement ranger with his police record and setbacks. And he didn't have the temperament or education to be an interpretive ranger. But the kid enjoyed calling him ranger and Johnnie gave up arguing.

Johnnie now knew everything about little Chase. His favorite color (blue), his dog's name (Chumlie–Wumbly), what he got for Christmas (an iPad), his favorite TV show (Star Wars: The Clone Wars), and what he wanted to be when he grew up (a scientist who studies sharks or an ice cream man).

Johnnie took a deep breath, pausing purposefully to slow the onslaught of more questions, "No, what did the cow say when he was tired of walking?"

Chase giggled. "I'm poopy pooped! Get it?"

No, he didn't get it. Johnnie looked behind him, doing a visual head count. "We have to stop and wait for the others." A gust of wind brushed his arms and a sizable black cloud above them darkened the path. He eyed it and wondered if the storm clouds would pass them by.

Chase stuck out his tongue. "But I need to go to the bathroom!"

Johnnie surveyed their surroundings. "See that clump of bushes? Go back there."

"No, I need to go number two."

Five of the adults walked up. Only two more were lagging.

Johnnie said to the arriving group, "We'll wait for the others. This would be a good time to drink some water."

Chase tugged on Johnnie's belt. "Mister Ranger, I need to go!"

Of course, the two missing adults were Chase's parents. The mom was wearing heeled sandals, and the dad was helping her, propping her up from falling in the slimy mud caused by the morning rain shower.

"Chase, why don't you go see where your parents are and report back?"

A woman in the group, short and overweight, with brown curly hair, dressed like Steve Irwin, chimed in, "Ranger John, you can't let a little boy wander the path alone! Are you crazy?"

Did she have to use the word crazy? He exhaled through his teeth. "Fine, do you want to go look for them?"

The short woman glared at him. "Fine." She turned to Chase. "Honey-pie, come with me. We'll go get your mom and dad together." Mrs. Irwin held out her hand.

Chase took the woman's hand and stuck out his tongue at Johnnie.

The pair walked up the hill, disappearing where the path made a turn.

The other four hikers looked at Johnnie. He needed a distraction. Something to occupy them while they waited. "So, how is everyone doing?" The second he uttered this, he regretted opening his dumb mouth.

An older man, maybe in his seventies, wearing a bright orange Hawaiian shirt, responded, "Well, my knee feels a bit inflamed. Took some ibuprofen before we left the hotel. How much further until we get to end?"

As if the day couldn't get worse, the God of Pain and Irony chose this precise moment to dump water from the heavens in a torrent. Not unusual for mid-day on the island. Rains came and went, most times lasting less than ten minutes. But the group screamed. From up the hill, more screams, probably from Chase, his parents and Mrs. Irwin. Some took off their backpacks, using them as cover. Others hugged themselves, shivering.

Chase's mom came running toward them, now barefoot, her legs covered in brick-colored mud. Her once white Bermuda shorts were slicked with more mud. "Ranger, help!"

Rain dripped off the bill of Johnnie's green Park Service ball cap.

"What happened?"

She walked up to him, beet-faced, gasping for air, slapping him in the chest. "The God-damned rain! Get us out of here!"

"It will pass soon. And don't touch me." He began counting, closing his eyes.

"What? Can't you call in a bus or jeep to get us out of this hell hole?"

He opened his eyes. She was still in his face, water matting down her hair, running down her nose. "Ma'am, the rain will probably pass in a couple minutes. We should continue on." In a loud voice, he called. "Everyone, we're moving on. Watch your step because the path will be slippery."

Chase cried, "But I can't!"

Chase's mom cuddled him close. "I know, baby." She yelled, "Hey, doofus! We need to get my son to a bathroom."

Johnnie spun around. "Lady, there are no bathrooms until we get to the shore. Now, you can hike back up the way you came for a mile to the port-a-john at the railhead or little Chase can take a dump behind a bush, or you all can continue the next mile and a half to the boat pickup point. Choose now."

Chase's face wrinkled and his cheeks turned fuchsia; he began to cry, his chest convulsing.

Mrs. Irwin pointed at him with her hiking pole, "What is wrong with you? Talking to a mother and little boy like that?"

He should have felt bad for making the boy cry. Maybe part of him felt remorse. But the practicality of the matter instructed him that standing around in a downpour wasn't helping anyone. Ironically, constant movement helped him forget the pain in his back. Stillness caused his mind to register the discomfort.

With narrowed eyes, Johnnie said, "The hike description went over all of this. Rain or shine. This is a three-hour nature hike, not a visit to Chuckie Cheese. Now, for those that want to continue, please follow me."

The group didn't follow. Mrs. Irwin said, "I think we should all go back."

Johnnie looked skyward, rain falling on his glasses. *Days at Hawksnest Beach were never like this.* He studied their stricken, wet faces. "By a show of hands, who wants to go back?"

One by one, all the hands went up.

Johnnie clapped his hands together. "I guess we're going back." He took out his whistle. [Tweeeet] "About face!"

The troupe turned around, grumbling. Hiking up the newly soaked path was treacherous; even he had mild difficulty with his thick-soled boots. The hikers slipped and grabbed onto thin tree branches and brush during steep ascents. Chase, leading the pack, followed by his parents, was simpering. "Mommy, I don't want to be here!"

Two minutes later, the deluge ended and the sun came out; intense rays warmed the air. Johnnie felt some vindication, but it did him little good. He still had another twenty minutes with this group. They mumbled between themselves and he heard the words, "report him" and "get my money back".

Another group of hikers passed them. He radioed headquarters to let them know the change of plans and the new pickup location. At least Chase wasn't pestering him anymore. That was a bonus.

When they finally arrived back at the trailhead, the Park Service bus was waiting for them. Little Chase ran to the port-a-pottie, holding his bum. But someone else was waiting. *Mark.*

The mega-douche was leaning against his SUV parked right next to the Pig. How did Mark find him? This couldn't be good. Especially after what Cud told him. But he couldn't deal with him now. He needed to get the visitors on the bus, safely out of the way, before he could engage.

The bus driver opened the door. "Good afternoon, Johnnie. Had some trouble today?" It was Candace from the Visitor Center. She was okay, but a little too cheerful for his taste.

"Good afternoon, Candy. Just the usual trouble." He chuckled, "I didn't murder anyone. Yet."

Candy wrinkled her nose and shuddered. Apparently, she didn't find it funny.

"It's a joke."

She smiled and laughed. "Ha! Johnnie, I'm just messing with you."

Johnnie exhaled with relief. "I think, after the boy gets out of the bathroom, they'll be ready to go."

Candy exited the bus, sidled up to him, and whispered, "A reporter came to the center today asking about you. We didn't tell him anything, but I think that's the same guy." She nodded her head towards Mark.

Shit. "What did he say?" Johnnie watched the hikers board the bus. *Not one 'thank you…'*

"He wanted to know if you'd be at the beach today. Said he wanted your side of the story. But when we asked for his press credentials, he just gave us a creepy smile and left. I don't think he's a real reporter."

"Oh, you think?" Johnnie shook his head and stared at his boots. "Sorry, not trying to be snarky. I just need to get these folks on their way."

"Roger Wilco!" Candy grinned. "Are you coming with us?"

"No, my scooter is here. Could you tell Kemper I'm not feeling well? Gonna go home early."

"Sure, I got you." She grinned and held her hand out for a fist bump.

He slumped his shoulders and raised his knuckles, quickly grazing hers and stuffing his hand in his pocket.

Chase ran across the gravel parking lot, smiling like he'd forgotten completely about the last few minutes of his moaning and crying. "Mister Ranger! Miss Bus Driver! What happens when a pig gets on an airplane?"

Johnnie cracked a smile. "Why would a pig go on an airplane?"

Chase stomped his foot and pouted his lips. "No! You're ruining it! You're supposed to say, 'No, what happens?'"

"Ok, I don't know. What?"

Chase started giggling. "You get...ha, ha..." He clutched his stomach, his face turned red, laughing like he'd explode.

Candy asked, "What? What do you get, sweetie?" She bent down to Chase's eye level and smiled at him.

Chase stopped laughing. "Um. I forget. But it was really funny."

Johnnie laughed. "Well, you enjoy the rest of your day."

Chase bounced up onto the bottom step of the bus, shouting. "Mooooommm! What do you get when a pig flies in an airplane?"

Candy clasped Johnnie on the back. "Good luck with your reporter friend over there." She entered the bus and closed the door.

Sure enough, Mark was heading his way.

The bus inched forward, turning its tall tires on the gravel, crunching and spewing small rocks behind it. As it left the lot, a bus window slid down. Through it, Chase yelled, "You get piggy flu!"

Amidst the rock dust, Mark walked up, cracking his knuckles, glaring. "Crosswell. I suspect you know why I'm here. We can do this the easy way or the hard way."

He sneered back. "Am I talking to Bob's brother, my lawyer, or a news reporter?"

"Who I am is not relevant. Give me the thumb drive and you won't see me again." He stepped closer, his face a foot from Johnnies.

Mark's scented body spray—or whatever it was—stunk like iguana dung. It would be so easy to punch this guy, but his ribs were still sore. The hike helped loosen his muscles, but he didn't want to risk another physical altercation. "I don't have it. Besides, there was nothing important on it. A friend said it had nonsense numbers."

"Wait—you read the contents? Where is it now?"

"My friend said he threw it away."

"When? Where?"

"I don't know. Maybe two days ago? My memory isn't great."

"What's your friend's name?"

He really wanted to punch Mark now. "None of your business, dick-breath."

Mark poked him in the shoulder. "I say what's my business, shit-head. And I'm very persuasive. Did you know I met your sister yesterday? Cute lady. It would be terrible if something happened to her."

Johnnie's eyes popped. Fury swirled in his brain like a sand-storm. "You touch her, you die."

"Ha! Are you going to kill me? Mr. Mumbles-to-Himself? Now, let's be civilized. We'll go to your place, jog your half-witted memory, and we're going to look for this damn thing together, capiche?" He growled, "Get in the damned car." Mark drew a gun from the backside of his belt and gestured toward the SUV.

A group of three hikers emerged from the tree line at the trail entrance, walking toward them. They waved. One called out, "Ranger? We have a question."

Mark hid the gun.

Johnnie used the opportunity, walking over to the trio. They asked him about whether certain berries were poisonous. He asked them several questions in return. *What size? Color? Where did they see them?* He knew the answer. They were talking about the sea-grapes, which were ripe when they turned from green to purple. Johnnie kept an eye on Mark, who looked annoyed, playing with a switchblade.

When the conversation with the hikers ended, he took a deep breath and sprinted back to the trail, hoping Mark was smart enough not to shoot him in the back in front of the hikers. The trail had good hiding spots and he knew how to double-back without being seen.

Mark remained in place and yelled, "Where you gonna go, dipshit?"

He didn't know exactly. But he wasn't going with Mark. And he needed to warn Robin and get her to safety. Charging along the path, he flew past other hikers—despite the ache in his sides—until he reached the first bend in the trail where he had a good vantage point. He took out his cell phone. Only one bar. Dialing Robin's office, the phone rang and rang before a woman answered.

"Good afternoon Johnnie."

This wasn't Robin. "Who is this?"

"Dot McPherson. Stay where you are."

"What?"

"Mr. Smith is getting ready to leave. I'll call you when it's safe."

"Who?"

"The guy wearing black. I can't talk right now. Just sit tight."

The line went dead. None of this made sense. But somehow, Dottie seemed so in-charge and commanding. He didn't know why, but he trusted that this was a good sign.

And he stayed where he was.

A long five minutes later, his phone rang.

Dottie said, "It's safe. Come back to the parking lot and I'll drive you home."

* * *

Thomas stuffed his gun back under his belt. *Why did they always run?* He hated running. This guy was such a pop-eyed dork. Trying to be nice always backfired.

He stabbed the tires on the idiot's bike. What grown man rides a scooter? This Crosswell guy was such a loser.

Rule Number 5, 'always engage on your own terms and choice of setting'. He jotted down additional notes about not running blindly into the woods after targets. Too many variables.

He placed a small tracker on the bike and checked the signal on his phone. At some point, loser boy would have to retrieve his lame toy scooter. And he would pinpoint him the second it moved. Rule Number 9, 'make technology work for you.

The sister comment really rattled sissy boy. Two birds with one stone. Threaten the sister and get approval for the project and the thumb drive in one operation. But kidnapping a high-profile person went against Rule Number 21. Too much attention by the government and press. No, that would be a last resort.

Which left him back to basics.

Who was this friend that threw away the drive? Did this moron even have friends?

The land-lady would know. And she was easy to get to.

He got back into his truck and entered a new calendar appointment on his phone. Midnight, Calabash Boom, Landlady.

A text came in. The boss-man. "Status, now."

He texted back. "Getting closer. Working a few angles."

Another text. "You have one week."

This was why he needed passive income. His clients' expectations were always so ridiculous. Bribery was a long game. A process of quid pro quo that took years to cultivate. If only they had brought him on sooner. And folks with hero complexes always mucked up the works. Like Bob, who stole the bitcoin for the government bribes and spilled his guts to that goody-two-shoes reporter. Sure, the results of the surveys were falsified, but a few corals, plankton and mollusks weren't worth killing hundreds of jobs.

The air smelled fresh and sweet after the short down-pour. A rainbow stretched across the sky to the east. Perhaps he would find the treasure there tonight. But first he needed gloves, duct tape, rope, and tarps. Then he needed to scout a couple abandoned properties. Ones with attached garages were best.

So much to do, so little time.

He turned on the ignition and gulped down the rest of his protein shake before putting the vehicle in reverse.

The Crosswell freak might run now, but he couldn't run forever.

Chapter 18

~Twenty-nine hours earlier~

With her new role as Robin's detective, Dot watched out the office window until Jacque Lords and Thomas Smith appeared on the sidewalk below and their vehicle departed.

Dot sauntered over to the police station. Arturo was eating a sandwich at the receiving station.

"Arturo dearest. How are you this fine morning?"

"Aunt Dot, nice to see you." He wiped his mouth with a napkin.

She wasn't his actual aunt. Arturo's mom had been a close friend for decades and part of their small, informal astronomy 'club'. When he was younger, Artie tagged along on their night-time viewings. Her own boy, Nick, had been close to his age.

"I need a favor. The street cameras outside. Can you get me a plate? It's important."

He grinned. "Anything for you, Auntie."

In the span of ten minutes, she reviewed the footage, easily spotting the dandy man and the guy resembling Ben Affleck in Boiler Room getting into a black SUV. The plate was easy to read.

"Another favor? The name on the registration?"

With a few clicks, Arturo told her it was leased from Virgin Auto Rentals.

"Thanks, hon, tell your mom to call me sometime."

This was almost too easy. She went back to her desk next door. Robin was on the phone and she decided not to disturb her.

Within fifteen minutes, she made five calls. Tracking Mr. Thomas Smith and the license plate to the resort was child's play, considering she knew all the concierges. In fact, they gave her his room number at the Tecoma Sands Resort and volunteered to call her when he returned.

The technology part was always the most troublesome for her. But after thieves briefly stole her pickup truck two years ago, she got a tracking device so she could always locate her vehicle with her phone. Parting with it for a few days wouldn't be a problem.

The next morning, she watched Mr. Smith's movements around the island. When he stopped at the National Park Visitor Center, she called her friend Candy.

"Candy, a guy just pulled into your parking lot. Dark hair, tall, mean looking. Be nice and play along, but call me after he leaves and tell me everything he says."

"No problem-o, Dottie. Hey, are you up for knitting circle on Saturday?"

"Maybe. I might be busy. I'll let you know."

"Right-o. Hey, I see him. Gotta run."

Dottie chuckled. This was so much fun. And the Smith guy didn't know who he was dealing with. Her circle was wide and deep. It felt like catching a photon in a black hole.

He didn't stand a chance.

* * *

Johnnie walked out of the woods, stepping out thoughtfully, scanning the parking lot. Mark's vehicle was gone. Dot leaned against her white Toyota pickup, wearing a saffron yellow dress that popped off her dark skin plus oversized round sunglasses like Jackie Onassis. Her cropped brown hair was pulled back off her face with a stretchy red headband. She waved.

"Dottie, what are you doing here? And why do you have Robin's phone?" He scratched his arm where it was inflamed from some thorns earlier.

"Johnnie love, I forwarded her phone to mine. I saw your interaction with Mr. Smith. What did he want? Why was he pointing a gun at you?"

"Smith? You mean Mark?"

She shook her head. "I've been tracking Thomas Smith since yesterday. He was acting strange at the meeting with your sister. But how are you involved with the bridge deal?"

He pursed his lips and blinked. "Bridge deal?"

Dottie sighed. "You don't know about that?"

"About what? Why was Mark visiting Robin? Did he threaten her? I need to warn her."

"No, he didn't threaten her. Just looked at her strange. Hold on...so you don't know about the bridge and airport and such?"

"I honestly don't know what you're talking about. But Mark threatened Robin just now. He wants something and if I don't give it to him..." *And if Cud really threw it away, what would happen?*

"What does he want?"

Johnnie took a deep breath and scraped a line through the blue rock with his boot. He didn't want to spill the beans. *Could he trust Dottie not to tell Robin?* According to Robin, Dot was the town gossip. Nothing was safe with her. Hell, when he had that incident at the ferry two years ago, naked and raving about aliens putting a bomb in his head, Dot was the first to tell Robin.

"Shit, Dottie. I think I'm in a heap of trouble."

She rested her hand on his arm and patted it. "Honey, ain't nothing in the world that can't be fixed. Why don't we go sit down over some waffles and talk it through?"

"I can't...I need to warn Robin, talk to Cud, find out where the...thing... is. Maybe buy a gun." His cheek twitched, and he slapped at it, trying to get it to stop. "Fuck me."

"Now, now. Calm down." She took out her phone and went through some menus. "Look, see? Mr. Smith is heading back to town. I bet Arturo would keep an eye on Robin. That boy has eyes for her, you know. I heard they are going out on Friday. I'll call him right now."

He stopped slapping himself. "What? You're tracking Mark, I mean Smith? How?"

"Little old ladies have their ways. Okay, waffles." She clapped and rubbed her palms together. "I always think best with some warm syrup and a cup of coffee. And we have lots to discuss."

Waffles sounded great, a change to dry clothes sounded better. "Can we go to Gertie's? I need to talk with Cud. Find something..."

"Great idea! I missed Gertie at the bake sale. Let me call her next."

Johnnie shook his head. *How did she know everyone?* And when did her job description include tracking dangerous men? None of this added up.

After a minute on the phone, Dot said, "We're all set. But we'll pick up some milk and batter mix on the way. And I like the fake maple syrup, so I'll get a bit of that too."

He didn't argue. Instead, he examined the Pig. Both tires were flat. "Jumpin' Joe, did Mark do that?"

"Sorry, love, yes. We can try loading` your scooter in the back of my pickup. Do you think it will fit?"

He did some mental estimations. "With the tailgate down."

Soon enough, they were on their way to Gertie's.

On the way, Dottie relayed the details of the bridge proposal. Johnnie chose to listen instead of sharing what he knew about the thumb drive. He needed to find out if Cud really threw it away. Because if he had, the Mark guy would probably seek a retribution of the highest order.

And the outcome could be life or death.

✳ ✳ ✳

Cud came in from weeding the garden and heard Gertie on the phone on the couch. He washed his hands in the kitchen sink and looked at her. "Waffles? Who was that?"

Gertie put down her phone and chuckled. "My friend, Dottie. She's with Johnnie. They're coming over to discuss something important. A man was making threats."

"Threats? Oh, no. I bet it's that Mark person. I knew he was going to be trouble."

"Mark?" She put away her needlepoint in a wicker box.

"The fellow pretending to be Johnnie's lawyer. He wants something that Johnnie and I took."

Gertie walked into the kitchen and picked up her apron from the hook. "So, give it back. You don't seem like criminals."

Cud winced. "It's worth thirty million."

Gertie crossed her arms. "I could see why he wants it back then. What is it? Jewelry?"

"A thumb drive with bitcoin information."

She tied the apron around her waist. "Well, just give it back. Maybe Mark will go away and problem solved."

"You're probably right, I hope it's that simple."

She gave him a shy smile and a side glance. "Although, wouldn't it be wonderful to have that much money? What would you do if you were rich?"

Cud's eyes went wide. Did she know and was fishing? And if she didn't know, what would happen when she found out? He gulped and wrung his hands. "I don't know. But I have all I ever wanted just being with you." *The truth.*

She kissed him on the cheek. "Yes, we are very blessed. Now, help me put out plates and get the kitchen ready."

He dodged telling her the *whole* truth, but he would have to tell her at some point. And what would happen then? Would Gertie still love him for who he was now? Or would she crave the life he could have given her and resent him for it?

He wanted to marry her, almost from the first time he saw her. Which was nuts, but his heart had taken over his senses. Should he propose first and then tell her? Or be upfront? Would they need a pre-nuptial agreement? Or would he give her everything after he was gone?

Money complicated everything.

He watched her move around the kitchen, taking out a skillet and mixing bowls. What if Gertie was play-acting? Trying to get him to confess about his fortune?

She walked to the dining table with spray wax and a rag, wiping down the wood veneer, preoccupied, humming a tune. Fear gripped his chest— he couldn't take the suspense.

"Gertie?"

"Yes, dear heart?" She continued cleaning.

"Um...technically...mind you...I don't..."

"Yes?"

He clenched his face. "I have three point one billion dollars...I mean...used to have."

She turned, dropping her rag. "But you gave all the up, correct?"

His eyes bulged. "You know?"

With a hand on her hip, she stared at him. "Be serious. Most everyone on this island knows!"

"Well, it's not exactly irreversible. My grandson manages the estate, but I'm still the owner of the company on paper. It was best at the time not to scare investors."

Gertie picked up her rag and spray bottle. She strode past him back to the kitchen, crouching down to put away her cleaning supplies under the sink. "So, why are you telling me this?"

"I want to know if it matters." His arms were by his sides. He scanned her face for any clues.

"Matters?"

"You know what I mean."

"I don't think I do. Why don't you just say what's on your mind?" Her brows narrowed, one hand on her hip as she rose to face him.

Did he dare? He had already stepped in it. "Money can change things…expectations. It affects people."

"Heaven's sake." She walked back to the dining table and pulled out two chairs. "Sit."

He held his breath and joined her at the table, clasping his hands together in front of him, staring at the gleaming wood grain.

She placed her hand over his. "Cudlow, are you worried I only care about you because you have money? Because if that is what you think…" Her eyes misted. She took her hand away.

"No! I mean, I hope not. But you understand why I could be concerned…"

Her face turned ashen, but her voice was angry. "You *hope*?"

"No. I meant…when I essentially gave control to Jackson, the rest of my family refused to talk to me. I'm simple, but not naïve. Money matters to people. Most people. Resentments build. But money corrupts, makes people insane—"

"You think it matters to me?" She said this slowly, her body growing still like a statue.

"You were the aggressor…I just need to know…" Hearing his own words, the forcefulness and bitterness in his tone stunned himself. Just talking about money made his mood shift, resembling that other person who lurked below.

"Excuse me?" She crossed her arms.

In a steadier tone, he said, "Your attraction to me…it took me by surprise. I've wondered why…" He couldn't look at her. *Were his innate fears ruining everything?*

She lowered her eyes. "I like you because you are sweet. Were sweet. Now…I don't know."

Something was different. He'd never seen her sad. But it was more than that. And it occurred to him. Her aura was gone.

In a soft voice, he said, "I'm sorry. I didn't mean…Gertie, I don't know what to say." He wrung his hands in his lap.

"Cudlow, at our age, it's not like we'll ever get married. I thought we had a connection. And maybe other people have hurt you…" She turned her face away. "Look what you did. And we're having company soon."

She wiped her face and took a deep breath. "I had everything I need in life. Long before you." Gertie stood, her wet eyes meeting his. "Because I adore you, I'm going to *try* to forget you said these things."

Cud watched her go, his heart in a pit in his stomach. The back door slammed.

That went as badly as possible.

Never get married? That part stung. Maybe he had no right to be with a woman given his state of affairs. How could he be an equal partner in any relationship when he lived like a hobo?

He wanted to crawl on all fours back to his beach—to give her space. But Johnnie was arriving soon and they needed a plan to deal with Mark.

Being useful was the only course. He put out the plates and silverware, trying to remember which side the fork goes on. He'd always had servants to do this sort of thing and never paid attention. When he put down the plate in front of the chair Gertie had just left, a three-millimeter droplet seized his attention. *One of her tears.* He touched it gingerly, wondering if he'd lost her forever.

His daze broke with the faint sound of Gertie singing in the garden. It was the Joan Baez folksong, "It Ain't Me, Babe". It was beautiful. He snuck a look out the back window. She was picking oranges. In the sunlight, he could see it. A lavender glow.

Despite her sad song, her aura had returned.

And he hoped she could forgive him.

Chapter 19

Johnnie walked through the front door behind Dottie. Gertie hugged Dot and the two began chattering about orange juice, brands of waffle-makers, and whether to heat some sausages as a side-dish.

Cud was in the far corner of the living room, quiet, a frown on his face.

Johnnie sat down next to him. "Hey, why the long face?"

"Oh, nothing ol' chap. I've put my foot right into it with Gertie, I say. I don't know when to keep my trap shut."

"What happened?"

"I told her about the money."

"What money?"

"My money. See, this is why I hate the bloody stuff so much. Always causing issue. But we need to focus on your troubles. What happened to you today?"

Gertie came over and handed a glass of orange juice to Johnnie. "Yes, what happened?"

Johnnie glanced over to the kitchen. Dottie was mixing batter and bobbing her head to her own beat.

"There's a guy named Mark, or Smith, that wants something. He followed me to the hiking trail today. Pulled a gun and threatened Robin if I don't give it to him."

Gertie said, "The thirty-million dollars?"

Johnnie squinted, "What?"

Cud said, "Sorry, Johnnie. I should have told you. The thumb drive contains the codes to thirty-million in Bitcoin."

"Wait, you knew what those letters and numbers meant the whole time? Why would you lie to me?"

Cud put his hand on Johnnie's knee. "I wanted to protect you. That amount of money spells danger. And I needed to put it in a safe place."

"Where is it?"

"Close. Hidden."

"Why would the dead guy have that much money and why does Mark feel entitled to it?"

Dottie chimed in over the sound of sizzling sausage. "I know why."

The three stared in her direction.

Dot said, "You'll have to wait until food is served."

The three groaned.

Johnnie's cell phone rang. It was Robin.

"Hey, Robin, I'm kind of busy right now."

"I heard you had a run-in with Thomas Smith and he wants something from you? How do you know him?

"It's a long story."

"Great. I'm coming over."

"No! I mean…dang. I'll take care of it."

"See you soon." She hung up.

"Shit."

Gertie said, "Don't use that language here, please."

Dottie laughed. "Right, Gert. Like you never cursed. Remember that time you tripped at church? I thought lightning was going to strike the building."

Gertie smiled. "None of us are perfect."

Cud looked at Gertie. "I think you're perfect."

Gertie put her hand on Cud's shoulder. "Stop sucking up, dear. I'm not done punishing you."

"God would forgive me."

"Like I said, none of us are perfect."

Johnnie shook his head. "So, what? Now we wait for my sister? This is crazy."

Dottie said, "No, we eat first. I'm starving. Johnnie, help bring these plates over. We can dig in."

Soon, the table was filled with stacks of waffles and sausage links. They passed around the carafe of freshly squeezed orange juice. Gertie poured coffee into mismatched mugs and said grace.

They largely ate in silence until Robin arrived.

And then the revelations began.

* * *

Robin pulled into the driveway, recognizing Johnnie's scooter, Gertie's blue ford sedan, and Dottie's white pickup. The front light on John's bike was cracked. He hadn't replaced it as she insisted. It was a quarter past six and the sun was nearly set. Still wearing her suit and heels, she hadn't wanted to delay a single second to find out what Dottie discovered about Thomas Smith and what it had to do with her brother.

She knocked on Gertie's door.

Johnnie answered. "Did anyone follow you?" He tilted his head, looking toward the road.

"What?" She stepped inside. The place smelled like sausage and the thought of food made her stomach dance.

Johnnie closed the front door, turned the deadbolt, put the chain across, and joined the party at the table.

Around the dining table, Gertie, Dottie and Cudlow trained their eyes on her, glued to her in unison like kittens watching a string toy.

Their steady stares instantly seemed suspicious. "What did I miss?"

Dottie said, "Make a plate in the kitchen. I was just showing them the photo I took of Thomas Smith at the trailhead parking lot."

"Trail?" Robin went to the kitchen.

Cudlow said, "It's definitely Mark, the one with the black aura."

Robin placed two waffles and three links on a plate and sat at the empty place setting to the right of Johnnie. "Who's Mark? Get me up to speed." She cut a waffle with the edge of her fork and started to eat.

Dottie cleared her throat. "Seems your brother met Smith a few days ago. Chief Tobias introduced them."

Robing gagged on a chunk. She involuntarily spat it out and it landed on Johnnie's arm. "What?"

Johnnie picked up the morsel with a paper napkin and folded it into a tight square. "Yeah, said he was Bob's brother. I didn't believe it for a second."

Robin took a sip of Johnnie's orange juice. "Why? What did Smith want?"

Her brother shrugged, "He was looking for something Bob had. Asked if I found anything."

Her mind raced ahead, then she punched John in the shoulder. "What the hell did you steal from Robert Taylor?"

"Ow."

She hit him again.

"Ow, a key chain."

She slammed her palms on the table. "So, you lied to me! Twice!" She raised her fist again to strike him, but Johnnie pushed back his chair and escaped.

"I'm going to sit over there." Johnnie pointed to the side chair in the living room, in the far corner.

Cudlow raised his hand, like a school boy asking a teacher for permission. "Don't blame him. It's my fault also. I took the item from the bank box."

Robin pushed her plate away. She couldn't eat under these circumstances. She held her head with both hands, staring into the table's wood grain, her nostrils flaring. "All of you. Hand me a dollar."

Cudlow asked, "What?

Stonily, without looking up, enunciating every word, Robin said, "HAND-ME-A-FUCKING-DOLLAR-AND-I-WON'T-HAVE-TO-TESTIFY-AS-YOUR-LAWYER!" She exhaled. "Shit. Someone get some paper and a pen."

Dottie rummaged in her handbag. "I only have a ten. Do you have change? Or do you take quarters…"

Robin slammed her palm again on the table. "Just slide it the fuck over!"

Dottie said, "Gertie asked us not to curse."

Gertie laughed, "No, it's fine. She's had a long day."

Robin looked up to see Cudlow slip some paper and a pen beside her. With a deep sigh, she set to work, hastily writing one of the worst letters of representation in world history that amounted to a paragraph with several run-on sentences. Robin shoved it over to Cudlow. "Now sign."

As she waited for them to pass it around and sign, she slipped out of her heels and walked to the kitchen. "Gertie, do you have any vodka?"

"No dear, just wine. In the fridge, there's an open half-bottle of white."

Robin grabbed the wine and shut the fridge. She screwed off the cap and guzzled straight from the bottle.

Johnnie, still across the room, said, "Hey, slow down."

She pointed, "No! You slow down."

He responded, "That makes no sense."

Cudlow slid the paper back next to Robin's plate. "It's done."

Robin pointed, "John, too." She took another swig, but it hit her pipes too fast and she gagged.

Cudlow walked the pen and paper to Johnnie and waited while he signed it. "Now I know where he gets it."

Robin came back to the table with the bottle, "Gets what?"

"His crazy temper."

Dottie laughed. "Ha, there was this time Robin got so mad, she threw her desk chair down the stairs. Milton didn't get out of the way in time—"

Robin shouted, "Stop! Everyone shut up." She huffed. "If I point to you, you can speak. Now," she pointed to Cudlow, "tell me about the bank."

For the next two minutes, he relayed the story about the bank manager and his not actually dead mother.

Robin said, "Damn, he believed you? Okay, moving on. What was on the drive?"

The interrogations went on for another half hour. The bottle of wine was empty. Finally, Robin was ready to ask Johnnie questions. She moved to the sofa, directly across from her brother. "Try to remember his exact words. You said Mark threatened to kill me?"

Johnnie fiddled with his hands. "Not in those words, but something like that."

She stood. Her head felt light. Maybe waffles would have been a better choice than the wine. "You need to give it back."

Johnnie shook his head. "Dottie told me about what they're planning. They'll ruin the island. I only came to St. John for the peace and quiet…"

"Listen to yourself. He KILLED TWO PEOPLE!"

"But—"

Robin bared her teeth. "I swear, John, if you don't return it tonight, I'll kill you with my own bare hands."

From the dining table, Dottie laughed. "He should definitely return it. But Robin, you can't even kill a spider. One time," she directed her voice to Gertie and Cud, "a cricket was bouncing around her office and she climbed on her desk and screamed so loud, people on the street heard her and called 9-1-1. Plus, she broke her monitor—"

Cudlow raised his hand again, "I could give Smith the money. Jackson could wire it in seconds."

Dottie said, "I thought you gave up your money."

Gertie shook her head and raised both her hands over her head.

"Cudlow will do NO SUCH THING! You saw what happened...throwing around millions only leads to more trouble."

Johnnie said, "I'll do it. I'll give back the thumb drive."

Robin's head ached. All that wine wasn't sitting well. She walked back to the dining table, dropped onto her chair, and noshed on a cold waffle.

Dottie reached her hand across and rested it on Robin's arm. "Are you okay, sweetie? I can drive you home."

It was true; she wasn't feeling okay. A wave of nausea hit and she clasped her hand over her mouth. Bolting up, she raced for the kitchen sink. The first heave released a torrent of liquid into the stainless-steel vessel. Dottie came up behind her and held Robin's hair and rubbed her back, "There, there."

Johnnie joined them. "Sis, I'm sorry..."

Her throat burned, but after two more waves, her stomach felt better. The whole situation was so humiliating.

Dottie handed her a paper towel. "*Now* can I drive you home?"

Robin righted herself and took a step away from the sink; she ran the cold water to clean the mess. "I'm better. I can drive. Dottie, would you follow me home? Make sure I get there?"

"Sure, honey."

Before Robin left with Dottie, she fixed her eyes on John. "Do it. Return it tonight. And don't die."

He scratched the back of his head. "I will. Promise."

"Good." She ran her hand along his head, next to his scar. "Butthead." In a wave of sadness, she put her arms around him and hugged him tight.

Johnnie hugged her back. "I'll text you after."

"You'd better." She gave a weak smile as she opened the door to leave. "Because if you die, I'm going to kill you."

Chapter 20

Thomas lay on his hotel room bed, propped up by pillows, his eyes closed. Rest was necessary, because midnight kidnappings always made him tired, and he'd need all his energy to focus for the task ahead. The abandoned house at Chocolate Hole was ready and he stocked his SUV with snacks and water, although he hoped the operation would go smoothly.

Still, his mind kept returning to his manuscript. Did he start the book with enough bang? If he couldn't grab the reader's attention in the first three paragraphs, it would never become the bestseller he desired. Thomas also contemplated pen names. A strong name, but something memorable too. Clive Manly? Boris Ironstock? Or should he remain anonymous, allowing for a future sequel?

He'd researched agents. Only the best would do. A New Yorker—someone connected. But instead of querying, he would use his innate talents of bribery and extortion. It didn't matter who you knew. It only mattered what dirt he could find on his dream agent. Stalking on the internet made this easy, especially when they posted pictures of their kids and dogs, or tweeted what conferences they attended.

Maybe he could turn his story into a graphic novel, with himself as a caped hero. And dingbats like Crosswell would meet their demise at his righteous hand. Thomas grinned and doodled himself as a Marvel character, with a tight costume that showcased his bulging groin and pecs.

When all this was over and he received his final consulting fee for the bridge project, he could buy a brownstone in Brooklyn and enjoy his days writing. No more traveling for work, or lifting weights, drinking protein shakes, and pacifying obnoxious clients. The life he'd dreamt of back in college would be his. Settling down, going for long walks, learning to cook gourmet meals, attending concerts, and vacationing in the south of France. Hot chicks always liked sensitive writer types. He could learn to play the part.

Or maybe after all this was over, he'd join that closeted gay militia in Arkansas for two weeks of recreation. Young guns with guns. What could be better? Thoughts of hefty bearded chonks holding their large bazookas always charged his weapon.

His last fling, Renaldo, chided that he would basically hump anything with a pulse. Which was not exactly true; his tastes were simply varied and his libido was healthy. Admittedly, Renaldo was the closest he came to a relationship in his years of fixing, when he was stuck without a passport for three months in Cuba. But he continued to live by Rule Number 10, 'falling in love is for pussies'.

Smith unzipped his pants and daydreamed about Ren before falling into a deep slumber.

* * *

After Robin and Dottie left, Johnnie patched and filled the tires on his scooter and removed the tracker Dottie pointed out.

Cud went to the garden and retrieved the thumb drive from under the garden gnome. "Just drop it at Mr. Smith's hotel room and go. It will be all right. We'll all be tracking your phone on Life 360, but call if anything goes askew."

Johnnie looked at the piece of paper from Dottie—Tecoma Sands Resort, Room 669. "What if he sees me? He might shoot me? Maybe I should bring a baseball bat?"

Cud shook his head. "Would you like me to go instead? I was the one who took the blasted thing."

"No, this is my fault. I put you up to this. My problem. I'll go." Johnnie donned his helmet and placed the thumb drive in his jeans pocket.

He arrived close to eight-thirty and the sun had set two hours ago. The Tecoma Sands was a well populated and well-lit resort. Mark was staying in one of their condo-style rentals on the back hill of the complex.

Johnnie didn't need another confrontation. He scanned the numbers next to each unit. *Number 669.* This was it. The lights in the unit were out. And he didn't see Mark's black SUV. A good sign.

Parked in line with the door, still seated on the scooter, he fished his hand into his pocket and retrieved the drive. He aimed and tossed the drive onto the doormat. It bounced, hitting the door and bouncing sideways into a nearby shrub.

Johnnie smacked his forehead. *Not smart.*

Releasing the kick-stand, he got off the scooter and rummaged on the ground for it, scraping the mulch in the shadows. The sound of a door closing inside Mark's condo set his teeth on edge. He felt around again and found it.

Johnnie placed the orange thumb drive squarely on the black rubber door mat and pressed the doorbell. He didn't hear a ring. *Was it out of order?*

He rang it again for good measure and raced back to the scooter.

The door flew open. "Crosswell!" Mark was wearing his black pants and a white undershirt, no socks or shoes. He bolted out.

Johnnie yelled. "I returned it! Look, the doormat."

Mark stopped and turned. "Ha! Well, looky there. You wised up, moron." He walked back and picked up the item. He took his gun out from behind his waist. "Crosswell. Stay here. I'm going to check this first. Make sure it's real."

With bared teeth, Johnnie growled, "It's real. I'm leaving."

"You know, it's ironic."

Johnnie stopped. "What's ironic?"

"If your sister plays along and votes the right way, she could get a cool half-mill from these accounts. You were stealing from your own sister."

Johnnie crossed his arms. "Who says she'll play along?"

Mark smirked. "True, she didn't say yes—yet. But since I know where you both live, I think she'll behave. Honestly, the company I work for is doing a great thing. The entire island will benefit from more visitors, industries and transportation options. Ha! When the next hurricane hits, they'll be able to rebuild ten times faster. I'm the fucking hero in this story. You know what, numbnuts?" Mark waved his gun, shooing him away. "Go crawl back to your beach and enjoy the quiet while you can." He tucked the gun in his waistband and went back inside, shutting the door, and turning on the lights.

Johnnie's nostrils flared and he sucked air through clenched teeth. *All those people.* More cars. More trash. More questions. Crowded stores. Crowded bars. It would be like Miami or worse. Or like Charlotte

Amalie with the dumb stores and dumb tourists descending like horse flies. Choking on vehicle exhaust. More noise. With St. John's usual population of five-thousand, a single large cruise ship would double the island's numbers when in port. Paradise would become a hell on earth. He didn't want to consider moving again.

In a blinding rage, he stormed over to a nearby flower bed where a wheel-barrow and an assortment of garden tools were left abandoned.

He knocked on Mark's door.

Mark poked his head out, "What do you want, shit for brains?"

Johnnie smashed him in the face with a shovel, knocking him backwards into the room.

Mark's face was cut and bloody. He tried to get up.

Johnnie hit him again, sideways against his skull. He raised the shovel, ready to slam it through the soft muscles of Mark's neck. But stopped.

The thumb drive! He dropped the shovel and dashed to the laptop on the bed. The thumb drive was in the port. He unplugged it and ran off, through the room, slamming the door, through the parking lot, getting back on the Pig and zooming away.

As he drove through Cruz Bay, his pulse slowed, the pounding in his head subsided.

What now?

Was Mark dead?

Should he throw the thumb drive into the ocean?

Instead of going home, he drove to the beach. *Hawksnest.*

Once there, he walked through the vegetation over to Cud's former nest. In the broken cooler, he found a bottled water and downed the contents, pouring the last part over his head to cool off. He lay down on Cud's boogie board, surrounded by vegetation, and admired the stars above. He couldn't go home. Not now. He was in such trouble now.

But he was too exhausted to think about it now.

Why couldn't he do anything right?

Was Robin going to die from his mistakes?

He curled into a ball and closed his eyes. Another migraine was coming on. Counting backwards from three hundred, he focused on his breathing, lowering his heart-rate.

A tickle at his back surprised him; he opened his eyes. Stumpy blinked at him, his front foot on his side, as if to say, [There, there,

Johnnie boy. I'll stay with you.]

He smiled at his friend. "Thanks. Goodnight, Stumpy." He closed his eyes again.

[Goodnight, Johnnie. Sweet dreams. I won't let that Green-tail bite.]

* * *

Still prone on the floor face down, Thomas ran his fingers along his temple. Blood. Thick and caked in his short hair. A stream ran behind his left earlobe. His jaw throbbed.

Who knew the brain-dead Boy Scout had it in him?

He chuckled, then stopped as a sharp pain radiated along his skull.

Thomas rolled to his back, contemplating his next moves. One, get off the floor. Two, inspect the damage. Three, kill that punk-ass bitch.

In the bathroom, he splashed the cuts on his face and skull with cold water, sending red streams across the counter and mirror. The pristine white embroidered hotel towels were ruined. But the least of his concern. Rule Number 17, 'keep a well-stocked medical kit'. His kit included needles and thread for stitching himself up. He hadn't had an injury like this in several years. Needles hurt, but antiseptic really hurt.

As he applied some tape over the stitches, his anger roiled. He imagined ways to make the man-child suffer. Cuts with a straight-edge in the most painful areas, letting him bleed out, crying in pain. That would be gratifying.

But Rule Number 4 said never seek revenge. Because revenge was sloppy and emotional—not the work of a professional. And above all else, he was a professional.

Recalling their conversation, he pin-pointed his mistakes. First, he engaged the creep in a discussion about the project, goading him. Second, he opened the door after he achieved his goal, too smug and self-confident. Perhaps this lesson would go in his book. A classic example of what *not* to do.

The tracker he placed on the half-wit's bike showed he returned to Calabash. *Did meat-head think he wouldn't find him there?*

He stuffed his tools and materials in a black canvas gym bag and checked the bullets in his gun.

It was time to get the damned thumb drive back for good.

Chapter 21

Johnnie should have checked in by now. Cud couldn't understand how Gertie was so calm. She was on her sofa concentrating on her small embroidery hoop, poking her needle through the unbleached muslin.

He grabbed her phone and dialed. Johnnie's phone went to voice mail—again. He left another message. "Man, where are you? Call and let us know you're all right!"

He stopped pacing and turned to Gertie. "Do you think I should go after him? The last coordinates from his phone shows he went to Hawksnest. What in blue blazes is he doing?"

Gertie's phone rang. It was Robin.

Robin said, "Did he make it home? His phone tracker shows…"

Cudlow said, "I know. He's not answering. I can go check on him…"

"No, I'll go. I'm feeling much better. Stay where you are and call me if you see him, okay?"

"Yes, absolutely."

"I'm heading out now. I'll keep you posted."

Cud gave the phone back to Gertie. "Robin's going to fetch him."

"Are you sure that's safe?"

He had to think about that. "I don't know. Could you call Dottie and see if Arturo could meet her there?"

She put aside her sewing. "That's a very good idea."

Cudlow paced the living room, listening to Gertie's conversation. The whole situation was out of control. His best friend was in hiding. A potential hit-man was on the loose. A senator was being threatened. And Gertie was still giving him a cold shoulder. His life was much simpler in the wild.

When Gertie ended the call, he said, "Well, what do we do now?"

"I don't know. We wait." She moved to a tufted chair, turned on the adjacent floor lamp, and opened a women's magazine.

"Are you still not talking to me?"

"I'm talking to you," she said, without lifting her eyes, "I'm just waiting for an apology."

"I said I'm sorry." He took a seat on the sofa across from her.

She dropped her shoulders but kept her eyes on her reading. "You know…I forgot for a moment why I was alone all these years. Men are impossible to live with."

There was a disgust in her voice that he'd never heard before. "If you want me to leave, say the word. I don't want to be the cause of your unhappiness."

She said nothing for a minute, staring at the magazine page, her eyes fixed, like she was lost in thought, not reading. Gertie took a deep breath and looked up. "Cudlow, you're a sweet man. But I don't know if I'm ready for something serious."

With a deep sigh, Gertie put down the magazine and took a seat beside him on the sofa. "I've lived alone for forty years. I'm not good with change. I don't want to hurt you."

He searched her eyes. "I've been a recluse of sorts myself these past ten years. I understand more than you could know."

"Maybe we're both bad at this."

"No, I've been a horse's ass. I do love you, Gertie. I was just scared…"

She placed her palm on his cheek, her eyes bored into his like a brewing storm. "Me too." Gertie shook her head and straightened her shoulders. In her usual sweet voice, she said, "Good. I propose we make up and put this behind us. Tomorrow we can have some time apart to re-evaluate."

"Time apart?"

"I think it would help. Don't you?"

He bowed his head. "I trust your instincts more than mine in these matters."

"Well, tonight isn't over." She ran her hand along his inner thigh.

A jolt went through him. "So, you *do* forgive me!"

"Oh, I'll let you know in the morning." She gave him a coy smile and tickled his earlobe with a kiss.

He teased her back, pretending offense. "You know, I'm not your plaything. I have feelings."

"That's not what you said yesterday." She kissed him on the mouth; her breath tasted like maple syrup.

God, was this woman sexy.

"What about Johnnie? We should make sure he gets home…"

"Hold that thought." She got up, retrieved her phone from the side table, pressed some keys, and threw it inside the bedroom. It landed with a soft thud on the mattress. She smiled. "If it vibrates, I'll answer it."

Cudlow rose from the sofa and bowed, tucking his arm behind his back. "After you, my queen. I'm your loyal subject."

Before he followed her inside, he grabbed a cold waffle off the dining room table and stuffed it in his mouth while shimmying his shoulders. Despite his delight at being forgiven, he didn't know what would happen next. Between him and Gertie, with Johnnie, or with the Bitcoin. All he could do was focus on the present moment.

And another waffle never hurt.

It was after ten at night when Robin found the Piaggio in the Hawksnest Beach parking lot. Wearing her pajamas, a pink terrycloth bathrobe and her slip-on white canvas sneakers, she walked onto the beach. A group of young people sat on blankets talking, drinking and smoking what smelled like marijuana. The drinking wasn't prohibited on the beach, but the smoking of any sort was.

She stopped at the group. "Have you seen a man, about five-foot-ten, round glasses, brown hair? Wearing jeans and a brown T-shirt?"

One of them pointed west. "About an hour ago, a dude walked past us going over there."

"Thanks." She walked the length of the beach. *Where was he?* Did he try to drown himself again? A shot of panic rose through her chest. "Johnnie! John!" She yelled.

A figure approached her in the dark. It wasn't John. *Was it the Smith guy?* She looked for an escape route. The bushes were dense on this side of the beach. Scrambling over the rocks along the coast would only lead to a dead-end. She squinted, trying to discern the man, ready to dive through the bushes if needed.

A voice called. "Robin?"

It was Arturo. She exhaled. "Art? What are you doing here?"

He was still in his police uniform. His badge caught the light of the moon as the clouds parted. "Aunt Dot called. I'm here to help you find your brother."

"Do you know about Thomas Smith?"

He nodded. "Auntie told me everything. But don't worry, I won't get John in trouble. Although, if Smith made threats, we'll need Johnnie to go on the record."

"Yes, thanks. Help me find him. His scooter is here. But in the dark, he could be anywhere."

"Did you try Cud's place?"

"What place?"

"The homeless guy. I think they're friends, correct? Over there," he pointed, "that's where he sleeps."

Arturo turned on his flashlight and they found a narrow path through the mangroves. About forty feet later, they found John, asleep. Snoring, in fact.

Robin kicked the boogie board. "Hey, wake up! You scared the shit out of me."

John opened his eyes. "Robin? Sorry. I..." He rolled up to a cross-legged position on the board.

She kicked the board again. "What? What happened with Smith?"

He fished into his pocket and held up the drive. "I couldn't do it."

"Are you shitting me? Why?" Robin wanted to slap him. Instead, she kicked sand on him, spraying it on his legs and midsection.

Arturo placed his arm between Robin and Johnnie. "Just let him talk."

Johnnie wiped the sand from his shirt. "Why do you think? The project will RUIN the island. I...I want things to stay the way they are."

"Stealing thirty-million dollars is still wrong. And that madman won't stop until he gets it back. I'm sure of it. Christ! You didn't spend all those months relearning to talk and walk just so some maniac could murder you! Understand?"

"I know. I know."

Robin shook her head; with her teeth bared, she growled, "Get the fuck up. You're coming with me."

John crossed his arms. "Robin, I'm a grown man. Don't talk to me like that."

"I *wish* you were a grown man." The second she said that, she regretted it. But her nerves were shot.

Arturo grabbed Robin's shoulders and pulled her to the side. He whispered, "You're not helping things right now. Look, I'll take the drive to this Smith person. He won't attack a police officer, and maybe he'll take the hint we're on to him. What do you say?"

Her eyes searched his. In a soft voice, she asked, "You would do that?"

"Yes."

Her pent-up adrenaline collapsed into a wave of gratitude. She gulped for air to contain herself. "Art, you are…so sweet. Yes, I would like that."

Art brushed a wisp of hair out of her eyes and chuckled. "Well, it's a better idea than you greeting him in your pink bathrobe."

Robin laughed. She'd almost forgotten the sight she must have presented. Glancing down at herself, she chuckled. "You have a point." Her eyes met his. Arturo's eyes had a twinkle and a kindness that overwhelmed her in the moment. Art was sexy and funny and adorable and good. *Why hadn't she realized this years ago?*

"No!" Johnnie yelled. "You don't get it! You can't give that baboon the money. It's not right."

Arturo bent, leveling his eyes with John's. "I understand how you feel. I really do. But right now, to save your life, and Robin's, we need to play along. Your sister won't cave in and vote for this project, right?" He turned to Robin.

"Absolutely not."

"See, John. It will all be fine. Now give me the drive." He held out his hand.

"No." He stuffed it in his mouth. "I'll swallow it."

Arturo laughed. "Okay, I'd love to see that. Go ahead."

Johnnie swished his mouth, his face contorted. He gagged and coughed, spitting it into his hand. "Well…wait!" He stood up and pointed toward the beach. "What's that over there?"

They turned. "What?" said Arturo.

Johnnie started running. *Fast.*

Arturo chased after him.

Robin's phone rang. "Hello?... Oh, God. I'm so sorry…Stay there…" She hung up. "JOHNNIE! ARTURO! COME BACK!" Both men were gone. She ran to the parking lot. Back to the Piaggio. *John couldn't go far on foot.*

And he needed to know what just happened.

Because it changed everything.

✳ ✳ ✳

Cudlow lay awake, spooning Gertie, appreciating the way her chest rose and fell with each contented breath, the smell of her skin and hair, the curve of her back. She had fallen asleep a few minutes ago, but he couldn't sleep… wouldn't sleep…knowing they would part soon.

He could sleep in his next life, he thought.

In a whisper, he said, "I love you, Freddy."

She didn't stir. Panic seized him. *Did he just call her that?* Cud's heart pounded. *Oh, no. Please, God…*

"How sweet," said a deep voice.

Cud bolted up, his chest pounding. A man wearing dark attire stood in the bedroom doorway. Cud positioned himself on the bed, arms wide, to shield Gertie. "You!"

Groggily, Gertie said, "What is it, dear?"

The overhead light came on, blinding him. "Smith! Stop!" He fumbled for the bedside lamp as a weapon. The cord wouldn't come loose.

Smith came toward him, with a black rope between his hands. In a split-second, Smith was strangling him.

Cud grasped at the cord pressing into his flesh, losing air. His eyes bulged with panic. He kicked, not landing any blows.

Gertie—out of view—screamed, "Stop!"

His mind blanked. He was going to die.

Gertie threw her cell phone at Smith, missing. She picked up and threw a glass-jar from her dresser, hitting Smith on the forehead; its contents—buttons of different colors and sizes—exploded across the floor. The rope loosened. Air returned to his lungs, but in spasms.

"Ow." Smith pulled a gun. "That's enough. Tie him up. Now, or I blast you both."

Gertie wiped her eyes and spit at Smith.

Cud felt a blow to the head from the butt of Smith's gun. His skull felt torn open. He fell sideways on the mattress.

"Stop! Don't kill him."

Cud came to consciousness again, not sure how much time elapsed, duct tape over his mouth, tape being wound around his hands, the stickiness pulling on his thin skin. Gertie was above him, working the tape, her eyes full of concern.

"I'm sorry," she whispered.

He blinked his response, "I know."

After his hands and feet were bound, the last bit of tape covered his eyes. The fingers pressing down were thick. *Smith's.*

Cud listened carefully, hoping whatever he heard would lead to finding her later. He heard feet shuffling out of the bedroom. The slam of the front door. Car doors, engine noise, gravel spraying.

A realization came. *Had he forgotten to lock the front door earlier?* He had.

This was his fault.

Getting the tape off his mouth and eyes was easier than unlocking his wrists and ankles. He wiggled off the bed onto the floor ungracefully, landing on his hip and shoulder. It smarted. He picked at his ankles first, finding an edge. It took a minute, but he could walk again.

He found Gertie's phone on the floor. He dialed 9-1-1, his hands shaking, and walked to the kitchen for ice for his forehead. But he hung up when the operator answered. On the front door, a message in black magic marker read,

"Call the police and she dies. I'll call her phone with instructions in one hour."

He scrolled through Gertie's contacts and called Robin.

Cud's next call was to the Bahamas. With his vast resources—if he could pull the right strings—he could end this nonsense once and for all and save the woman he loved.

And if it cost a billion dollars, so be it.

Chapter 22

Gertie blew on the black fabric over her head, puffing it up like a balloon. "Thomas, is this really about money?" Sitting on a metal folding chair, her wrists bound behind her, she tugged against the duct tape.

He took off her hood. "Lady, I have a job to do. All Johnnie had to do was give me back what he stole. Instead, he hit me with a shovel." He pointed to the gauze taped to his forehead.

"You know what they say, money can't buy happiness."

He bent over, his face inches from hers. "It's not my money. But if my bosses don't get it back, I don't get the wages I earned. And what good is capitalism, then?"

"Johnnie does get headstrong."

"I'd love to chat, but I have to get ready for the exchange. Let's hope, for your sake, the bug-eyed freak comes to his senses. If he has any." He unwound another strip of duct tape and approached her.

"Please, I'll be quiet. No need for that."

He gave her a sneer. "Fine." He put down the tape and began checking the items in his black utility vest.

Gertie looked around the grand residence. Probably a second home, because there were white canvas coverings on all the furniture. The floors were marble, twenty-foot ceilings with wood beams, mid-century furniture—the real high-end stuff, not imitation—and gorgeous drift wood chandeliers. She wondered if Cud had once owned homes like this. Maybe with servants. It was a home that would be fun to live in for a few days. But it seemed sterile. Also, very wasteful. Thousands of residents lost their homes in Irmaria. Still, years later, homesites were vacant lots. Yet, here was a pristine home with no one living in it. Capitalism was cruel.

She estimated it took them a half hour to reach their destination. Meaning, they were likely on the west end of the island. She wondered if the tracking device was still on Smith's car and whether Dottie could locate them.

Her mind wandered to the upcoming Easter service at church. She and Dottie were on the schedule to set up on Friday, two evenings from now. Would she be free by then? Who would fill in for her? Pastor Lillian had picked some great hymns this year. Gertie began to sing softly *How Great Thou Art*.

Thomas was sitting at a desk in the corner of the living room, his back to her. "Stop that."

"Does it bother you?"

Thomas spread out what seemed to be a map. "Yes. Shut up."

"Does the television work?" She nodded toward the far wall of the living room.

"Shut up. No television." Smith seemed to be marking up the map with a ball-point pen.

"Sorry. I'll be quiet."

He kept his eyes on the map, "You keep saying that."

"I said sorry. I'm just trying to make the best of the situation."

"How in Hades am I supposed to concentrate if you don't shut your trap?"

"If you need help, I'd be happy to listen and collaborate. Two heads are better than one, they say."

Thomas stood, shoving his chair away. "Lady! That does it." He strode over, raising his hand above her head, aiming to strike her. His phone chirped.

He answered it, walking back to the desk. "Hello, sir...Yes...What? A hostile what?" A long pause. Smith shook his head. "You're shitting me, right? Son of a... Goodbye." He threw his phone against the wall.

"What happened?"

He sat back down, holding his head, leaning his elbows on the glass desk. "All that work..." He slammed his fist on the surface so powerfully the impact dislodged a cup of pens onto the floor and knocked over silver frames of the owner's family pictures.

"This is BULLSHIT!" he screamed.

"Anything I can do, dear?"

"SHUT UUUPPPP!" He stormed out of the room.

A minute later, he was back, pointing his gun at her. "I should fucking end you..."

"I wouldn't." She looked down at the beautiful white Oriental rug, gesturing with a nod of her head. "Think of the mess."

Smith shook his head. "Lady, you crack me up. Shit. It is a nice house, isn't it?"

She nodded. "Yes. Very nice."

Smith's phone rang. He retrieved it from where it landed after bouncing off the wall. He squinted at it, like he didn't recognize the number or maybe the screen was broken. "Yeah? Who's this?" After a pause, "Johnnie! How the hell did you get this number?" Another pause. "Yes, she's right here...no, she's fine." Another pause. "Hold on." He hit a button on his phone and asked, "Lady, what song did you sing in the garden yesterday?"

Gertie's heart leapt. It meant Cudlow was with Johnnie, because only he would know about the garden yesterday. "First, ask Johnnie if Cudlow is all right."

"Your boyfriend? I'm sure he's fine. So, what did you sing?"

"I don't remember. I hum and sing all the time."

"Yeah, no shit. They want to know you're alive. Give me something."

"I could just talk to them."

"Right." He said sarcastically. "Nope. Rule Number 28. Come on. Something only you know."

"Well, Cudlow has a tattoo of a ladybug on his right buttock."

Thom relayed the information, adding, "But I need that drive...Yeah, I know...I can still kill her...don't bring the cops...a simple trade...one hour. Got it." He ended the call.

Gertie cocked her head. "What happens now?"

Thom turned off his phone and stuffed it in his pocket. "I get paid and you go back to lover boy."

She smiled. "See? I knew it would all work out. God always has a plan."

"I don't believe in God. Now, shut up and let *me* plan."

Cud drove to Hawksnest in Gertie's car, arriving fifteen minutes before the midnight exchange. Arturo, Robin, Johnnie and Dottie were in the parking lot, standing around, waiting.

He parked and walked over to the group, ready to spit. "What is this? Arturo can't be here! Smith will kill her!"

Johnnie put his hand on Cud's shoulder. "I'm sorry. I messed up. We'll get her back."

Cud grit his teeth. "I'll never forgive you…"

Robin clapped her hands. "Stop. We need to plan this. Listen." She turned her head, staring at each of them in turn. "Arturo, tell them."

Art cleared his throat. "Dottie, Robin and I are tracking Smith's SUV. We'll drive half a mile up to the next parking lot at Peace Hill so he doesn't see our cars. Johnnie is going to exchange the drive for Gertie. For real this time. As soon as Smith leaves and Gertie is safe, I'll track him down, call for back-up and arrest him. Simple."

Cud shook his head. "I need to be here. I'm not leaving."

Arturo said, "If Smith sees anyone but Johnnie, he may kill her. Do you want that on your head?"

"No. But I've lived on this beach for ten years. I know how to stay hidden. I'll use Gertie's phone to let you know what's happening. In case things go badly."

Robin stomped her foot. "Cudlow, I know you want to be her knight in shining armor, but let the authorities handle this."

He yelled. "I'm not leaving!"

Arturo said, "Alright. Calm down. Mr. Loughton. You see the problem, right? He can't see your car here. I'm ordering you to follow us. Don't make me arrest you."

Cud scratched his head. "What if he kills Johnnie?"

Johnnie sighed. "After all my mistakes, I need to make things right. Besides, Arturo gave me his Kevlar." He lifted his T-shirt, showing the black vest.

"Are you sure?" Cud said.

"I'm sure."

Robin said, "Now, we all need to take our places." She hugged Johnnie. "Be safe out there."

Dottie said, "He's on the move. About fifteen minutes out. We need to skedaddle."

Cud shook Johnnie's hand. "See you on the other side, mate."

The group dispersed, getting into their vehicles. Cud wasted no time, beating the rest to his car and speeding away, with little concern for keeping the vehicle to the left of the center median. He had little time. Because there was no way he was staying put.

At the small dirt parking lot at the Peace Hill Trail, Cud stretched his calves, waiting for the next car to arrive. It was Robin. She waved.

"Robin, I'm going to go take a pisser. I'll be back."

She said, "Sure," then turned her attention to the next car pulling in: Dottie's.

And he was off, ditching his flip flops. He knew the quickest path back to Hawksnest, knowing every rock and tree and curve of the shoreline. The moon came out, making the job easier. Could he cover the serpentine half-mile in ten minutes? He focused on his breathing. *In...out...in... out.* A branch whipped him in the face but he kept going through the lush vegetation. His legs were sturdy from daily walking. Still, his calves and thighs burned.

A private residence between the beach and North Shore Road appeared. He was getting closer, now running fully on the sand, close to the water line.

Then a scramble on an incline behind some rocks. And he finally saw Johnnie in the distance, standing alone on the sand. *No sign of Smith yet.* He'd made it in time.

Cud crept through the scraggly shrubs and trees, trying to regain his breath. He stayed off the footpaths and made his way to his nest on the west end. Under his cooler, he found the belt with the knife sheath and donned it. Then made his way back toward the edge of the parking area, crouching to remain unnoticed.

A minute later, Thom's black SUV took a slow turn into the lot, it's headlights off, inching along to a stop near the path to the pavilion. Smith got out and released the back hatch of the vehicle. He pulled Gertie's arm to exit. She had a bag over her head, and he guided her roughly toward the beach.

She's alive! Thank the Heavens!

Cud prayed under his breath. *God, don't let Johnnie screw this up.*

When they were out of sight, he stabbed the rear tires of Smith's vehicle. He called Arturo and whispered, "She's here. They're heading to the beach."

"What? Where are you?"

"I'm at Hawksnest. They can't see me." Cud moved toward the sand to witness the exchange.

Arturo muttered something angrily, but he didn't care.

Smith and Gertie now stood forty-feet from Johnnie.

Smith said, "Throw it. Now."

Johnnie and Smith appeared like two men in western movie gunfight: wide stances, tall posture, daring each other. But now, Smith had something dark in his hand—probably a gun—pressed against Gertie's side.

Johnnie countered, "No. You let her go first."

Smith sighed audibly. "How about this? Simultaneously, you throw it half-way, and I let her go, and she walks toward you. The standard routine."

"Okay." Johnnie threw something small. Probably the drive. *Hopefully the drive.*

Into the phone, Cud whispered, "He did it. Johnnie threw the drive to Smith…"

Smith still held onto Gertie. "Sucker." He kept the gun on Gertie and walked toward the drive, pulling her along by her elbow. "I'll let her go when I'm out of here safely. Maybe tomorrow."

"Oh, no," Cud gasped.

Johnnie yelled, "You can't do that!"

Then something very odd happened. Cud screamed.

Arturo shouted through the phone, "What happened? Tell me!"

Cud didn't know what to say. Or how to describe it.

Because all hell broke loose.

Chapter 23

Stumpy heard the nice man's voice. It had been days. Many days without his favorite crunch-crunch. He gazed down from his high perch in the tree. Was it treat time? Or did he have to wait until day-break?

The human tossed out a small orange oblong item onto the sand, saying, "Here."

Could it be? His heart went pitter-patter. Yes! Yum time!

He licked his upper lip with his forked-tip tongue and dashed down the tree, running across the sand. A woman tripped in front of him, landing face-down in the sand, but he leapt across her. The cheesy puff was his!

Scooping it in his mouth, he noticed his foe, Green-tail coming in his direction. He took the prize and ran back to the underbrush.

He turned, ready to defend. Green-tail was closing in, but a tall strange man was also chasing them, yelling. Yelling something angry. He bit down on the orange noodle, but it didn't taste right. No pockets of cheesy air. He spat it out. Green-tail could have this stale nasty thing if he wanted. He dashed away from the onslaught.

On the beach, the bulging-eyed man was helping the woman sit up, taking something off her head. Not his concern.

But he wouldn't be denied. He ran back to the goody man.

He needed to get the man's attention. Inserting himself between the humans, he rested his two front feet on the woman's knee, bobbing his head at his friend, blinking, insisting he pay heed.

Stumpy asked again, "Cheesy puff?"

Thom watched the arc of the thumb drive as it landed on the sand, twenty feet in front of him. He held the gun on the landlady. The four-eyed butt-munch believed him. *What a lobotomite.*

He forced the woman to walk beside him. The pussyboy whistled and shouted something that sounded like 'Rum time'. Obviously, the mental patient was having a nervous breakdown.

Only three more feet…

Something dashed out of the brush toward them. *An iguana?*

It stole the thumb drive!

Did that just happen? Mother…

Without thinking, Thom released the woman and chased the reptile into the bushes. Finding an iguana in the dark beneath dense bushes was difficult. The moon came out from behind a cloud and he saw some branches rustle. As he got closer, a second iguana stole it. He stepped on its long tail. What kind of whack-o reptile farm was happening here? As he pried the drive out of the hissing animal's mouth, it snapped its jaws, cutting him in the fleshy bit between his thumb and forefinger. *Great.* Now he'd need antibiotics.

He kicked the animal and it ran off.

The drive was his! He clenched it in his right hand, pumping his left fist in the air.

He jogged to his vehicle. Soon he'd be done with these amateurs and could leave the island forever.

Thomas couldn't believe what he found next. The old man—the wrinkled-skin, bony-ass lover boy—was leaning against the hood of his SUV, holding a cell phone. He didn't have time for this shit.

"What do you want? Your girlfriend is fine. I'm leaving."

"You have my thirty-million quid."

"Yours? Ha!"

"I purchased the company you were working for." He gestured air quotes when he said 'working'.

This guy was funny. "You? Right. You couldn't even purchase a decent bath." He brushed past Cud and got into the driver's seat.

The old guy got off the hood. "I properly fired your employer. The ill-conceived bridge project is quite bollocked, to be sure."

How would he know that? Thom rolled down the window. "Hold on. So, I kidnap your girlfriend and in under an hour you buy a multi-million-dollar real-estate investment company? That's not even possible."

"You messed with the wrong bloke."

Thom brandished his gun. "Maybe. But I'm done and I'm leaving now." He put the SUV in reverse, swerving away, gunning it across the lot. The back tires made flopping noises. *What the hell?*

Flashing lights appeared in his rearview mirror and to the side of him. Thom slammed on the brakes. *Boxed in.*

`He whipped open the door, ran across the two-lane highway, his arms pumping, up through the brush, climbing the hill to the south.

Police called out, "Stop, we'll shoot."

Thom fired two shots behind him, not aiming, continuing to climb. It was so dark he could hardly see the ground in front of him. But he knew where he was going. The map he studied earlier showed a route, if he could only find it. Rule Number 8, 'always have three exit strategies'.

After five minutes, he no longer heard radios or sirens, knowing he was clear.

With the Bitcoin, he could get off the island and start his new life.

His passport was in his vest pocket.

All he needed now was to lay-low and get to his boat.

* * *

When Smith ran off, Johnnie rushed to Gertie.

"Are you okay?" He took the cloth off her head.

Gertie nodded.

"Come, we need to move, in case he comes back." He grabbed her waist and helped her up; they dashed across the sand to the tree line near the east end. Near some rocks, they crouched in a dark spot. Sirens and yells pierced the air. A good sign. *The police had arrived.*

Cudlow emerged onto the center of the beach shouting, "Gertie! John!"

Johnnie held Gertie's hand firmly as they rose. "We're here."

Gertie broke free; the lovers jogged toward each other. Johnnie followed but let the two have their reunion.

Cud nearly tackled Gertie. "I'm so relieved. Are you okay? Did that gorilla hurt you?"

"I'm fine. Somehow, I wasn't worried. Maybe being outnumbered by seven-year-olds for twenty-five years made me impervious to bullies."

More kissy stuff. Johnnie patted Cud on the back, "Did you see Stumpy? That was hilarious."

Gertie brushed sand from her knees. "Can we just go home now?"

Cudlow kissed her hand. "About that—"

The lights and the sirens in the parking lot held more interest than the soap opera in front of him. Johnnie headed that way. More police vehicles arrived with their flashing lights. Like a stormtrooper, Tobias marched toward him.

Tobias barked, "What the hell happened? Officer Bell called me fifteen minutes ago about a kidnapping. Where's Miss Brown?"

Gertie and Cudlow walked up, arms around each other's waist. "I'm here," she said. "All in one piece."

Tobias' face seemed happy. Johnnie discerned what seemed to be a smile on the Chief's face. This was a first time Johnnie perceived the Chief had any facet of human compassion or caring. Maybe Tobias *wasn't* actually the love child of the Terminator and Genghis Khan.

In what might be described as a soft voice, although still with a baritone that could summon elephants, the Chief said, "Ms. Brown, the EMTs will be here shortly to check on you."

She said, "Honestly, I'm fine. Can I just give a statement and go home?"

"Sorry. But we'll try to be quick. I'll walk you over to Officer Cage and she'll ask you a few questions." He turned to Johnnie and Cud. "And you two, I'm not letting you out of my sights. Come along." Tobias' usual tone of contempt mixed with constipation had returned.

They followed.

Cud whispered to Johnnie. "What's our story?"

Johnnie shrugged and whispered back. "I don't know. Maybe the truth?"

"I don't want to go to prison. I have urgent business back home. Like you said, stealing from a dead person…"

"I'll say I found the thumb drive on the beach the day after Bob."

Tobias stopped and turned his head. "What are you girls talking about?"

They both replied in unison, "Nothing."

At the parking lot, the police interviewed everyone. Formal statements could wait and be provided at the police station later. Cudlow and Gertie were talking with Officer Cage a few feet away.

When Tobias began questioning Robin, Johnnie leaned against the park entrance sign and couldn't stop grinning. As he listened, Stumpy ran up the sidewalk, seized something on the pavement in his mouth and brought it up to him like a puppy bringing a slipper.

Johnnie crouched. "Whatcha got there?"

Stumpy dropped it at his feet. [Here Johnny!]

Who had taught him this?

It was a small red-leather notebook, smaller than a cell-phone, with lined pages. He skimmed through it. There were lists of rules and stuff about how to kidnap people effectively. *Did Smith keep a diary?* What were the chances?

The iguana rested his front legs on his sneaker. [Treat?]

"Sorry, Stumpy. I'll get you next time."

Stumpy wandered off.

Tobias was only three yards away. He could just hand the book to him. Easy, peasy. *But no, Tobias was a tool.* Johnnie made a mental note to give it to Arturo later. There had to be some really incriminating shit in there and maybe some clues on where Smith might go.

Tobias, his feet apart, arms crossed, asked Robin, "So you met with Thomas Smith about a bridge project and had him followed?"

Robin crossed her arms, mimicking him. "Unlike you, when someone is acting suspicious, I investigate them."

"What are you implying?" Tobias put his hands on his hips.

"Apparently you were so easily conned into believing Smith's story about being Mr. Taylor's brother, you escorted him here to harass Johnnie. You know, I'll be putting that in my statement later. The FBI will also be curious—"

His eyes threw daggers. "You don't have to be spiteful."

Robin pointed to herself. "Me? You jailed my brother purely on speculation. I think he has a good civil suit for defamation, battery and unlawful imprisonment. In fact, I know Mr. Greaves is champing at the bit for a juicy case like this."

Tobias shook his head and growled, "Look. You win. You and your merry band of amateur detectives can go home." He waved at them dismissively and went to talk with another group of officers.

Robin shouted after him, "Call me when you find Smith. Although I doubt you could find your own navel."

Johnnie hit Robin in the shoulder playfully. "Nice one, Sis."

She said, "John, promise me you'll stay out of trouble for a while. Please." For emphasis, she grabbed his shirt with both fists.

"I will. Pinky promise." He held out his pinky, just like they did when they were kids. Although, maybe he needed to be more adult. Gertie could have died. Maybe not the best time to tease.

She rolled her eyes and hooked her pinky in his. She stuck out her tongue at him, "Butthead," and walked to her car.

Cudlow and Gertie were finished with Officer Cage. Cud gave the car keys to Gertie. "I won't be coming with you."

"Why? Are we staring our break? After everything that happened, I think you should stay."

"I want to stay. But I can't. I'll be in touch." Cud kissed Gertie on the cheek and chased after Robin. "Can you give me a ride to the car ferry dock? A helicopter is meeting me there."

Gertie sidled up to Johnnie, watching Cud get in Robin's car. "What was that? Did Cudlow say where he's going?"

"Something about business back home. Maybe the Bahamas? That's all I know. Wait, he also said it was urgent."

"What could be so urgent he has to leave in the middle of the night?"

"I honestly don't know."

* * *

Dear Diary,

Another boring day.

Ha! Psyche! Fooled you. I just got home and it's after 2 a.m. Tobias interviewed all of us, but was still an ass. And Gertie has to go give a written statement tomorrow. The whole police force is out looking for Smith. Robin called the FBI.

I made some really bad mistakes. Maybe I should have killed the creep with the shovel and avoided all this. But Gertie is safe now and Thom the butt-hole is out of our lives.

It pisses me off that he got away with all that money, considering he probably killed two people for that stinky bridge project.

In other news, Cud left and went back to the Bahamas. I really don't know what is going on with him and Gertie, but I'm staying out of it.

Also, Robin and Arturo seem very friendly. I'm glad for her. He's a good guy.

I'm supposed to give another guided trail hike tomorrow and need to report in five hours. It's been a long day, so I'm heading to sleep.

Goodnight Diary,

Love, Johnnie

P.S., I should bring Stumpy a bunch of treats. He's deserves a year's supply.

Chapter 25

Thursday morning, Robin took a taxi to Mary Taylor's temporary residence near Smith Bay on St. Thomas. She didn't recognize her at first with her dark sunglasses and flowered bucket hat.

"I want to hear everything," Mary said.

"Me, too." Robin held the door for her. "We'll go to the legislature building. The FBI will meet us there."

Mary nodded.

Once inside the taxi, Robin said, "Thanks for sending me Robert's email."

Mary clenched her hands together on her lap. "I couldn't believe it. When my brother-in-law showed me at the funeral, I nearly collapsed."

"I'm sorry for not calling you earlier."

Mary turned to face Robin. "Did Smith really kidnap someone?"

Robin sighed. "Yes, Ms. Brown is fine. But Smith, if that is his actual name, got away with the money."

Mary's face turned hard. "I just want to see him rot in jail."

"Me, too."

They arrived to the legislature building at nine. After passing through metal detectors at the security screening, they went to the assigned conference room. Arturo met them outside and opened the door for them.

The FBI was setting up shop there. The room looked like any other government conference space. Beige walls, ugly carpeting. The three folding tables looked like they were an afterthought, the tops were a worn wood-look laminate. The metal-framed padded chairs looked as old as they looked uncomfortable.

Hard-shelled equipment cases and a maze of cords rested on a table in the far corner.

A man and woman, both wearing suits, sat at a center table with laptops open. The man rose to greet them first. "Good morning. Senator, I'm Agent Deckman and this is Agent Morris." He looked at Mary. "You must be Mrs. Taylor. Sorry for your loss."

The group got down to business, exchanging information about the development deal, the killings, the kidnapping, and Smith's escape.

Deckman said, "We tracked Smith's phone to Cruz Bay after his escape, but then the signal didn't appear again, meaning he's probably ditched it. But he can't go far. There's a bulletin issued by Interpol, the coast guard as well. We'll find him, if not now, then soon. Officer Bell will be our local police liaison on St. John."

Mary Taylor asked, "What now? I can't live in fear forever."

Agent Morris looked at her. "We understand. But men like Smith are pragmatists. With untraceable wealth at his disposal, he's likely setting his sights on South America or a jurisdiction with lax extradition laws. Nothing is certain, but I believe it's unlikely he'll bother you again."

Mary shook her head. "I hope you're right."

Arturo said, "I'll escort you home later and the department will patrol your street for the next few days. But I think Agent Morris has a point. Smith is likely long gone."

Robin said, "I have another meeting upstairs, but please call me with any updates." She shook hands with the agents.

Arturo walked her out to the hall, closing the door behind them.

"So much for our dinner date," he said with a lilt.

With all the commotion of the last few days, she'd forgotten their Friday dinner plans.

The look in his eyes, like he was unsure of her feelings, was too much to bear. "I'm sorry. I'll be back Saturday night. Maybe we could have brunch on Sunday?"

He brightened. "I would love that. How about Lucy's Kitchen? They have the best stuffed French Toast."

She furrowed her brow. "No, wait. Isn't Sunday Easter? I completely forgot. We'll never get a table."

Arturo grinned. "Lucy's an old friend of the family. I can get us in."

Robin smiled. "Sounds heavenly. See you then." She stood on her toes and gave him a goodbye kiss on the cheek. Still, sadness washed over her, having to postpone their date. She walked down the hall toward the building lobby, her briefcase and overnight bag in hand.

A few seconds later, Arturo's voice called out behind her. "Wait."

She stopped and turned.

He jogged toward her, closing the ten-yard distance. "You forgot something."

She searched her memory. *Did she leave her phone on the table?* She felt for it in her pocket. "What?"

He took her face in his hands and bent to kiss her. A delicate kiss, like velvet mousse on her lips, making her spine go limp and her heart pound. She dropped both bags and reached for his tall, uniformed shoulders.

"Wow," Robin gasped.

"A *good* wow?" Arturo asked, stepping back, one eyebrow arched.

"The *best* wow."

"Good." Arturo winked, his dark eyes dancing with mischief. He spun on his polished black shoes and strode back into the meeting room.

A million thoughts and desires ran through her brain. *Should she cancel all her meetings?* Run away with him to a deserted beach and make out with him in the wet surf? Arturo was a stone-cold fox and an excellent kisser. *How could she leave now?*

She blinked and looked around the hallway, noticing her fallen briefcase and overnight bag. No, she had a job and commitments. For now, she would have to be content with daydreaming.

Robin picked up her bags and shook her head.

Concentrating on zoning and infrastructure plans in stuffy meeting rooms for the next two days was going to be a living hell.

* * *

Merv leaned against the post of the pavilion and checked his bank balance on his phone. *Overdrawn again.* He hadn't counted on the Boston Celtics losing to the New York Knicks. Who knew their star player would sprain his ankle in the first half? His bookie had already made threats. Something about cutting off his right ear. And he liked his ears.

Hopefully the iguana would come through. Merv puckered his lips and gave a long whistle.

Like clockwork, the skanky iguana with its crusty skin appeared, hopping up and down and eyes wild.

"Get!"

The animal stared at him.

With a sigh, Merv reached in his pocket for a goldfish cracker. He held it between his thumb and forefinger, lowering it to the iguana's level so it could smell the treat. "Get!" he called out again.

As trained, his partner in crime raced away. He wanted to follow; to see where he went. What amount of treasure had the creature amassed?

The last item, a woman's diamond ring, only fetched $500 due to a chip on the side. And he couldn't use the gold-buying store on St. John anymore, as the owner began asking too many questions.

On the dark web, he found a better connection. But it required a trip to Puerto Rico, which ate into his profits.

A man walked up to him wearing swim trunks and too much white zinc oxide sunscreen on his nose. "Ranger? I can't find my wallet. I had it tucked under my towel. Has anyone turned it in?"

"Oh, are you sure you didn't leave it in your car? We always recommend people leave valuables locked." Merv pointed to the large wood sign by the entrance.

"I'm sure I had it. Did you see anyone messing with my stuff?"

Out of the corner of his eye, he saw the reptile waddling toward him with a gold chain in its mouth.

Merv steered the man to face the opposite direction. With a hand behind his back, he waved at his klepto-friend in a way that meant 'not now.'

"Sorry, I can't police individual belongings. But if anyone turns it in, it will show up at the Visitor Center Office lost and found. I suggest calling there tomorrow." Merv glanced back quickly, confirming that the iguana had slunk back below the foliage.

The man's face turned ashen. He shouted, "But we're leaving tonight! I had my license in there."

Merv frowned. "I wish there was something I could do. Tell you what? I'll radio the office to keep an eye out for it. What's your name?"

After some back and forth, he provided the man's name and cell phone to Candy at the center. With great reluctance, the man with the white nose sulked away.

Merv's thoughts danced with glee. *A wallet!* He rubbed his hands together. No need for a middle man where cash was concerned.

Now alone, he whistled again. His buddy approached and dropped the chain at his feet. It was thin and maybe not real gold. Merv sighed. He threw four goldfish on the concrete.

After the reptile scarfed them down, Merv said, "Get!"

His friend scampered away on his mission.

How much longer could he sustain the constant debt and threats of bodily harm?

Maybe he needed to face his gambling addiction and get help.

The thought quickly faded, knowing he would lose his job in a heartbeat.

Merv's mouth dropped open with a new thought. Perhaps he needed a trained iguana *army*! One on every beach. He could *quadruple* the income from his side-hustle.

Buoyed with this new revelation, he knew his next step.

And it would involve a shit-load of cheesy puffs.

Cudlow loosened his bow tie, facing the gilded mirror at his family's manor on Grand Bahama. His hair, now quite short, made him look like his late father. He ran his hand across the top. *Who was this person? Serious people need serious hair…*a line from a movie.

Their butler, Hugh, asked, "Sir, can I get you a spot of tea?"

"No, thank you. After our guests leave, could you send my lawyer in?"

"Yes, sir."

Alone in the room again, Cud noticed not a single thing had changed in his office over the last decade. It was a time capsule. His wife, Winifred, had decorated the grand room in a mix of Jacobean style and British Colonial furniture, with green silk toile curtains and throw pillows. *How many years ago was that?*

Beautiful Winifred.

Freddy, to him once.

He ran his hand over the curtains. Freddy had the fabric made custom. Instead of farm scenes or horses or dogs in the toile pattern, she wanted palm trees, sea turtles and corrals. The pattern was subtle, but charming. He hadn't appreciated her or her decorating efforts at the time. No, he was too consumed with business and increasing the bottom line. It wasn't until she was dying of cancer that he learned from his mistakes. And by then, it was too late to make amends. The week after her funeral, without telling his family, he instructed his helicopter pilot to drop him on St. John.

Now, the same ghosts haunted him. On the fireplace mantel, a framed photo caught his attention. Their wedding, when they were in their early twenties, without a penny, in love, like nothing else mattered. She wore a white dress she'd found at a London second-hand shop. He wore borrowed tails with sneakers.

As he met Winifred's happy eyes, he whispered. "I'm sorry."

The thick mahogany door opened with a creak, waking him from his sweet memories. A slender, white-haired woman walked in; she had a crew cut and wore a loose-fitting black linen suit with a white silk scarf tied in a wide bow. "Welcome back. Are you ready?"

He wiped his eyes. "Please sit, Felicity. Yes, fine then, let's go over everything."

She took file folders out of her case and spread them on the conference-size, antique cherry table. Gesturing to a row of five, "These are the incorporation papers for your new acquisition. You need to sign all the tabbed pages. These," she gestured to a stack of two folders, "invalidate the previous power of attorney you bequested to your grandson, and restores all your bank accounts and holdings."

Cudlow pointed to a red folder. "Is this…?"

"Yes. As you requested."

He put his glasses on and opened the red folder, staring at the front page. *Was he being foolhardy?* "Right. Let's do this before I change my mind." Grabbing a gold-tipped pen, he signed the items in the red folder. "Of all the things I want to give her, this pales…" He rubbed his forehead. "Do you think she'll hate me?"

"Why would she hate you?" She affixed a notary stamp and signed the lines below. "After what you did? Risking everything?"

He fiddled with his hands. Gertie didn't know about him buying the company to save her. And he intended it to stay that way. "Send it now. I don't want to discuss this again."

"I understand. Give me a moment."

His lawyer left. Cud signed more pages from the other stacks. Five minutes later, Felicity returned. "How are you making out?"

"Fine. Is it done?"

"Yes. The account is transferred. Do you want me to mail a notification to her?"

"No, please call the bank manager, Mr. Jameson, and have him relay the message personally. I would go myself, but there is so much to do."

"As you wish."

He let out a long yawn.

"We can pick this up tomorrow if you'd like." She reached to gather the folders.

"No, best to carry on." He rubbed the bridge of his nose. His ten-dollar, fake wood-grained, plastic reading glasses he'd purchased last week probably looked incongruous with his decade-old black pin-striped five-thousand-dollar suit. But he didn't care. Hopefully, he'd complete his work soon enough…

Cudlow continued signing. In the last ten years, he hadn't signed his name on a single piece of paper—until last week with Samuel for the twenty dollars. Now, after signing a few dozen papers, his wrist ached. And his feet hurt. He shuffled off his dress shoes under the table, rubbing the sore parts around his ankle with his socked toes.

His former life was once again his current life. With meetings and legalities and stockholders and bankers. All the things he despised. But until he could turn his new acquisition around and find a new buyer, he was stuck. Which meant he would need to find new development deals to bolster the company's value to break even; or refinance the hard money loan to more reasonable terms. The livelihoods of ten thousand employees were at stake.

Cud owed them and Jackson to make it right. *Especially Jackson.*

He couldn't dwell on the discomfort of his feet or the cold emptiness of his bed. He had to focus on the big picture.

Gertie was worth waiting for.

He only hoped she would wait for him too.

Chapter 26

Johnnie returned to forest hike duty the day after the kidnapping. Kemper said he could take the day off, but he needed some normalcy and he was up at sunrise anyway. The afternoon hike went as well as he could hope for. No dumb questions. Everyone had proper shoes. No rain. No complaints. He even smiled twice without being self-conscious of coming off phony. Yes, it was a good day despite needing to keep a look out for Thomas Smith, because there was no telling when that asswipe might resurface.

At the end of the trail, a Park Service boat transported their group back to the Visitor Center. Once there, he walked inside and up to the desk.

Candy waved to Johnnie, infused with energy, like she was hailing a cab. "Good afternoon, John! how did it go today? Did you battle any international assassins?" She beamed at him from behind the tall, yellow, L-shaped customer desk. The ceiling fan provided welcome streams of cool air across his damp back.

"Ha. Funny. The hike was fine. Hey, I called Robin a couple times. Any word on Smith?" He took off his ball-cap and wiped sweat from his brow, rubbing his wet hand on his pant leg.

"Yes, Kemper came by an hour ago. She heard that the police raided his hotel room this morning but no signs of him. From cell phone tracking, they believe he took a boat off the island during the night."

"Thanks, Candy. I'm heading home. See you in the morning." He walked out and checked his cell phone again. A text from Robin reminded him she was away for a three-day storm resilience conference on St. Thomas, and would be back Saturday night. He wondered if that was wise, now learning Smith could be anywhere. He texted her to be careful.

Johnnie rode his Piaggio across the island toward Calabash Boom. Gertie had plans with Dottie that evening at the church—getting things ready for the Sunday Easter service—and Cud was away on his mystery trip. He was all alone, which was just as well, and maybe he could do some fishing, fry up whatever he caught, and go to bed early with a good book.

Before fishing, he stopped home to change into board shorts and a T-shirt. Then he continued south to the beach at Johns Folly, an area where he could legally use his spear to fish.

The sky was blue and the wide sandbar near the rocky southern portion of beach was deserted. His favorite spot. Around the corner, the terrain climbed to a rocky cliff, becoming impassible. The lone house perched on the hillside—with its sleek lines and walls of glass—looked deserted; he never saw anyone or any lights on. If he owned a house as beautiful and remote, he would never leave.

Johnnie took off his T-shirt and sneakers, put on his snorkel and flippers and walked backwards into the water as short powerful waves broke across his legs.

It felt great diving under the surf, searching for dinner. A snapper or a mackerel would be ideal. Fish were part of his 'clean diet' that Dr. Lou always recommended for better brain health. She'd given him instructions: whole foods and cut the sugar. He tried, but sometimes emotional eating got the best of him. Like those Mallomars he finished in forty-eight hours. And, of course, cheesy puffs.

He scanned the ocean, swimming past schools of small Parrotfish. A dark moray eel scared the shit out of him. Eels freaked him out. Ironically, sharks and stingrays were fine. But eels looked at you funny, like they were reading your mind and they hated you. No, he couldn't abide them.

When he surfaced, treading water, he took off his snorkel mask and looked back at the shore. A hundred and fifty feet away, a man, wearing black, stood alone on the sand bar. Even from the distance, he could make out the bandages.

Thom the Douche. But how?

The man in black yelled, "Hey, Crosswell. You can't stay out there all day. Come face me like a man."

Did Thom track his scooter or his cell phone? It seemed inconceivable. Johnnie considered his options. He could out-swim this guy. So, he stayed put, treading water and grinning. "Come and get me."

Smith retreated to a high spot on the sandbar and sat down. And he waited.

Johnnie swam closer, waves now crashing on him. He had to yell to be heard. "You have your stupid Bitcoin money. Shouldn't you leave?"

"It's not the money. It's the principle."

"What principle?" This whole conversation was so strange, shouting over the 25-yard distance.

Thom screamed, "That you're a punk-ass whiny bitch that needs a beat-down. You fucking ruined my face."

"I'm sorry about hitting you with the shovel. Does that help?" He smiled, which was not the right move. His face was incapable of sincerity, because deep down, he wasn't sorry. And unfortunately, his tone of voice was equally unconvincing.

Thomas snickered and cracked his knuckles. "You're a weirdo. And I'm going to punch your skull in."

"That's totally unnecessary."

"*I* say what's necessary." Thom shook his fist at the sky. "Yeah, shut up number four!"

Number four? Who was he talking to? "Damn. And I thought I had anger issues." Johnnie paddled closer toward the sneering Frankenstein monster jug-head. When the water was shallow enough, he found his footing and stood, water up to his waist, waving at Thom from a distance of thirty feet. "Okay, bro, come get me. Or are you scared of the water?" He clucked like a chicken and wiggled his arms. He glanced up again at the house on the hill. *No signs of life.* Their showdown would not have a witness.

Thom stripped off his black dress shirt, balled it up and left it on the sand. "Right. Screw rule five. Let's go." He clapped his hands and strode through the water.

What was rule five? Johnnie rethought his plan. Bare-chested, Thom was jacked, with muscles like the Rock. *Maybe he should just swim away?* Instead, he took off his flippers and tossed them toward the beach; they spun like wobbly Frisbees, missing his target and crashing into the surf.

Allegedly, according to his former buddies, he was once good at hand-to-hand combat, sparing with his bunk mates for fun and winning often. Did he even remember how to fight? Were his reflexes up for this? He did best Chain Boy, even with bruised ribs. But Chain Boy was a poser.

Yes, maybe this was a terrible idea.

Thomas closed the distance quickly.

Now in striking range, Johnnie said, "We can work this out—"

Thom whipped his fist at Johnnie's jaw, sending it sideways.

Johnnie's goggles, perched on his forehead, flew off. He fell backwards, below the surface. In freefall, water entered his lungs. *Get up,* his inner voice screamed. His backside hit the sandy bottom and he rolled to the side to get his legs under him. Breaking through, he popped up, coughing, spitting out salty water.

But Thom was on him, grabbing his neck, squeezing, pushing him down under the water again. Johnnie couldn't breathe, couldn't release his grip. *Was this the end?*

He knew what had to happen…how to execute his plan. If he could only reach...

Kicking Thom's legs had the intended effect. His opponent fell, his face below the water. Thomas involuntarily released his grip around Johnnie's neck. Johnnie twisted, reaching for the handle on the ocean floor where he had left it. With a quick flick of his wrists, plunging it forward, he stabbed Thom in the torso with the fishing spear.

Thin streams of blood oozed out of the holes in Thom's abdomen.

A look of surprise crossed Thom's face. With this window of opportunity, Johnnie punched him in the jaw, twice in succession with all his strength, and chopped him in the Adam's apple. These reflexed fighting moves surprised himself and he wondered where he had trained; they felt like pure muscle-memory, as if he'd done them a thousand times.

Thom gagged, fell, eyes shut, and sank below the shallow water. His foe was defeated.

For a moment, he was proud of himself. Like he wasn't a total incompetent. He clenched his fists with a sense of joyful vindication. But this gratification was short-lived.

In an instant, Johnnie's brain flooded with fear and regret.

He wasn't a killer. As much as Smith deserved it, he couldn't let the creep drown. Even on patrols during Village Stability Operations— before his injury—he had never killed anyone, even when it might have been justified as self-defense. At least as far as others told him. Did his friends shelter him from a grimmer truth? Whatever the truth had been, he knew he couldn't live with himself if he let Smith die.

And—like Dr. Lou always said—he didn't have to let rage control him.

Johnnie reached down, grabbed Thom and pulled him to the surface. He blew into Thom's mouth, expanding his lungs. He checked for a pulse. *Smith was alive!* Although still passed out. The wound below Thom's ribs was bleeding, but in small streams as the entry points were tiny.

He had to think. Keeping Smith's dead weight propped up in the ocean wasn't sustainable. The beach was still deserted, thankfully. No boats in sight. They had drifted a few more feet from shore, and now the water came up mid-chest. The tide was going out. Despite his fatigue and stress, he had to move Thom far away where he'd have little chance of coming back soon...if he survived.

Leduck Island rose out of the water about a half-mile away. It was his best option. Not that he was thinking clearly. What he had in mind was insane and could kill them both.

In between the black, jagged boulders on the southern shore-line, he spotted a faded, busted-up blue boogie-board. From his Marine training, Johnnie knew how to use a lifesaving stroke, he didn't have the muscle strength these days. Using flotation was the only way, no matter how strange or uncomfortable.

He dragged Thom to shallower water, then headed south, clutching his foe's arm with one hand while he trudged toward the rocks to snatch the Styrofoam board. The board had a nylon cord attached. Johnnie untied the knots, using his teeth, then placed Thom chest down on the board, his face to the side. He tied Thom's hands behind his back, just to be safe. Uncomfortably, to propel their craft forward, he had to keep his arms around his nemesis and lean against Thom's rump. He could only imagine how it looked, but it kept them both breathing in the choppy water.

After the first quarter mile, his kicking slowed down. His heart felt ready to burst from the strain, his legs were numb like icy rubber, and salt water stung his eyes. He could easily dump Thom and no one would be the wiser. Or he could turn around and call the police. The stabbing was in self-defense. Tobias wouldn't arrest him again...would he? But what if Tobias was on the take? On Smith's payroll? He could ask Robin to contact the FBI. But he couldn't land another one of his disasters on her shoulders. She'd been through enough. Involving her was out of the question.

As the pair floated, in a bizarre fashion like bareback lovers—the water below them deep and cold—Thomas groaned, then whispered, "I'm gonna kill you."

Johnnie splashed water in Thom's face, toward his slack mouth, and shouted, "Shut up or I'll let you drown."

Thom gagged, closed his eyes and he grew still. *Did he pass out again?* Or was he biding his time, lulling him into a false sense of security for a later attack? The boogie board had red ooze on one side. *How much blood had Smith lost?*

Johnnie resumed the journey, his body freezing and his hands numb. John's Folly receded to a fuzzy line in the distance. Another fifteen minutes and they reached Leduck Island—an uninhabited wildlife preserve. But there were too many rocks to bring Thom ashore. He kept paddling. A couple minutes later, around a corner, a patch of sandy beach appeared. A safe area to land.

He pulled with all his might, digging his bare heels into the sand, gripping Smith under his arm pits. Johnnie pulled, straining, until Smith was fully on dry land, and rolled him to his side. Johnnie checked again for Smith's breathing. It was shallow, but there. Part of him wanted to check Smith's pockets for the thumb drive. But he resisted. *Rule number 1*, no more taking things off bodies on the beach.

Did he dare untie Smith? No, the bastard could figure it out.

A Laughing Gull, with a black head feathers and red beak, perched on a boulder ten feet away, and cawed at him relentlessly like a rabbit in distress, upset at the intrusion.

"Yeah, I know," he told the gull. "But he's your problem now."

With his muscles aching and his hands and feet tingling, he returned to the water, flopping chest down on the board. He paddled methodically back toward Johns Folly, a speck in the distance. An apt name given his situation. Before he rounded the inlet, he glanced back. Thomas hadn't moved.

Johnnie didn't know what time it was; the sun was setting behind the hills. Long shadows crept toward him, turning the surrounding water black and ominous. *Keep paddling, keep paddling...you can make it.*

Time slowed. He rested his arms for a spell, bobbing in the water, doing his breathing exercises, wondering if he would die. The Sabbat Channel was sixty feet deep in this spot. Would anyone really miss him?

Robin would get over it. Gertie could find another renter. Cudlow might not come back. And iguanas only lived twenty years, and Stumpy had to be at least fifteen.

Sheer exhaustion taunted him with thoughts of sleep. The waves lulled him; his body relaxed into the cold.

His friend Zach, wearing his desert gear, held his head, his face pleaded, "Hold on, JJ. The medic is coming. Stay with me, bro." Through broken glass and bloodshot eyes, he reached for Zach, but his friend disappeared into vapor. In a white room, Darla was sobbing, her face red and puffy, "Stay with me, John. You have to stay…" Regret filled his brain, wishing he could do things over. As he began to say, "I'm sorry," her face morphed into Robin's, looking down at him as she pushed his wheelchair. Taking a lap around the hospital courtyard in the noon day sun, she was telling him a story about their childhood pet— Tommy the yellow lab—and how he trained the dog to chew up her Barbie dolls. They both laughed. But now Darla appeared again, this time her face was red with anger, "I won't take it anymore. I've tried. You know I have. You won't talk to me…"

Through half-lidded eyes, he saw her. *The Goddess*. Paddling out toward him, the low sun illuminating her golden hair. The next second, she was kneeling on her board next to him, whispering, "You can't give up. We'll meet again soon."

Johnnie opened his eyes, seeing only water, the cold in his legs like needles, unsure of how much time had passed. No Darla. No Goddess. Only hallucinations.

A sailboat passed by, sending a wake over him, enveloping him in a coffin of water. He woke in a panic and gripped the board in his hands. No, he had to live.

Johnnie remembered he promised to work on Gertie's shutters this weekend. And he owed Stumpy a bunch of cheesy puffs. These seemed like good enough reasons to stay alive. And what Robin had said yesterday, "If you die, I'm going to kill you." His tears mixed with laughter at that one.

After twenty-minutes of slow paddling, he rode the two-foot-tall waves onto the sandbar. Johnnie hobbled, like a hunch-back, to the spot where he left his belongings. He grabbed his T-shirt, keys and flip-flops and trudged to the center of the main beach, onto the soft sand. Johnnie collapsed, laying face up, bare-chested, prone like a snow angel. He wiggled his toes and hands into the topmost layer of loose warm sand, hoping to bring feeling back.

A family walked past him, holding a picnic basket. It was Chase and his parents.

Chase stopped and hovered over him. "Mister, are you okay?"

Johnnie chuckled, staring up at the clouds—now pink above the darkened beach. "Just dandy."

"Guess what? I found a star-fish! But mom said I couldn't keep it. Mister, what did the mama cow say to the baby cow?"

"What?"

"It's pasture bed time!" Chase giggled and clucked his tongue. "Get it?"

"Ha. Nice."

Chase's mother pulled the boy away and the trio trudged off.

Johnnie yawned. Time to go home and have a sandwich for dinner. Yet, his muscles refused to move. He vaguely remembered a time as a young Marine when he could swim that distance and still have energy for a five-K run. As he lay there, willing himself upright, wondering if he should take a day off tomorrow, he heard Chase shout, "Mom, I found a jellyfish!"

Then her voice, shrill with terror, "No! Stop! Put that disgusting thing down!"

Johnnie laughed and couldn't stop laughing, his ribs registered pain, his mind delirious, imagining what Chase *actually* found.

The sky turned dark purple and lights from distant houses appeared across the hillside. It was time to go home. As he rode the Pig up the winding road, his thoughts wandered. If the evil Thomas lived through the night, would he leave him alone now? Perhaps appreciate the fact that he was still alive? Tomorrow was Friday. He was supposed to call Dr. Lou to check in. Would he feel some guilt by then? He didn't think so.

He'd done many bad things in his life.

Stabbing and stranding the douchebag Mr. Smith wasn't even in his top ten.

* * *

Smith tugged at the knots behind his back. *It must be a bad dream,* he thought. The sun was going down fast.

It was his own damned fault.

The rules were there for a reason. Had he gotten too complacent?

Right now, he had three goals. Untie himself. Bandage his wound as best as possible. Get off the damned island.

None of it made any sense. Why hadn't Johnnie killed him? Was he supposed to be grateful to that piece of shit?

His pruned fingers caught an end of the rope, allowing him to trace it back to the knot and force his fingers underneath. The cord loosened. Soon, his hands were free.

The sun was gone now, but his eyes adjusted. In the moonlight, he couldn't see the extent of his chest wound, but he still felt dizzy. With no fresh water, his clothes wet, and no phone, his prospects looked bleak.

He stripped off his wet pants. Living the commando lifestyle, he now sat with his bare tush against the coarse sand and pebbles. With his teeth, he ripped strips of fabric from his pants and wound it around his torso.

In the distance, he saw a sailboat. Yelling made no difference.

Waiting until dawn was the safe option. The other was to swim the half-mile in the dark. He felt for the thumb drive in the buttoned back pants pocket. *Still there.* But what good did it do in this situation?

As he sat on the sandy slope admiring the twinkling lights across the channel, a strange thought crossed his mind. *What if he was actually dead?* And this island was some type of purgatory?

That made more sense than the piss-head leaving him alive and swimming him to a desolate island.

Maybe he was a ghost.

A grin crossed his face. Ghosts were pretty cool. They could haunt their enemies for decades.

Yes, he decided. He would be Johnnie Crosswell's ghost.

If it took fifty years, he would make sure Crosswell felt his presence—his evil presence—until the moron's dying breath.

* * *

Dear Diary,

I'm so tired I can't function. You'd be proud because I ended up doing the right thing. At least as right as I can manage. I'm not telling Robin about what I did to Smith. She would never understand. Heck, I don't understand it.

I watched The Simpsons tonight even though it was one I think I saw before, but it made me miss Cud. He's only been gone a day and Gertie asked before when he's coming back and I don't know. He said it could be weeks.

Kemper left me a message saying I could go back to maintenance work next week now that stories about the actual killer are in the news. Today's hike wasn't bad, but I'll be glad to not talk to anyone for a while.

I cancelled my appointment with Lou because I don't know what to say to her. Would she despise me if I told her the truth? Probably. If I lost Lou as my doctor, I'd be in trouble and that thought is terrifying.

And what if Cud never comes back? And if Robin spends more time with Arturo?

But I'll always have you Diary. And Stumpy.

Goodnight,

Love, Johnnie

P.S. Remind me to buy a new fishing spear, hang Gertie's shutters, and fix my headlight.

Smith's 30 Rules for Excellent Fixing

1–Charge your client double the expected cost.
2–Get half payment up front.
3–Use multiple aliases.
4–Don't seek revenge.
5–Engage your enemies on your own terms and choice of setting.
6–Disguises work.
7–Hacking up bodies is time consuming, messy, and pointless.
8–Have three exit strategies.
9–Make technology work for you.
10–Falling in love is for pussies.
11–Never work with a partner or in a team.
12–Don't take on asshole clients even when the money is good.
13–Don't skimp on self-care, exercise, and naps.
14–Avoid drugs and alcohol. Never accept free drinks.
17–Keep a well-stocked medical kit.
18–Travel light; black goes with everything.
19–Don't get caught with expired identification.
20–Flying coach leads to murder. Don't do it.
21–Kidnapping high-profile persons or kids causes more problems than it solves.
22–Eat all your meals standing up.
23–Pack bolt-cutters and duct-tape.
24–Strike first and make it count; don't show mercy.
25–Diversify your client base.
26–Save your money for a rainy day.
27–Owning a pet is beyond foolish.
28–Never let a hostage use the phone.
29–Torture works, but threats work better.
30–Live long enough to retire.

ABOUT THE AUTHOR

 DS Whitaker is a New Jersey author who loves quirky, contemporary stories with oddball twists. Johnnie Finds a Dead Body, the first of the Johnnie Series, is her fourth novel.

Her debut novel, Antigenesis, was a finalist in the 2020 National Indie Excellence Awards. Johnnie Finds a Dead Body is a 2021 NIEA Finalist for comedy.

Follow her on Twitter at @ds_whitaker and subscribe to her mailing list through her website at www.dswhitaker.com.

Check out book two of the Johnnie series, Johnnie the Pirate King, to see what happens next!

Other works by DS Whitaker:

Antigenesis
Planet of the Creeps
Shower of Lies

Dear Reader!

While I have your attention,
please consider leaving a book
review on Amazon or Goodreads!

Thank You!